ALIVE AND KILLING

DAVID WOLF BOOK 3

JEFF CARSON

4296

CROSS ATLANTIC PUBLISHING

CHAPTER 1

"My DAD and I used to hike up there a lot. I love it up there ..."

And there was number four.

Wolf went back to blocking out the drone of the greasy-headed underachiever in front of him and stared up at a spider web in the corner of the ceiling. It was high up, gently swaying on the breeze of the air-conditioner vent. Too high to stretch up and swipe it away, even with Wolf's six-foot-three reach.

At least Wolf liked that about his new office. The politics? The fact that he had to be interviewing this candidate? *Those* were things he didn't like about his new position, which had put him in this new office. But the ceilings? He loved the airy and light feel of the tall space.

He could probably scoot a chair underneath it and get at it. Wolf blew a puff of air out of his nose as he realized how much thought he was putting into the whole thing.

"Sheriff Wolf?"

Wolf snapped back to attention and looked at the interviewee.

He was smiling at Wolf, like he wanted in on the joke. He looked to the corner of the ceiling. "Whoa, got a doozy of a web up there. Don't they clean this place?" He laughed too loud and sat back with one arm hooked to the back of the chair. Then he wiped his nose with a sniff and crossed his leg, displaying a smudge of dirt on the knee of his jeans. The sudden movement pushed another wave of body odor across Wolf's desk.

Nineteen-year-old Kevin Ash, son of the new chairman of the Sluice County Council, Charlie Ash, was a shoo-out, and Wolf had just about heard and seen enough.

The only points Wolf could give the kid on self-presentation were for the collared shirt. Unfortunately, it looked like he'd been storing the shirt in a tennis-ball can for the past year, and demerits for ill-fitting jeans and beyond-broken-in muddy hiking boots negated said points.

Kevin winked conspiratorially. "I'll tell my dad they need to get someone on that."

Then there were the shameless mentions of his father in order to help his chances of getting hired. That was *the fifth*. And that was enough.

Wolf stood up and held out his hand. "Thanks, Kevin. I've got your résumé, and I'll be in touch."

A confident smile stretched across Kevin's face as he stood.

Wolf shook his hand, walked around his desk, and

pushed him gently toward the door. He opened it, and pushed him a little harder into the hall.

"Uh, I guess I'll check in with my father, or whatever, or I'll just wait and see—"

"Yeah, don't worry. I'll be telling your father what I think. I'll definitely be in touch with him."

Relief replaced worry on Kevin's face and he strutted his way through the squad room in front of Wolf. Kevin nodded and slapped his hand on the corner of Deputy Baine's desk on the way by.

Baine raised an eyebrow and looked up from his paperwork.

Wolf walked Kevin Ash through the door into and through reception, and then propped open the outside door with one hand. He waved Kevin out, sending him into the cool early June morning, and out of his life.

"Thank you so much Sheriff W—"

The door clicked shut and Wolf walked to the glass-enclosed reception desk where Tammy Granger sat glaring.

"Tammy, if you let another—"

Tammy coughed, pointing a discreet finger toward the seating area behind him.

Wolf glanced behind him and saw a woman in her early twenties sitting stiffly, gaze fixed straight ahead out the window. Wolf noticed that her feet weren't touching the ground, and estimated her at no more than five-foot two-inches tall. Unlike Kevin Ash, she wore business casual, dressed in dark slacks and jacket.

She turned to him and smiled with a curt nod, a

gesture that portrayed confidence and poise, and then went back to staring outside, looking like she was doing a particularly tough calculation in her head, and solving it.

Wolf turned back to Tammy and gave another glance over his shoulder, intrigued by the interaction.

He caught Tammy's scowl and felt his face flush. He shouldn't have kicked Kevin Ash out of the building like he had. But the process of hiring a new deputy was getting to him, and the presence of Ash's son was a flick in the ear he hadn't needed from the council chairman. It was one thing that they were pushing him with an unreasonable deadline to choose a new deputy to hire; it was quite another to force him to look at candidates like Kevin Ash—complete wastes of his time.

Wolf leaned a forearm on the reception counter and raised an eyebrow.

Tammy kept a blank face and scooted a manila folder across.

He ignored it and kept staring at her, failing to read any tells on her face.

Tammy Granger was the forebrain of the department, manning the phones and any walk-ins, and she was also a motherly presence. She looked out for all the deputies, keeping abreast of their personal lives, as if to make sure they were living right. If a deputy came in hungover, she'd know about it, and browbeat said deputy into promising better behavior in the future. If a deputy had wronged a spouse, or a town member, they would have Tammy to answer to when she heard about it through the grapevine.

At two hundred pounds, she was built like a mountain

woman who'd spent as much time cooking as chopping wood to heat the fires she cooked with. She was imposing, but smart, and also compassionate. In Wolf's estimation, it was a combination that made her one of the best employees in the entire department. He likened her to a worthy assistant football coach.

And since Wolf was the head coach now, having been sheriff for a little over eight months, he valued his assistant coach's opinion. Wolf knew she had an opinion about the candidate sitting behind him. Tammy had studied the applications harder than he had, and the all-important first-impression rating was in the books, no doubt supporting what she had gleaned from the résumé.

True to classic Tammy Granger-form, however, she wasn't letting on anything. Maybe Tammy was too disappointed in the entire process to play the game. They both knew that the woman sitting in the lobby was Wolf's final interview, and then time was up.

He needed to choose a new deputy by Thursday, in two days, or the money would not be coming from the state of Colorado. The Sluice County Council had made it clear to Wolf—they needed that money. Either he made a choice, or they would make it for him.

As the days of Gary Connell, the deceased former council chairman, and his bottomless pockets, receded in the rearview mirror, the council's money-grubbing was beginning to take on the personality of a hungry bear. They were ripping through the county, and the town of Rocky Points, upturning every opportunity to get any sort of funding, every cent from every source.

First they had concocted the idea of the Rocky Points Music Festival, which was taking place this weekend, kicking off Friday, and now there was the new hire.

It was clear to everyone that Wolf and his deputies were being proactive, and were ready for the upcoming music festival. But as far as the new hire went, the council thought Wolf was dragging his feet. He wasn't. He just wasn't going to hire some lackey to fill a quota. And he wasn't going to hire Kevin Ash, the new council chairman's moronic son, just to fill the position and to score some political points.

However, and what Tammy knew just as well as Wolf, the seven candidates he'd seen so far had fallen woefully short. And, now, here was the final contender. She was also a "recommendation" by a council member, Margaret Hitchens.

Chairman Ash's nepotistic hopes were certainly going to be denied by Wolf. If he had to disappoint two council members—well, that was probably going to make things sticky for his future.

Wolf took a breath and slapped the manila folder on his leg, and then turned with a smile. "Heather Patterson?"

She scooted forward until her feet were flat on the ground, and then stood up and faced Wolf. "Yes, sir."

Wolf was startled by her short stature, and he knew he was showing it.

Her glacial pool-blue eyes were unwavering as she stepped forward with an outstretched hand. Her shoulder-length dark-brown hair had a tint of auburn in it, and it was pulled back on one side, fastened with a series of silver hair clips.

Her handshake grip was small, firm, and confident, like the rest of her seemed to be.

"Nice to meet you," Wolf said.

"Likewise, sir."

Wolf waved a hand toward the door. "This way."

She stepped past Wolf, wafting a soft, flowery aroma into his nostrils. The smell of Kevin Ash was finally a memory.

The door clicked and they entered the squad room.

CHAPTER 2

EVERY DEPUTY in the room stopped what they were doing and stared like dogs. Wolf cringed and barely stopped himself from screaming at the top of his lungs for them to get back to work. Instead, he ignored them and walked, and she did the same, bouncing fast alongside him. Her hair swayed side to side as her legs did double time to keep up. She held her chin high and ignored the persistent glares burning into her.

"This way." Wolf led her down the hall and into his office. "Take a seat."

She sat down and eyed the sparse contents on Wolf's shelves, and then the framed CSU football pictures hanging on the wall.

Wolf followed her eyes and slapped the manila folder on the empty desktop. "Heather, thanks for coming in today."

She looked him in the eye and sat still and straight. "Thank you for having me, sir."

He pulled the manila folder closer and opened it. "I've taken a good look at your application and résumé. Tell me why you want this job."

Her confident look wavered for an instant, and she furrowed her eyebrows. "You mean why do I want this particular job? Or why do I want to be a cop?"

"Let's start with why you want to be a cop," Wolf said.

She didn't blink. "I come from a long line of lawyers. My grandfather was a lawyer. My father is a lawyer. My mother and my two older brothers are lawyers. To say I've been raised with an intimate familiarity of the law would be an understatement. I've always been fascinated by it. My father is a corporate lawyer in Aspen, works in entertainment, but my grandfather was a public prosecutor. And he used to tell me county court horror stories, as he liked to call them, about how this guy got off for murder, or this guy got off for raping a woman ... all because of technicalities that lawyers exploited to get their clients off scotfree." She narrowed her eyes and shrugged. "Usually things that were done wrong during the investigation. Preventable stuff."

Wolf nodded.

"Anyway, I realized early on that the way to combat this was to make sure that the investigations were done more thoroughly, and intelligently. Then one wouldn't have such holes in cases to be exploited by some scumba"— she widened her eyes and straightened—"by a lawyer who was out to bolster their reputation and willing to do anything to win a case, no matter whether justice was served or not.

"Ever since I was a little girl, I've just known I wanted to be a cop. An investigator. I've always been fascinated with forensic science, and putting together the pieces of the puzzle. And it's a lot more exciting than being a lawyer, in my opinion."

Wolf nodded and smiled nonchalantly, but the truth was that he hadn't interviewed a candidate yet who had sparked his interest like this young woman had. Her passion was as infectious as her confidence.

He tilted her résumé and gave it a glance. "Tell me about your qualifications."

"I graduated third in my class at Aspen High School"— she rolled her eyes when she said third—"and then went on to the University of Colorado at Boulder, where I trained in criminology—DNA analysis, fingerprinting, and the like —getting my Bachelor's degree in forensic science with a specialty in investigation.

"In Boulder, I interned with the Boulder County Police Department under the tutelage of the CSI department's Sergeant Jim Duclon. I gained a ton of experience in the field and in the lab. The whole internship exceeded my expectations. By the end, I had zero doubt that I was headed in the right direction."

Wolf had talked to Sergeant Duclon on the phone the previous Friday. The words the man had used were "Pattie kicked ass. She's as smart as they come. If you don't hire her, you're an idiot. I don't know why she doesn't want to work here." Duclon had seemed genuinely upset about the whole situation. Couldn't shut up about her.

Wolf flipped to her fitness-test page. Despite her physical stature, her score was outstanding—ninety-fifth percentile across the board. Her run time, pushups, sit-ups, and pull-ups could beat out pretty much anyone in the department he had now. Her broad jump would have been remarkable for a man a foot and a half taller than she. And then there was her bench press. She had the relative strength of an ant, able to lift well over her body weight.

She narrowed her eyes and shifted in her chair. "I ... know I'm not the largest woman on the planet, but my fitness-test score is satisfactory, as you can see. I'm a black belt in karate, and I'm more than capable of defending myself."

Wolf had noticed that. Most of his men were well versed in self-defense and hand-to-hand combat, but not many had taken it to the level she had.

That, however, wasn't what was most exciting about the firecracker sitting across the desk. It was her forensic-lab experience that distanced her from the other candidates. For years, any time the Sluice County Sheriff's Department had needed specialized lab work done, they had had to farm it out to the Summit County crime lab. Heather Patterson had the experience to change that.

Wolf also noted that Heather Patterson had not mentioned her relation to Margaret Hitchens, a prominent member of the Rocky Points town council and Sluice county council. And, unlike many of the other council members, Wolf liked Margaret Hitchens. Heather Patterson would have known that coming in here, yet she was relying on her own merits to get her through the interview.

So far. She hadn't heard the next question.

"All right. Now tell me why you want this job. Why Rocky Points?" he asked. "We aren't big. We don't have the high crime rates of a city like Boulder. So, why here?"

"As you know, I grew up in Aspen, and I absolutely love the mountains, and Colorado. I've actually spent some time here in Rocky Points with my family over the years. We have relatives here in Rocky Points, and we used to ski here. I really love the town and the ski resort." Her eyes glazed over as she chuckled. "I still remember when I was young how we used to come here during Christmas time. We loved the festival, and my oldest brother, who's a really good skier, used to do the horse-drawn skier race."

Wolf smiled and nodded. "The Ski-Joring race."

Every year the town gathered to watch the fastest horses in town sprint down Main Street with skiers on ropes behind them. He and his brother had raced it many times. Wolf had broken a pinky finger one year doing it. He'd also won it, twice.

"Yeah, the Joring!" she said. "Anyway, I have great family memories here, and when I saw there was a job opening for the Sluice County Sheriff's Department, I knew you guys were headquartered in Rocky Points ... and then when I got the call to interview I was very ..." She snapped back to the present moment and regained her job-seeker composure. "I was excited for the opportunity to interview for the job. I realize this may not be a high-crime area, but I also know I have a lot to learn."

Wolf smiled.

There were three knocks on the door.

"Yeah," Wolf said.

The door opened a crack and Deputy Tom Rachette poked his head in. He did a double take and his eyes popped wide at the sight of Heather Patterson. "Hey, uh, sorry, I'll come back."

Wolf waved him in. "Heather, this is Deputy Tom Rachette. Rachette, this is Heather Patterson."

She stood up and held out a hand. "Hi, nice to meet you."

Rachette stood tall, stretching his stocky build as much as he could without getting on his toes. He took off his Sluice County Sheriff's Department baseball cap and ruffled his closely cropped blond hair underneath, sending something that looked like piece of dried leaf onto the floor. He looked her up and down, narrowing his eyes to unseeing slits, and then pursed his lips.

"Hey," Rachette breathed more than said, as he gently grasped her hand.

She furrowed her brow. "Hi."

Wolf flushed watching the exchange. He wanted to meet the guy who had taught Rachette how to talk to women and give him a punch in the nose.

"You're not from here, are you?" Rachette asked.

Heather Patterson gave a small snort, and then mimicked his tone. "No."

Rachette gave a warm smile and placed his other hand on top of hers. "Well, good luck. It was great to meet y—"

Rachette squinted and gritted his teeth. He sucked in a

breath and pulled on his hand, which was now white in Heather Patterson's grip.

After a few tense seconds, his hand slipped free and whipped back with a thump against his stomach.

"It was great to meet you, too." She turned to Wolf with raised eyebrows, and Wolf gestured for her to sit back down.

Rachette's face was brick red and trending toward purple. He stuck out his lower jaw and glared down at her. "You've got a lot—"

"What is it, Deputy Rachette?" Wolf asked.

Rachette looked at Wolf with genuine confusion.

Wolf sighed. "Why did you come here to my office?"

"Oh, yeah." Rachette put his hat back on and flexed his hand. "I just wanted to talk about the team assignments today up at the festival grounds. It can wait until after your interview." He backtracked to the door.

"Stick around," Wolf said, then looked at Heather Patterson. "Ms. Patterson, you're hired if you want the job."

She smiled wide and stood, thrusting a hand at Wolf. "Yes! Thank you."

Wolf hesitated for a second after seeing what she'd just done to Rachette, and then smiled and took her hand. "You'll be a great addition to the department, Deputy Patterson."

It was her turn to blush now. "Thank you, Sheriff Wolf," she said.

Wolf nodded. "As you probably know, we have the first

annual Rocky Points Music Festival coming up this weekend. Putting on such a big event is stretching us to the
limit, to the point where we're bringing help in from Vail
PD, Glenwood Springs, and deputies from Summit
County to help out. In other words, we need boots on the
ground. So, I hope you understand when I ask, can you
start today?"

"I ... yes, I could." Her eyes sparkled and she took in a
shaky breath.

"Yeah, okay. Easy," Rachette said.

She flicked a glance at Rachette, and then raised
her chin.

Wolf smiled. "You're sleeping at Margaret's, right? So
you have a place to stay until you find a place of
your own?"

Her face went red again, and then she nodded. "I
didn't know you knew I was related to Margaret."

"Lesson one, sister," Rachette said. "Sheriff Wolf
knows everything."

"If you need to take a few days," Wolf continued, "and
go back to Aspen to get a few things, I understand. But
we're really going to need your help later this week, and it
would be nice to get you up to speed for the next few days,
then have you working the festival this weekend."

She shook her head. "I'm packed for weeks if need be.
Consider me on the job right now."

"Great. Rachette, send Baine with Wilson for the rest
of the week. You're with Patterson."

Rachette went wide-eyed and pale. "Uh, yeah, okay."

He cleared his throat. "Are you still going up to Grimm Lake with Jack?"

Wolf pushed in his chair and walked around his desk. "Yep. In fact, I'm outta here now. I'll see you guys tomorrow afternoon."

Rachette turned to Patterson. "Jack's his son. They're going camping today."

Patterson gave a large nod. "Aha."

Wolf opened the door and ushered them out. The squad room was completely empty except for Deputy Baine, who squinted at his computer screen, pecking at his keyboard with his index fingers.

Patterson smiled at the sight of Baine, and so did Wolf. It was rare in this day and age to see such a display of computer ineptitude. Even Wolf could type circles around Baine, who was a couple of years younger than Wolf.

"Hey, Bill Gates," Rachette said, "you're with Wilson today."

Baine looked up. "Wilson already left with Hughes."

"I guess we need to call him back then."

Baine gave Patterson a quick nod, and looked up at Wolf.

"This is our new deputy, Heather Patterson," Wolf said, and Baine stood and shook her hand.

"Nice to meet you," Patterson said. "That your son?" She pointed down at a few pictures on Baine's desk.

"Yep. That's my little man," Baine said.

Rachette sniffed. "You want to call Wilson? Or me to?"

"I'll call him. He's on the parking team. We're on traffic. Which team are Wilson and I gonna be on now? Which team are you guys?"

They all looked at Wolf. Wolf slapped Rachette and Patterson on the back and walked away. "You guys have this covered. See you tomorrow night."

CHAPTER 3

WOLF SCRAPED his boots along the gravel of the department lot, kicking small stones in front of him. Crunching
tires rumbled behind him, and he turned to see the glaring
sun reflecting off Chairman Ash's black Range Rover. Ash
slowed, and then sped past him and parked in a vacant
spot, sending a cloud of dust into the air.

He sighed inwardly and walked to meet Ash as he
stepped out of his truck.

"Sheriff," Ash said with a sly smile.

"Chairman Ash."

"I just spoke with Kevin. He said the interview
went"—Ash pushed up his gold-rimmed glasses and looked
to the doors of the station—"very well." Ash smiled gratefully and held out a hand.

Wolf shook his hand and gave a nod, and then walked
away toward his SUV.

"Hey, I came to talk to you," Ash said.

Wolf turned around. "Oh? What about?"

"Well, about Kevin."

"What about Kevin?"

Ash frowned like Wolf's question was ridiculous. "What did you think? When's he starting?"

Wolf looked into the trees for a moment, picked the right words, and then looked back at Ash. "I didn't hire Kevin."

Ash's face went blank. He shrugged, straightened his suit jacket, and passed one hand over his pink tie to smooth wrinkles that weren't there. After a few more seconds of contemplative thought while grooming himself, he said, "That's disappointing."

"The interview was disappointing, yes," Wolf said. "I'm sorry. I've found a better candidate, and I hired her."

Ash tilted his head back and scoffed. "So you hired Margaret's niece?"

Wolf took a deep breath and walked away. "I hired the best candidate for the job, Chairman. Now, if you'll excuse me, I've gotta get going."

Ash stepped up and pulled on Wolf's shoulder.

Wolf stopped dead and looked down at Ash's hand.

The chairman removed his hand like he'd rested it on a hot stove burner, and then took up position in front of Wolf.

"You know it's just a matter of time before Sluice County changes, right? Pretty soon we're all going to have to join the twenty-first century and county officials are going to be voted into office. The state's fed up with our antiquated appointment system. That's why we had to jump through hoops and this hire happened in the first place so we could get our money. The next step is a complete overhaul of our county government structure, and you know that means law enforcement, too. They're even talking about merging us with Summit or Park Counties."

"I've heard the rumors."

Ash scoffed. "Rumors? These are plans being considered, not rumors. You have any friends in Park or Summit? I mean, besides those lowlifes you know from your high-school football days, digging ditches by day and swigging beer by night."

Wolf said nothing.

"I do." Ash stretched his mouth in a self-satisfied grin. "I know quite a few people in Park and Summit. People in high places."

"What are you saying, Chairman? That I should compromise my integrity to ensure I'm keeping you happy, so I can keep my job in the future? You trying to corrupt me?"

Ash stared with ripening cheeks, and then pleaded to the sky. "I'm just saying, you're going to need friends to keep your career on track when that day comes. And it's coming." He lifted his glasses to his forehead and continued, "You shouldn't forget that."

Wolf turned and walked away. "Goodbye, Chairman." Ash's car door slammed and his tires sawed into the gravel on the way out.

CHAPTER 4

JACK LOOKED up and stopped in his tracks as he and Wolf heard the loud thump. Wolf stepped around him to see what the commotion was.

"Whoa, oh my God," Jack snickered quietly, just like any twelve-year-old boy would do when a man face-plants somewhere nearby.

Wolf could hardly blame his son for laughing, the unexpectedness of the whole scene was startling. It was the first sign of seeing another human being since they'd began their hike at the high-alpine parking lot an hour ago. Walking through the trees, up the remote mountain valley, a few elk and soaring hawks overhead had been their only companions. Now, out in the clearing along a trail cutting through the expanse of knee-high grass and high alpine flowers, a man struggled on the ground under an upside-down backpack. He was shoulders-down, the top of his head on the ground and the rest of his body twisted like a pretzel, trying to right himself without any luck.

"Is he okay?" Jack asked.

Good question, Wolf thought. He stepped forward, his concern growing for the man by the second. "Hey, you all right?"

"Ah! Fuck! Goddammit!"

Wolf's blood pressure jumped as the man's outburst echoed down the valley behind them.

"Stay behind me," he said to Jack.

The man couldn't get up, as if an industrial-strength magnet in the top of his pack had latched onto a car buried underneath the trail. He squirmed for a few seconds, and then finally rolled out of the straps and got up, swiping the dust from his green shell jacket and camouflage canvas pants. He took off his baseball cap and slapped the backpack, and then rose up with a start at the sight of Wolf and Jack.

The man's eyes sprung open and he set his feet wide, as if he'd just woken up on a set of railroad tracks, staring at a diesel engine speeding right at him.

Then the guy relaxed and jerked his head around to look behind him. He stood still like that for a moment, and then turned to Wolf and Jack, and bent down and pushed his backpack over.

In the still mountain air, Jack and Wolf heard the contents of the bag scrape and clunk, and listened to the man grunt like he was wrestling with a backpack full of bricks.

The man's camo pants and lace-up boots looked military to Wolf, standard army combat uniform, ACU, but the green parka was a light ski jacket, a combination of civilian and military attire.

"He ate it hard," Jack whispered behind Wolf.

Wolf held up a hand for Jack to be quiet.

The man squatted and hung the pack on his shoulders, then teetered to a standing position, his teeth baring as he did so. He pulled his baseball cap low, and wobbled fast toward them. His breathing was hard and loud, like he was on the verge of hyperventilating. In the first twenty yards, he looked over his shoulder three times, which sent his body into a slight twist that threatened to topple him again.

The more Wolf watched, his unease grew. Not only were the guy's actions puzzling, so was his presence at all. For one, it was a Tuesday afternoon, in such a remote area of National Forest that even mid-summer weekends rarely saw hikers. Second, when they had started their hike at the trailhead parking lot, Wolf hadn't seen any other vehicles. Third, that parking lot sat atop an unforgiving road. Wolf and Jack had spent over an hour bouncing and scraping their way up Grimm Lake Road at a snail's pace. The skid-plate underneath Wolf's old Toyota pickup had slammed, scraped, and pinged against rocks as they inched their way over huge washout gullies dug into the steep incline. Most people turned back after the first two switchbacks.

So where did this guy come from? Was he on a long trek from the other side of the mountains? If so, why such a large pack, with so much weight?

Wolf's pulse accelerated as he watched the guy scramble toward them with out-of-control speed. When he saw what was dangling on the guy's backpack strap—a wood-handled .357 revolver in a leather holster—his body tensed for action.

Wolf had a gun, too, as was his habit after spending so much time rubbing elbows with the seedier population of the world. Only, while backpacking he always carried his paddle holster in the side pocket of his pack rather than on his hip.

Wolf turned and glared at Jack. "Stay behind me."

Jack nodded, now with wide eyes.

"Hey, you all right?" Wolf called out as he unbuckled his hip belt. He put both his thumbs underneath his pack straps and slid them an inch outward, envisioning exactly how he'd remove his pistol in the fastest move possible.

The guy ignored Wolf and kept walking toward them. His head was down, face obscured by his Boston Red Sox cap, and he was digging in the collar of his jacket for something. After a few steps, he fingered out a dark-blue handkerchief with a pattern of white logos on it, and then pulled it up over his face.

An instant later, he tripped again on a jagged rock in the trail, and went down hard. This time he twisted before being tackled by the crushing weight on his back. The man landed on his side and the backpack clanked like a huge sack of ingots.

Wolf shook his head and stepped forward. "Hey, whoa! What's—"

"Fuck!" The man's scream shook the air.

Wolf flipped his pack straps off his shoulders, turned around, and unzipped the side pocket of his pack the instant it hit the ground. With a quick move he pulled his personal pistol, a Glock 17 identical to his department-issue piece, and turned around, stopping short of pointing it at the guy. Wolf put his finger on the trigger and held it at his side. "Hey."

The man grunted and struggled to his knees, then planted one foot.

"Hey!" Wolf said. "What the hell is going on? Are you running from something? You'd better start talking."

The guy got to his feet and started walking again.

Now, from only ten yards away, Wolf could see a streak of blood oozing from underneath the man's cap. It was dried where it ran underneath the neckline of his jacket, like it was a wound from hours ago.

"Are you hurt?" Wolf asked.

The man kept coming, like Wolf and Jack were ghosts.

Wolf racked the slide of his gun, stepped in front of the man, and raised it for effect, keeping his aim to the woods in the distance. "Start talking. Now!"

The man stopped at the unmistakable sound of the gun and lifted his head, revealing wide brown eyes, dilated from excitement. He wore a medium-length brown beard, which was thinner on one side. Wolf realized one side of the man's face had been burned. One of his ears was smaller than the other, wilted into scar tissue, like Wolf had seen on severely burned veterans in the past.

The man raised his hands. "Whoa! What the hell?"

Wolf stared. "Good question. What the hell is going on? Are you hurt? Are you running from something? Start talking, now."

The man opened his mouth, and then his eyes

narrowed to slits and he made a face like he'd just smelled the worst thing in the world. "Whoa, man, I've got rights. You can't just pull a gun on someone in this country. I've got rights." He pecked himself in the chest, then pointed at Wolf, and then at Jack. "You've got rights, little man—"

"Don't talk to my son," Wolf said. "Fuck your rights. What's going on?"

The guy stared at Wolf and swallowed.

The man was crazy. And probably a little drunk, maybe a lot drunk, though Wolf couldn't smell anything. Or maybe he'd been eating magic mushrooms.

Wolf shook his head and lowered his gun. "I'm not going to hurt you. I just want to know why you're running. Are you running from something? Because it looks like you are. Do my son and I need to be worried?"

The man swung slowly under the huge weight, and looked back up the trail.

Wolf tightened his grip on his pistol and kept his eyes on the man's hands.

After a beat, the man turned back with a strained smile. It could have been the man's facial injuries that gave the illusion of strain, but Wolf didn't think so. The man was scared.

"No man, I'm not runnin'. Just enjoying the day, like you two."

"I didn't see your vehicle down at the Grimm Lake trailhead lot. Where're you coming from?" Wolf asked.

"What, you a game warden or something? I'm not hunting."

"No, but I'm the sheriff of Sluice County," Wolf said. "Where are you coming from?"

"Just up there, camping. I parked at the other lot." He pointed past them, down the trail and to the west. "I came from Aspen, past Ruedi Reservoir, then on up a hairy road. The trailhead is a couple of hours down. You have to know where to look for the cut-off."

They stared at each other for a few seconds. Wolf didn't know about the other trail, and he had been coming here for years.

The man stood still and shrugged, a gesture that failed to move his heavy pack a millimeter. "Well, have a good day."

Wolf nodded and gave him a sour smile. "Yeah. Have a good day." What could Wolf do? He couldn't exactly arrest the man for lack of social skills.

The guy nodded to both of them and walked away at his same frenetic pace.

As he left, Wolf caught a glimpse of a tattoo on the side of his neck—a bomb pointing straight down with crossed lightning bolts through it. Underneath the bolts were curled-up branches, resembling the shape of a handlebar mustache from a distance. Wolf had seen it many times before and recognized it as the Army Explosives Ordnance Disposal badge.

Now Wolf's pulse jumped again at the thought of the metallic clank from the man's backpack as he'd slammed against the ground. Was this guy trudging through the high alpine Rockies with a backpack full of heavy bomb parts?

Freaked out because they were about to blow up on his back?

Wolf didn't dare blink as he watched the man waddle down the path, welcoming the distance opening up between them.

Jack kept quiet, shooting glances up at Wolf. When the guy finally bobbed out of sight for good, Jack looked up at Wolf. "What the heck?"

Wolf looked down at him and forced a smile. "Who knows? What a weirdo."

Jack's worried look melted away. "Seriously. Oh my God, did you see that first fall? He face-planted so hard."

Wolf shook his head and smiled. "Yeah, I did. Okay, enough standing around. We're losing time. Let's get going." Wolf nudged Jack and let him go first. His nerves were zapping from the encounter and he didn't want Jack out of his sights for a second. Wolf tucked his paddle holster on the hip strap of his pack and followed close.

CHAPTER 5

"WHAT POSITION DID YOU PLAY?"

"Center field. Hey, one more time," Wolf said.

Jack stopped and turned around.

Wolf did too, scanning the trail behind them. They now stood almost at the top of a steep south-facing mountain slope. The path they'd climbed switched back and forth down an open scree field, and then flattened on a long valley that stretched out south for miles ahead before turning to the east and out of sight. He looked up past Jack. Ahead a short distance, the trail wound up and out of sight, and onto the cirque valley where their destination waited —Grimm Lake.

Wolf slowed his breath and listened. The tips of the pine trees swayed and howled in the breeze below, and a marmot barked in the rocks somewhere nearby. The sky was clear, except for some saucer-shaped clouds created by the winds flowing over the snow-covered peaks. Two crows cawed as they circled above the valley in front of them. Nothing out of the ordinary.

Wolf raised a hand to block the late-afternoon sun and a freshening wind cooled the sweat on his neck and armpit. He squinted and methodically followed the trail with his eyes until it turned out of sight. There was no movement or glints of metal in the sun.

"Is it much further?" Jack asked.

Wolf looked up. "One, two ... looks like four more switchbacks, then we're there."

Jack smiled. "Cool. It's just over the ridge, then?"

"Yep. Let's go."

Ten minutes later they crested the mountain slope.

Grimm Lake was a frigid pool of melt-water three quarters of the way up a peak that was a thirteener, as Coloradans would call it—not quite a fourteen-thousand-foot peak, but formidable nonetheless. Steep mountain walls surrounded the water on three sides, which were strewn with slushy veins of snow, reflecting the orange light of the fading day.

Wolf loved this spot. The place was always deserted—the burly condition of the road at the trailhead made sure of that. He could count on one hand the times he'd seen another human being in this part of the mountains, despite its relatively close proximity to the large populations of Vail to the north, and Glenwood Springs and Aspen to the west.

The camping was exceptional. Since the lake sat below timberline, it was lined on the west side by pines that twisted and leaned toward the mouth of the valley, bent by the relentless wind over time. They were thick in a few places, creating a few nooks to camp in.

Then there was the water. The shallow edge of Grimm Lake was almost as clear as the mountain air, allowing one to see the rocks, logs, and swimming fish, and the deeper interior of the lake glowed an emerald green.

But Wolf's biggest reason for loving the area was the memories of him and his father camping here every year for as long as Wolf could remember. Even the year his father had died, they'd come here earlier that summer and fished for two days. It had always been just the two of them; not even his little brother had come along. It had been their private spot, and now Wolf was continuing the legacy.

"Wow!" Jack's smile glowed in the orange light. "This is wet." He bounced his way down the trail toward the water.

Wolf looked at the lake and heard the trickle of the groundwater sliding from the slopes into the lake. "Yeah, I guess it is. Lots of melting this time of year," he said with a shrug.

Jack stopped and turned around. "No. Like, you know, dude, that's wet."

"What?"

"Yeah, like, it's awesome up here." Jack rolled his eyes and kept walking.

Wolf sighed and followed. *Good God.*

Jack ran all the way to the edge of the lake, looked down the shoreline, and darted to a place with a ring of rocks blackened by fire.

"We should camp here!" Jack yelled.

Wolf's smile widened. "Yeah, sounds good to me." It was the same spot Wolf had camped at every time he'd come here with his father. Probably every single person that had come here had camped there. It was naturally inviting, with a clump of pines surrounding a fire pit, blocking the winds that frequented these altitudes of the Rocky Mountains.

"All right, let's set up our tents," Wolf said as they reached the spot. "Make it quick. Then we'll get some grub cooked up."

Wolf and Jack set down their bags and got started unpacking the tents.

A few seconds later, Wolf froze as the boom of a rifle rolled up the valley, and twisted into the distance.

"What?" Jack said, seeing Wolf's alarm.

Wolf held out a hand and looked to the blue layers of mountains out the mouth of the cirque valley.

Another shot rang out, this time a little louder, perhaps riding a different pocket of wind. It was definitely a rifle and not a pistol or a shotgun.

"What's wrong?" Jack asked.

Wolf shook his head and waited for the next shot. It never came.

"Nothing. Just a hunter." Wolf flipped his backpack and unzipped the main pocket.

"It's not hunting season for months, right?" Jack asked.

No, it wasn't. Hunting season for any sort of game, big or small, wasn't for at least two months.

Wolf shrugged. "Probably just practicing. All right, let's get set up."

"You wanna do a tent-setup race? I bet I beat you." Jack was dead serious.

"Pfffft. You don't have a chance." Wolf ripped into his backpack and pulled out his tent, setting off the latest in a line of increasingly frequent father-son competitions.

Wolf feigned interest, all the while thinking about the shots. He would have bet his life that those reports had come from a rifle shooting supersonic rounds. The sound had that extra punch that echoed far and long through the terrain. What really bothered him was that the frantic man wrestling his backpack they'd passed hadn't been carrying a rifle.

Wolf's stomach churned as he pictured the scarred, bearded man, trapped under the crushing weight of his overstuffed backpack, taking his final breaths as he bled out somewhere far below.

Wolf inhaled deeply and calmed himself down. The fact was, those shots were close—at least closer than the man they'd passed would have been. If that man had continued at his same frantic pace, he would have been miles down the trail, near Wolf's parked truck by now, around at least two bends in the valley.

No, Wolf and Jack wouldn't have been able to hear the shots with such clarity had that man just been shot at. *Unless he had turned around and headed back toward us.*

Was Wolf's imagination redlining? Or had whatever, or *whoever*, that man was running from finally caught up to him? And what did that mean for Jack and Wolf?

CHAPTER 6

A HALF-MOON HUNG just above the eastern wall of the amphitheater valley, bathing the western shoreline of the lake with a soft glow, casting ink shadows of all shapes and sizes across their campground. There were no clouds above, only the stars, planets, galaxies, star clusters, and other relics of the recent and ancient past gleaming in every nook and cranny of the sky.

The flickering flames of the fire licked straight up in the calm night.

"I definitely want to play football again this year." Jack stabbed yet another hot dog on his pointed stick and stuck it in the fire.

Wolf groaned inwardly. "Yeah?" He got up from his chair and crouched next to his camping stove, giving it another pump on the gas tank.

"Yep."

"We'll see," Wolf said, hating the words coming out of his mouth as he spoke them.

Jack turned to him with arched eyebrows.

Wolf patted him on the back. "Don't worry. We'll talk about it in the fall."

"So I don't get to play? Is this because of Mom?"

Wolf shook his head and turned up the hissing flame of his camp stove underneath the simmering pot of water. "No, no. It's just that you're kind of in a transition period. Right now, the kids are getting a little too big, and you haven't hit your growth spurt yet. Your Mom *and I* don't want you getting hurt."

Jack studied his twirling hotdog.

Wolf's stomach sank, feeling like he'd just whipped his son with a leather belt.

Jack was almost thirteen, and despite his smaller size compared to some of the other kids, he was a hell of a player. Wolf had been an all-state quarterback in his day, earning himself a full-ride to Colorado State before deciding to go into the army. But Jack had his own set of strengths on the football field, seemingly opposite his father's. He was fast, caught nearly everything thrown his way, and moved through the defense like a rabbit. But the fact was that right now he was also five-foot-nothing and weighed less than half of many of the boys out on the field.

Wolf thought back to the previous fall season, and a kid on one of the Denver teams they'd played against. The kid had been taller and heavier than Wolf—a twelve-year-old behemoth whom Wolf had sworn he'd seen eyeing mothers on the sidelines in between plays.

Wolf had cringed that day for an hour and a half, watching Jack catch the ball repeatedly, just avoiding the man-child, who bowled over less fortunate kids like empty beer cans, leaving them whimpering in his wake wherever he went.

The reality was, there were kids like that all over the state now. They were sprouting feet over night, gaining pounds, a bushel of body hair, a deep voice, and a shot of untamed testosterone that made them love smothering little grunts like Jack into the turf all the more. The scary part to Wolf and Sarah was that Jack seemed to enjoy it all too much. Although Wolf was secretly proud of Jack for being such a daredevil, he also felt like he was playing Russian roulette with his son's safety.

What was the world coming to when an ex-collegiate-level football player was telling his son he didn't want him playing because it was too dangerous?

Wolf shook the thoughts out of his head and looked up at the stars.

For a few minutes, they crouched next the fire in silence. Jack's aromatic hotdog sizzled, dripping hissing juices into the fire while Wolf's gas stove blasted, struggling mightily to boil water in the oxygen-starved environment.

"I guess waiting until I get bigger is no big deal," Jack said, seeming to be completely over the argument.

Wolf studied Jack for a few seconds. "You know, you don't have to play football just because I did. If you don't want to play, then don't."

Jack looked into the fire for a moment, then up at Wolf. "I just want to be like you, you know? Nate says you were an awesome quarterback. Everybody says I'm a wet receiver. I bet I could play college like you did."

Wolf rubbed his eye with his palm. "Buddy, you have to stop using that word. You guys just go around using that as an adjective now?"

Jack looked embarrassed, like he realized he wasn't getting a joke that everyone else was laughing at.

Wolf couldn't suppress his smile any more. "Eat your hot dog—it's getting black."

"I like 'em charred." Jack made a psychotic face as he twirled the hot dog, and then he laughed.

Wolf laughed too, feeling a wave of pride for his twelve-year-old son. With his brown hair, grown out to the typical unkempt flop style of youth, and his wide pine-green eyes, he was a good-looking kid, too. Wolf had always marveled at how his own brown eyes and Sarah's sapphire blue could create such a striking color in Jack's.

Jack looked at Wolf. "What?"

"Nothing." Wolf turned up his stove a little more.

Wolf tensed and froze when he heard the next sound. A snake wriggled in his gut when he realized that the sound was the creak of straps and fiberglass rods stressing under the weight of someone sitting in his camping chair.

CHAPTER 7

"Аннн," the man sighed as he leaned back in Wolf's Coleman chair. "Hello."

There was a revolver in the man's right hand, shining liquid in the firelight. Then there was a soft metallic click of the man pulling back the hammer. It was barely audible over the rushing blood in Wolf's ears, but the sound was a clear enough signal to them. *Stay put.*

In the man's other hand was the barrel of a rifle, pointed to the sky, propped with the matte-black stock in the dirt. Affixed to the top of the rifle was a night-vision scope.

With a sinking feeling, Wolf recognized the revolver. It looked like the one carried earlier by the man from the trail. Only this certainly wasn't the same guy.

Wolf shuffled to his left to shield Jack.

"Don't move," the man said. His voice cracked and he cleared his throat.

"Who are you?" Jack said defiantly.

Wolf winced and put his hand up. "Quiet, Jack."

"Hey there, fella," the man said. He scooted forward on the camp chair with a grunt, and his face came into the light of the fire.

The man's eye color was indistinguishable, points of reflecting fire light surrounded by shadow. Three dark moles sat underneath his mouth, black voids in an otherwise ghostly pale skin. He didn't blink, and his light colored, almost invisible, eyebrows were bridged with concern. His upper lip was pushed down, like a child about to cry.

Wolf couldn't tell whether the man was mocking them or was actually sad. Or maybe he was even crazier than the guy they'd seen on the trail earlier.

Wolf took in the rest of the man at a glance. He was dressed lethally, wearing a black wool cap, black coat, black pants, and black leather boots. There was only one thing that outfit was for—sneaking up on people at night. The man had done a good job of that.

Wolf cursed himself for not noticing. "What do you want?" he asked.

The man stared unmoving, then slowly leaned the rifle up against the chair armrest behind him. Then he took a deep breath and exhaled, scratching his face while looking at them. He reached into his coat pocket and produced a radio. Twisting the knob, two staccato beeps pierced the silence.

"I'm here," he said into it.

The radio crackled. "So?"

"Just some guy and his kid." He kept his finger pressed on the button and sighed. "Just some guy and his kid."

"He isn't just some guy, mister." Jack's voice was defiant. "He's the sheriff of—"

"Keep quiet," Wolf said, keeping his eyes on their intruder.

Jack did.

The man looked at Wolf like he'd just run into an ex-girlfriend. "I guess this guy is a sheriff." He clicked off the button and pressed the radio to his forehead. "Where you sheriff of?" he asked Wolf.

Wolf narrowed his eyes. "I asked you a question. What the hell do you—"

The radio scratched. "Well," the voice hesitated, "doesn't matter. You know what you have to do." The man on the other end used an unmistakable tone. It was the tone of a father telling his son he had to take the dog out back and shoot it.

The man sat up a bit and looked at Wolf. He seemed to turn even paler. "No, I can't. You know that."

There was a long pause, and Wolf watched the man in the chair fight his thoughts.

"We'll be down. Keep them there."

Wolf had heard enough. He twisted and grabbed the wire handle of his nearly boiling water pot and stood. Like a collegiate softball pitcher, he threw the pot underhand, and then charged behind it with as much ferocity as he could muster.

The man was caught completely off guard. He screamed and crossed his arms in front of his face, dropping the radio and pointing the revolver at the moon as the water exploded against him in a puff of steam.

Wolf dove, landing an elbow in the man's face and clutching the guy's wrist at the same time. As Wolf landed on the man's upper body, the chair tipped back. The man tensed under Wolf with surprisingly strong muscles, and pulled Wolf over the top of him. After what seemed like minutes, Wolf finally landed, still with a tenuous grasp on the wrist of the hand that held the gun. He pulled himself onto the man in an instant. Then Wolf's teeth clicked together and his whole head thumped as the man connected with an uppercut punch out of nowhere. He rolled sideways, and Wolf's grip slipped.

Wolf exploded into frenzied action, twisting to get on top, seeking the revolver with his hands before it went off.

But the man was bigger and stronger than Wolf had anticipated, and turned on top of Wolf, mashing him into the ground under his pressing weight. Wolf found the man's wrist again, clamped both hands around it, and pointed the gun toward the lake.

"Get him, Dad!" came Jack's frantic voice from somewhere. "Get him!"

Now inches from Wolf's face, the man sprayed warm spittle through clenched teeth, his eyes wide with murderous intent.

The gun went off, and the recoil jolted Wolf's arms. Hot gas from the muzzle stung his hands and forehead, and his hearing cut out to a single screaming tone.

The bullet had sailed somewhere toward the lake. Harmless. This time.

Wolf dug his thumb into the pressure point on the man's wrist, so hard that he felt warm blood trickle down his nail. The revolver dropped out of the man's hand, and he screamed in agony. Wolf punched the man's forearm, and it cracked with the sound of an exploding ember in a campfire.

Wolf felt the guy go slack, and he took full advantage. He smashed him in the face with another punch and pushed him off, then picked up the gun in a lightning move, aimed, and pulled the trigger.

The .357 Magnum flashed and the air shook with a deafening boom.

Though he couldn't see through the blue floaters in his vision, Wolf had pressed the barrel so close that there was no doubt he'd hit his target. Any concern over whether he'd missed evaporated as acrid smoke filled his nostrils, mixed with the metallic smell of blood.

Wolf stood straight and was startled by Jack, standing no more than three feet away.

Jack stared down with wide eyes and a gaping mouth, holding a jagged rock the size of a cantaloupe.

Wolf realized what had happened. Jack had slammed the guy against the side of the head. That's why the man had abruptly gone slack.

"Good job," Wolf said. His own voice sounded like it was muffled with pillows.

Jack kept his eyes down. His mouth was gaping and shiny with saliva.

Wolf followed his gaze. Dark liquid pooled underneath the man's head, and a tendril of smoke curled its way out through the back of his wool cap. It looked like the man's face was half buried in the ground, but in fact the front of his was gone. Wolf knew that a .357 Magnum exit wound would do that.

Wolf put his hand on Jack's shoulder and shook gently. "Hey, buddy. Look at me, not at that. You okay?"

Jack stared at Wolf.

"You saved me," Wolf said.

Jack closed his mouth and said nothing.

Once again, Wolf felt overwhelming pride for his son. Then he looked back down at the man and felt shame grip his heart. Why? He'd had no choice. He hadn't wanted to kill the man, but he had been forced to. It was kill or be killed. Kill or have this bastard kill his son.

But he'd hoped, countless times in his life before this moment, that Jack would never have to see such things. And now he'd killed a man no more than three feet from him. In the most violent way Wolf could have imagined.

"Jack."

Jack was staring at the body again. "Yeah?"

"You okay?" Wolf gently turned Jack's face away from the bloody mess.

"Yeah." Jack dropped the rock and swallowed, then turned to the bushes and heaved.

The radio crackled, and a tinny voice came through it. Wolf picked it up and put it to his ringing ear.

"... on? You there? What's going on?" The voice was excited.

Wolf stared at the radio for a few seconds.

There was a blast of static. And then silence.

Wolf put a finger to his lips and made eye contact with Jack. Wolf cleared his throat and pushed the button of the radio. "It's done."

Wolf cringed at the voice he'd used. It was all wrong, the wrong pitch.

Five agonizing seconds of silence passed. Wolf twisted the radio. Had he pushed the right button? Yes, he had.

They had to know it wasn't their man talking.

The radio crackled. "We'll be right up," the voice said.

Wolf stared at the radio, then turned to look up the slopes of the surrounding cirque valley.

CHAPTER 8

WOLF PICKED up the man's rifle from the ground and inspected it. It was a lightweight, black Steyr Scout with a ten-round high-capacity magazine. Mounted on top was a night-vision scope.

He turned to the west. The steep mountain slope above was awash with moonlight. To the naked eye, details of the terrain were muddled and faint. He stared for a moment, looking for movement in his periphery. There was none.

He flipped the power switch on the night-vision scope and pressed the rubber eyepiece to his eye. The area was transformed into a bright black-and-white image, like an ultrahigh-definition monochrome computer monitor with the contrast cranked high.

The scope was a white phosphor display, rather than the green he had experience with in his army years. Wolf twisted the magnification knob and his vision was pulled closer into the terrain.

All the cracks and depressions of the mountain were revealed in the scope. Still nothing moved.

He scanned back and forth, high to low. Then he started from the bottom and scanned back to the top. He didn't worry about the sheer cliffs to the right and left, just the navigable slopes. He scanned all the terrain surrounding them on three sides and saw no movement.

He lowered the rifle and crouched to study the ground. He flipped on his headlamp and looked for shoe prints, hoping if he could figure out the direction the man had come in from, maybe it would give him a definitive clue as to where the other men were.

Jack watched on in silence as Wolf studied the dirt, brittle grass, and rocks around the camp. It was no use. The tracks led to the woods, straight toward the steep slope to the west. But that proved nothing. The man could have come from the mouth of the cirque, to the south, and circled around them, and Wolf didn't have the time to look.

Wolf turned his attention to the man himself for clues. The guy had a top-of-the-line rifle that was just as effective in combat as big-game hunting, with a quality, expensive night-vision scope and a high-capacity magazine. What did that say about the man? He could have been military, but he was dressed and equipped more like a well-to-do hunter, with Cabela's and Carhartt labels on his clothing. No military-issue knife, boots, or camo either. No military-issue anything, really.

"What are we going to do?" Jack asked.

Wolf looked through the night-vision display once

again and scanned the low saddle on top of the pass to the west. Nothing.

The cirque entrance, where they'd entered on the trail, was devoid of movement, too.

Nobody.

Wolf had to make a call, and the stakes had never been higher. Fear for his son raced through his veins with a stomach-quivering intensity. He wasn't used to feeling such emotion, any emotion, in battle. And he wasn't kidding himself for a second—he was deep in the battle of his life at the moment. Clenching his jaw, Wolf let his fear morph into a calm hatred for the men threatening his son. In this spot of all spots.

He shouldered the rifle and bent down over the dead body one last time. He dug his fingers underneath the man's coat collar and pulled it down, looking on the pale skin of his neck. Then he looked on the other side, swiping away the warm blood to see the skin underneath. No tattoos like the man they'd encountered on the trail earlier. Wolf wiped his hand on the man's jacket and stood.

"We're going to leave our stuff here and get down to our truck. Then we're going to go home."

Jack wiped his mouth and nodded absently.

Wolf grabbed his shoulders and glared at him. "Did you hear me? We are going to get to the truck and go home."

Jack narrowed his eyes and nodded faster.

"Get your headlamp. Put on your gloves, hat, and your heavy coat."

Jack breathed heavily as he did as Wolf told him.

Wolf put the Glock on his belt, and looked down at the man's .357 revolver lying on the ground. He picked it up, tucked it in the rear of his pants, took off the Glock, and then walked to Jack.

Jack swayed and stutter-stepped as Wolf tucked the paddle holster into Jack's belt line.

"You've shot this before."

Jack swallowed and nodded.

"Remember, there's no safety." He stepped close to Jack and hugged him tight. "Don't worry, bud. I'm not going to let you get hurt." Wolf pushed him back and looked him in the eye. "If someone attacks us"—he glanced down at the Glock on Jack's hip—"use that gun. Don't think about using it. Use it."

Jack nodded with a look that was somewhere between horrified and excited.

"Okay, here's what we're gonna do. They're coming down from up there." Wolf nodded to the surrounding slopes.

Jack shook his head. "But the guy on the radio just said they'd be right up. I heard it."

Wolf nodded. "I know. But before, they said they'd be right down. They were lying the second time. They knew it was someone else besides that guy. I think they were trying to trick us. They're trying to flush us toward the mountain slopes, where we're slow and vulnerable. So we're going to go back down. Fast."

Jack looked around, then nodded.

Wolf looked back toward the trail, and then up at the steep walls surrounding them. "But I could be wrong.

We're going to have to be ready if we're running straight into an ambush. So take the pistol out of the holster."

Now Jack looked positively horrified.

"Remember. No safety. Shoot, then think about it later."

Jack nodded and pulled out the Glock. He stared down at it and then held it at his side.

Wolf pulled out the smooth wood-handled .357 from his waist. "Let's go."

CHAPTER 9

"Shit. Do you think he's dead?" the first man whispered. "He's just lying there. I think he's dead."

The second man ripped the night-vision binoculars from his companion's hands and pressed them against his eyes.

The bright display clearly showed the man and his son talking next to a sprawled, motionless body. "Looks pretty dead." Just then the man below turned toward them and raised a rifle. "Keep still. He's lookin' toward us through the night scope."

They sat motionless, the second man studied the two milling figures below. The guy sure was proactive. They'd been ready to head down the slope when they'd heard the shots, which had blasted no more than a few seconds after the radio conversation.

"Okay, he turned around. These two have just become our only remaining obstacle. And I don't like the looks of this guy. A sheriff? And he's gotta be ex-military. Ryan was no pushover."

The first man shuffled next to him, scraping rocks, which sounded like a xylophone in the still silence.

"Careful!" he hissed. "Be quiet."

"Yeah, yeah."

The first man settled into a firing position. He flipped the night-vision scope on top of the rifle and exhaled. "Goddamn. I can't believe he's dead."

The second man felt a pang of guilt, but the sensation passed like a mild gas cramp. "You got this shot?"

The first man blew out a cloud of air in response.

"Seriously. You got this?"

"Yeah. They're at four-hundred and twenty-one yards now, and as soon as they get out of the trees, they'll be at least fifty yards closer, and pretty much coming right at us."

The second man looked down at the valley and concurred. He and his colleague were at the top of the slope, halfway between the edge of the cirque valley below and the campsite—a perfect spot from which to intercept the two figures, who would pass right underneath and into a zone where they'd make for easy pickings.

"And if they go up the other side? Up the mountain?"

"Yeah, right. They'd be crawling up, slow as turtles, and I'd pick them off. They won't do that."

"They're on the move," the first man said. "Headed straight toward us, through the trees."

The second man eyed the campground below through the night-vision display, seeing the bright pinpoint of the campfire and their other man lying motionless on the ground.

He tracked his lenses down and to the right, and caught the movement of the two walking. They were creeping slowly through the trees, taking refuge behind trunks. The man was putting the rifle to his shoulder, and then giving signals to his kid. Then they would move to the next set of trees. But they were quickly running out of cover.

"No more trees," the first man said in a sing-song voice.

"As soon as they—"

The second man stopped his sentence as he watched the two figures scatter below. He tracked his lenses up and down. The two had split up, and were zigzagging across the meadow in a full sprint.

"Shit. Go. Shoot!"

The night lit up as the first man's rifle exploded. Then he fired again. And again.

CHAPTER 10

As WOLF CREPT to the edge of the trees, he caught a glimpse of something so subtle it almost didn't register. It was the blink of a plane at the top of the mountain. But it wasn't moving. And then it was a solid red light, faint, and Wolf realized exactly what he was looking at.

"Run!" Wolf broke from the trees first, determined to draw fire his way.

A shot blasted and echoed for a long few seconds. There was no sign of the bullet hitting near Wolf. *Jack.* He almost fainted instantly at the thought.

Just then, Jack thumped past Wolf at full speed, then veered left and then right, then back left, making himself a hard target, just as they had discussed when they'd crept away from the camp.

Wolf blinked and carved a hard right turn. A bullet smacked into the ground, just where he would have been if he'd kept his course, and a rifle report rolled through the valley.

"Shit," he breathed, and upped his pace. There was no sense in slowing down, gawking at Jack, and getting shot in the process. He needed to stay alive to keep his son alive.

He ran as fast as he could, swerving between imaginary defenders on a football field.

And he prayed.

He couldn't remember the last time he'd prayed. The last time had undoubtedly been for his son then, too. And now he repeated a mantra through his bouncing breath as Jack flew through the meadow ahead of Wolf. "Please, God, protect my son. Please, God, protect my son. Please ..."

A flurry of shots rained down as they ran. Then Wolf heard two shots fire almost simultaneously. It was a subtle difference, but he was sure of it—there were two rifles now.

A clump of grass behind Jack's heel erupted into brown dust as the reports filled the air, drowning out the sound of Wolf's footsteps below him.

Jack kept on, still zigzagging, still at full speed.

Please, God. Wolf repeated the chant and reminded himself to stop watching Jack, and get his own ass to the edge of the meadow and down the trail.

Wolf's vision blurred and bounced as he pushed himself as hard as he could. The sound of his breath and rustling clothing filled his ears, and then there was another thump nearby in the ground, then another bang.

Jack was twenty yards ahead of Wolf now, almost to where the trail dove over the edge. As he neared the end, he veered right, then juked left, and dove over the hill and out of sight.

As Jack was in the air, Wolf thought he saw him twist in a strange move.

An instant later, the air shook with a final burst from a rifle high above, and Wolf dove over the edge after his son.

CHAPTER 11

"You IDIOT!" The second man grunted and put his smoking thirty aught six on his shoulder, then stepped close to the first man. He thrust his hand in front of the night-vision scope.

The first man looked at the second man's hand, now with a dancing faint red dot on it.

"Get out of my face." He slapped the hand away and switched off the infrared illuminator on his scope.

"That guy saw it and bolted."

They faced one another and stared for a few seconds. It was a defiant gesture, one they'd made to one another many times over the years.

In unison, they broke their staring war and looked down the slope in front of them.

"Shit," the second man said.

Their situation had just become dire, and they both knew it.

"They saw Jeffries," the first man said.

"And now Ryan," the second man said, finishing the thought.

"That's enough to figure everything out. And this guy's a sheriff. Obviously has a brain. They have to die."

"Yeah, they do."

They both turned on their headlamps.

"All right," the second man said. "You go after them. You're a better shot, anyway." He bent down and fumbled for a shell casing wedged in between two rocks. "I'll catch up!" he yelled to his already-gone companion.

The second man searched every slot and crack between the rocks, pocketing the brass shells in his jacket zip pocket. He kicked over the little rock tripod the first man had made and scanned the area one more time for any sign of them having been there.

Satisfied the area was clean, he looked over the edge and saw his companion bouncing down far below in a cloud of moonlit dust. He clenched his teeth, cursed their luck, and launched himself down the hill after him.

CHAPTER 12

WOLF'S LUNGS stung when he dove over the edge of the hill, but the pain of struggling for oxygen was quickly forgotten as he landed hard on his left shoulder. A pain he hadn't felt in a long time radiated down his arm and up to the side of his neck, and at that moment he knew he'd been shot.

As he righted himself and slid ten feet down a dirt embankment, he blocked out the pain and focused on finding Jack.

Jack was lying face down, twenty feet from Wolf. His back was heaving as he sucked for breath.

"Jack!"

Jack lifted his head and turned to Wolf.

Wolf was flooded with relief. "Are you all right?"

Jack nodded with wide eyes. "Yeah. I almost got hit when I dove over the edge. I heard it go right past my head."

"Thank God you didn't." He felt a rivulet of blood

reach his middle finger, dripping off at a fast tempo. He couldn't for the life of him remember getting hit.

He raised his hand and looked, feeling the warm stream now travel up his arm.

"Jack, I need you to tie my T-shirt around my wound."

Jack slipped and slid across the steep hill to Wolf.

Wolf pulled his arm out of his coat sleeve, and held up the fabric of his T-shirt. A steady stream of blood poured down his arm from a two-inch-long wound in his bicep. The left side of his shirt was already blotched with warm blood and stuck against his abdomen.

Wolf winced as he pulled the sleeve down over his wound. "Ah, shoot." Every move, every flex, sent a wrecking ball of pain through his arm.

Jack shook his head. "Forget it. Stop." He ripped off his own coat and shirt in a quick move, then put his coat back on over his bare torso.

Wolf nodded and leaned forward, hanging his arm out to the side. His lower arm throbbed, like it was being pulled by a tractor. "Okay, wrap it directly over the gash and tie it tight."

Jack threaded the shirt beneath his arm and wrapped it over the wound.

Wolf winced, and Jack hesitated.

"Just do it. Don't worry. It's fine."

Jack nodded. He made a knot, tightening it after he'd ensured the shirt covered the wound.

Wolf turned away and blew out of his clenched teeth, spraying saliva across his chin. The pain was enough to bring stars to the edges of his vision, but he knew Jack was being too delicate.

"Jack, you have to pull it as hard as you can, then double-knot it."

Jack didn't hesitate. He pulled much harder than Wolf had thought him capable of, bringing much more pain than Wolf was ready for. He clamped his eyes and jaw.

"Okay, all done." Jack's voice and jaw were shaking. Mild shock was setting in.

Wolf ignored the deep pain as he pushed his arm back through the coat sleeve and pulled up the zipper. He looked at Jack with steel eyes. It was time to get down, and to do so without freaking his son out any further.

"All right. We run as fast as we can all the way down. Ready?" Wolf looked down the valley. It was lit brightly by the half-moon directly overhead, but not brightly enough to be safe at a full sprint down the mountain.

He reached up and felt his headlamp. "Headlamps on. We're gonna have to go fast. They'll be coming after us."

Jack rolled his eyes and took a deep breath.

Wolf had seen that look before; it was the look of someone giving up in the face of extreme adversity. It was a look he'd seen on a few soldiers. And most of those soldiers were now dead. "Hey. Listen to me. We're going to get through this." Wolf gave him a firm slap on the cheek. "You hear me?"

Jack sniffed and wiped his eyes. And then he nodded. "Yeah."

Wolf looked up the hill. There was a rhythmic sound coming from over their heads, like a steam engine.

He flipped his headlamp off and peeked over the edge. He waved a hand at Jack, who was scraping up behind him. "Stop."

Wolf realized the sound he was hearing was footfalls crashing down the scree covered mountain side. He watched a headlamp bouncing down the slope on the left side of the cirque, and at a speed that suggested a man with great athleticism.

Wolf raised the rifle with his right arm only and looked through the night-vision scope. The image wobbled and swayed, loosely following the man as he descended.

Wolf lowered the rifle and brought it to his left hand. Then he gripped it with all his might and raised it with both arms, aiming better this time. His left arm felt like it was getting punched by a heavyweight boxer at the rate of his heartbeat.

The man avalanched down the hill in Wolf's scope. Wolf led him with his aim, took a deep breath, and pulled the trigger.

The recoil of the rifle jolted his upper body, sending a fresh explosion of pain through his arm. Wolf steadied the rifle, caught the man back in his scope, and fired again.

The man tumbled. Wolf watched as he somersaulted further and further down the hill. Just when Wolf was sure the man had been hit, he sprang to his feet and ran faster still down the mountain.

Wolf took another shot, and this time kept the rifle steadier; he saw a puff of dust in the white phosphor display mushroom up behind the man.

Their pursuer disappeared behind the tops of the trees, and a moment later the sound of his footsteps stopped.

Wolf slid down the hill toward Jack. Just then a gunshot rang out, echoing for seconds through the long valley in front of them.

"Let's go!"

Jack and Wolf stepped across the steep hill until they reached the trail; then they ran as fast as they could.

CHAPTER 13

THEY'D JUST PASSED the point where they'd had the run-in with the crazy man, and Wolf estimated they were now thirty minutes away from the truck. He could feel his body growing weaker as the warm slick continued to ooze down his arm. His wound still hadn't clotted, and surely the tourniquet had loosened, but there was no way they were going to stop to tighten it.

Wolf hoped the speed they were going would be fast enough. Then he hoped he'd stay conscious. If all that went well, he hoped a perfectly functioning truck would be waiting for them in the parking lot below.

Their pursuers hadn't made their presence known yet, and it had been over thirty minutes of running downhill. At the beginning, when Wolf and Jack had reached the valley floor, he'd seen one of the men come over the lip of the cirque high above. Wolf had opted not to stop and shoot at the distant light; the other man might have been lying in wait, aiming, waiting for a still target.

Since then, there'd been no radio activity, so Wolf was reasonably certain that there wasn't some other person waiting for them below.

"We're almost ... there," Wolf said in two breaths. He jogged behind Jack, holding the .357 in his right hand, the rifle strapped on his shoulder. His arm was numb now, and he felt weak, like he was suffering from a blood-sugar crash. The blood loss was taking its toll, getting worse with all the exertion and pumping of his heart.

"Any reception?" Wolf asked.

Jack looked down at his glowing cell phone. "No."

They continued on for the next twenty minutes. When they finally reached the truck, all hell broke loose.

...

They came through the final stretch of forest, and to an opening ahead, where Wolf's old Toyota truck shone in the moonlight.

Wolf now had the .357 in his belt line; his car keys were in his right hand, and for the past few minutes he'd been mentally rehearsing inserting them into his door lock, starting the engine, and driving away.

When they reached the truck, Jack went to the passenger door on the right, and Wolf to the driver's on the left.

Just then the rear window of his pickup shattered and dropped in a million pieces into the truck bed. Then a second bullet zipped past him, and bark from the side of a pine tree exploded. A third bullet, accompanied by another loud report, closer this time, hit the side-view mirror right next to Wolf's shoulder.

For several agonizing seconds, he pushed the key toward the driver's side keyhole, missing each time.

"Quick!" Jack said from the other side of the truck. "They're right there! Dad!"

Wolf's vision was tunneling down. He tried again with the key, this time feeling the smooth insertion into the lock.

Another bullet hit the truck with an earsplitting slap, just as Wolf lifted the handle. He reached in and pushed the automatic lock on the inside of his door, and jumped in.

The other door didn't open; Jack wasn't on the other side of the truck anymore.

Wolf turned just in time to see Jack near the rear of the truck, pointing the pistol, which was kicking and spitting fire in his hands. He fired four times, and then opened the door and got in.

"Jack, what are you doing? Get down!"

"I got one of them!" Jack slammed the door and jumped onto his knees on the seat, looking through the back window and using the headrest as a shield.

Wolf started the truck, and was relieved when it roared like it had countless times before in its one hundred fifty-thousand-mile lifetime. He pushed the clutch and crammed it into reverse, then grabbed Jack's shoulder.

"Get on the floor."

Jack slumped down.

Wolf backed up and cranked the wheel to the left with his right arm to exit the lot, a move that put Jack's door directly in the line of fire. He held his breath as he lurched the truck back, pushed the clutch again, put it in first, and sped away.

The truck jumped over rocks and ruts and barreled out of the lot, sending Wolf's head into the ceiling, and Jack against the underside of the dashboard. Ten seconds later they were around a bend and into thick virgin forest.

Jack climbed back onto the seat and buckled his seatbelt.

Wolf drove with one hand, feeling revived with every second that passed. He pushed the limits of the truck's suspension for the drive down the perilous road, covering the distance that had taken them over an hour to ascend in under fifteen minutes.

"Holy shit," Jack said, as they finally reached cruising speed on the dark highway far below.

Wolf turned to Jack and looked him up and down. His son was completely fine. "Yeah," he said. *Holy shit.*

CHAPTER 14

DEPUTY TOM RACHETTE pushed his foot to the floor. The department-issue Explorer lurched as it downshifted, then caught and sucked them back into their seats.

"Can you please slow down?" Heather Patterson squirmed in the passenger seat, gripping her tiny hand on the ceiling handle.

Rachette ignored her.

The siren screamed and the engine revved so high he thought it might explode, but it shifted back up a couple gears and mellowed out as they reached a downhill straight section of road, the odometer dial passing the one hundred ten miles per hour mark.

The drive from Rocky Points to County Hospital was just over a half-hour's drive south on a normal day. Rachette aimed to make it in half the time this morning. Simple math: double the speed, half the time.

He moved into the left lane and passed a semi-truck

and a car that didn't have enough reaction time to move to the right shoulder at the speed they were going.

"Please, Deputy Rachette." Patterson's eyes were clenched tight, and her teeth were bared, like she expected her life to end at any moment.

"He's in trouble."

Patterson wouldn't quit. "He's fine for Christ's sake! They said he's fine. Slow down!"

She just didn't get it. After one afternoon on the job, without even spending time with Wolf, there was no way she could understand how much the man meant to him, to the whole department, to the town. Now this new chick was telling him he needed to chill out? To not worry about the only man he'd ever looked up to in his whole life? To take his time while his mentor sat in a hospital bed with a gunshot wound, with tubes sticking out of him, and machines beeping, and God knew what else? *Screw that.*

They climbed a hill at the end of the straightaway and he let off the gas. At the apex, a caution sign with a right arrow and 45 *mph* written underneath rose into view.

He mashed the brakes, sending him and Patterson forward in their seats against the restraints. The whole vehicle shuddered. The tires squealed and the barrier cage behind their heads rattled with the vibration. Another vehicle was halfway through the turn ahead, coming the other way, so he had to crank the wheel to keep in his own lane, or risk a head-on collision.

He clenched his teeth and held his breath as the left wheels screeched and the right wheels lifted. With just the right combination of physical force applied at just the right time, they missed the other car. The instant the blur of paint was out of his peripheral vision, he compensated, steering to the left to avoid rolling, sending all wheels back to the pavement and the Explorer drifting into the other lane.

With pulse pounding, he let the SUV coast as he jerked back into the right lane, and watched the speedometer needle dip below ninety, eighty, then sixty-five. He let out a deep breath and felt himself go nova in the face.

At the same rate that his pulse abated, Patterson's presence seemed to grow next to him. It was probably the veins popping from the thin muscles of her forearm as she gripped the center console, or the death clench on the ceiling handle, exposing her rock-hard arm muscles.

When she kept silent for another few seconds, he stole a quick glance at her to make sure she was still conscious.

Her face was pale, and her lower lip jutted out. She stared out the windshield with cold, solid-ice eyes, and then, with a slow, deliberate movement, she swiveled her head and glared at him.

"Sorry," he said, thoroughly creeped out by the near collision, and now the deadly vibe he was getting from Patterson.

With a sudden move, she let go of the handle, sending it smacking against the ceiling on its springs. She leaned back, crossed her legs, and stared out the passenger window without blinking or moving another muscle.

Rachette swallowed, and slowed to the sixty-mile-an-hour speed limit. He kept that pace for the remainder of the trip.

CHAPTER 15

WOLF CAN HARDLY IMAGINE A LESS habitable environment than the heat of a Sri Lankan jungle before a
breaking monsoon.

He looks at the line of people shuffling forward onto
the CH-47 Chinook, and is at least grateful for their
mission objective—to get in, get the embassy employees,
and get the hell out. If it weren't for the twin rotor wash of
the giant helicopter, he's certain he would have melted out
of his ACU by now.

Sweat is pouring out of his helmet as he gazes into the
thick jungle at the edge of the embassy lawn. He knows
there is real danger out there. That's why they were called
here. They're only called to places with real danger.

"South, check," a voice calls in his earpiece.

"West, check," he responds.

"North, check."

"East, check."

Wolf continues to scan the edge of the thick lush growth. There are leaves hanging off trees that probably weigh as much as him, full of gallons of water. He looks to the sky, which is a muddy haze, ready to dump warm buckets of rain any second.

The line of people is getting smaller back at the Chinook, only ... seven more to load. Seven more people waiting to escape the latest flame-up of violence from the local faction of Tamil Tigers. Then they'll be on their way, and into an air-conditioned building on the Indian mainland. Then, if the rumors were right, a week in Diego Garcia for his team, a tropical paradise Naval Support Facility nine hundred miles south. And some much needed R & R.

A movement catches Wolf's attention to his right, against the line of vegetation, between the helicopter and him.

"I have movement on the west jungle wall." Wolf narrows his eyes, and confusion overtakes him for a moment. It's a child, no older than eight. "It's a kid. Stand by."

Wolf moves toward the child in long, fast strides through a patch of hip-high grass.

The child is barefoot, wearing a brightly colored backpack, and approaching the helicopter with a fast walk. It's a boy. He's holding something in front of his face, in his hand, like a popsicle or something, and he wants to show the people on the helicopter what he has.

Then Wolf freezes, and the blood drains from his face. As the little boy gets nearer the helicopter, he looks over his shoulder to the jungle, toward the trees with wide eyes, like he's searching for approval, like a kid in a soccer game looking over to the sidelines for encouragement from his parents, and Wolf takes in the truth of the situation in an instant.

The popsicle in the child's hand is a bomb-detonation device, a black rod with a thumb poised over a red switch, and the kid is wearing a backpack, filled with explosives. He's looking over his shoulder at men who have just ducked down and scurried away into the jungle, leaving swaying leaves in their wake.

Wolf shoulders his Colt M4 carbine just as a grasshopper lands on his face. Ignoring the clawing of the insect's legs on his cheek, he takes aim and fires without hesitation. The boy's head wrenches back and he falls at an awkward angle, dead before he hits the ground.

...

Wolf opened his eyes and sucked in a breath through his mouth.

After a few seconds of disorientation, he realized he was slumped in a hospital bed, staring at a cot next to him where Jack lay. His son was snoring softly under a gray blanket, a stream of drool coming out of his mouth.

Wolf released an exhale and panted trying to catch his breath. His heart was still racing, and a trickle of sweat fell down the side of his cheek. He reached up to wipe it off, and it felt like a nail had been hammered into his left arm.

He winced and looked down, saw the bandage and

sling, and memories flooded back to him. *More recent memories.*

They were in one of the rooms of County Hospital. Sluice County Hospital, with Rocky Points just over the pass to the north.

How? He didn't remember driving; nothing past reaching the main highway. Did Jack take over? Did Wolf lose consciousness? Did he get in an accident?

Memory fragments flashed like a strobe light inside his mind. Jack had driven. Wolf had walked inside the emergency room, propped up by Jack, practically carried inside by his son. Or was it a cop? Did a cop carry him? An IV. Blood bags. His arm being stitched. And then sleep. Fitful sleep.

Wolf checked his watch. It was 7:32 a.m. He remembered speaking to a couple of cops last night, though he couldn't remember who they were or what was said.

There was a soft knock on the door. Wolf turned to see a man in a green uniform on the other side of the rectangle of glass.

Wolf nodded and scooted off the bed. He planted his feet on the cold floor, picked up his jeans, which sat folded on a plastic seat, and awkwardly pulled them on with one arm. He kept the hospital gown on top, as his T-shirt was nowhere to be found.

He glanced at Jack, who hadn't moved a muscle, and stepped out into the hallway.

"Sheriff Wolf?" A uniformed deputy Wolf vaguely recognized stood in front of him with an extended hand.

"Deputy Sergeant McCall, Garfield County Sheriff's Department."

McCall stood a few inches below Wolf, looking up with pine-green eyes, almost the same shade as Jack's, Wolf thought. His hair was closely cut and light brown, and he had a solid beard of matching color and trim. He was muscular, though not bulky.

"Hi," Wolf said. "Did I talk to you last night?"

"No, sir. That was a state patrolman and another one of ours."

"You come all the way from Glenwood Springs?"

"I did. Yes, sir. Our deputy was at the county line last night, heard the 911 dispatch request for an intercept."

"Intercept?" Wolf asked.

"Yes. Your son called 911. Told the dispatcher his age, and the dispatcher called out for the nearest law enforcement. Our deputy and the state patrolman were nearest. My deputy caught up with you guys first, and then ended up driving you guys to the hospital."

"Oh." Wolf shook his head. "I don't remember that at all." He didn't know what else to say. It must have been quite the adventure for Jack.

"You were pretty out of it last night, with the loss of blood and fluids. Your son told us what happened, and we took an official statement when we figured out it had taken place in our county. Up at Grimm Lake, your son said."

Wolf nodded.

McCall held up a pen and paper. "And here's where I come in. I'd like to get your statement, now. If you don't mind."

Wolf nodded. "No problem. I could use some coffee."

"Good idea," McCall said, and they walked down the hall to a coffee machine. McCall appraised Wolf's bandage and shook his head. "As if you guys don't have enough going on in Rocky Points this week."

Wolf looked at him. "The music festival? Yeah, this isn't going to help."

"I'd actually been pushing my boss to let me volunteer for that. But we've already got three other deputies going over. Maybe next time."

"Really? I would think having to come to Rocky Points to run security for a couple of nights would be a crap assignment."

McCall shrugged. "I like Rocky Points, and I was thinking I could use a change of scenery."

"Your boss Sheriff Greene?" Wolf asked, already knowing the answer.

"Yeah."

"Well, I'd put a word in for you, but you'd probably be fired shortly thereafter."

McCall chuckled and raised an eyebrow. "You two don't get along?"

"You could say that."

"Then I guess I should let you know he'll be coming here in the next few minutes, and he'd like to speak to you as well."

"Oh, good."

McCall chuckled again.

They grabbed a styrofoam cup of coffee and walked back to a group of chairs outside the room.

Wolf checked through the window to make sure Jack was still asleep and sat down.

McCall was an attentive listener as Wolf rehashed the adventure from the night before. The Garfield County deputy contorted his face and made noises of exasperation as he took notes.

When Wolf ended the story with Jack shooting one of the men, and their narrow escape, McCall sat back and shook his head. "Good lord. We gotta get these two guys." He widened his eyes and looked down the hall. "We have deputies up on the trail now. They're saying there weren't any vehicles in the lot, and they haven't seen anyone. We've also checked every hospital in the surrounding four counties. Nobody had a man come in with a gunshot wound last night."

They turned at the sound of approaching footsteps.

"Sheriff Wolf," bellowed a deep voice.

Wolf winced as he bumped his injured arm against the chair and stood up. "Sheriff Greene. Good to see you again."

Sheriff Greene stopped on thick trunks for legs and held out a flesh-pillow hand. "Yeah, right."

Wolf had no clue what that response meant. Going on thirteen years now, Greene had never liked Wolf, and found it necessary to pretend that Wolf didn't like him back. Why, exactly, was a mystery Wolf had never solved.

Greene wheezed as his cold hand shook Wolf's with the vigor of a dead squid. "Sounds like you got into some trouble last night, boy."

Wolf nodded. "You could say that."

Greene was worse looking than Wolf had seen him last. Redder and larger, were two words that came to mind.

"Didn't think I'd see you down here," Wolf said.

"Why's that?"

Wolf shrugged. He knew that Greene, due to retire within the year, had already mentally checked out, just like Hal Burton had prior to Wolf's stepping in as sheriff. On top of that, Sheriff Greene had always been a delegator, preferring the warmth of his office to the world outside.

"I've just gotten word that we have a double attempted murder and a possible homicide in my county. Why the hell wouldn't I be down here?"

"I stand corrected," Wolf said. "Thanks for coming down. I appreciate it."

Greene glared at Wolf and heaved his barrel chest.

"I had just finished telling Deputy Sergeant McCall about what happened last night."

Greene nodded. "I'll read the report. Spare you telling it again."

Wolf nodded, taken aback by the small kindness. "Thanks."

"Coffee," Greene declared, turning around and walking down the hall.

He watched Greene's ample frame teeter from side to side and wondered what had been wedged between himself and that man over the years. It wasn't like they'd seen each other more than once or twice a year, but when they had, Greene had always been on the defensive. Wolf suspected it was something his father had done, years ago, and Wolf had inherited Greene's hatred.

Wolf went to the room door and looked in the window again. Jack still slept, now sprawled face down on the cot.

"My son saw one of them"—Wolf turned to McCall, remembering another snippet of time from the night before —"and says he can give a decent description."

McCall nodded. "That's what I hear. We have a sketch artist we use in town."

"Good, because we don't."

McCall nodded. "I'll get you a number." He fished for his phone in his pocket.

"What's that?" Sheriff Greene had returned.

"I was just telling Sheriff Wolf that we have a good sketch artist we commission. Glenn Meyer? I was getting the number." McCall held up his phone.

Greene eyed Wolf as he sipped from his cup. "You don't have a sketch artist in your employ?"

"Afraid not," Wolf said.

"So, we'll just send ours over."

Wolf nodded. "Thanks."

"Add that to the two other deputies we're sending over to help you guys out this week. For that music festival."

Wolf blinked. "Thanks."

"Your son was shooting a Glock 17 at the man when he saw him?"

Wolf nodded.

"In the dark."

"I had my reverse lights on. He says he got a good look at him, right before he shot him in the arm."

Greene nodded with a skeptical smirk.

"We, uh"—McCall cleared his throat—"also have the

description you gave last night of the man you saw on the trail. I'll notify the Glenwood Springs FBI field office. With an EOD neck tattoo like that? We're checking the NCIC database, but it would be good to get FBI eyes on it too. They can also check with the Department of Defense for any hits."

Wolf nodded. "Good call."

"I'll be heading up to the trail myself, as soon as we're done here."

"And I'll be going with you," Wolf said.

McCall nodded. "Where do you want your pickup? Your facilities or ours?"

Greene grunted. "That'll be going to us as well. They don't have the forensics department to handle that. They outsource it."

"He's right," Wolf said. "So, I'll probably need a ride back to Rocky Points when all is said and done as well."

McCall didn't skip a beat. "No problem. I'll give you a lift."

They all turned at the sound of more footfalls coming down the hallway. It was Rachette marching fast with Patterson jogging to keep up in the rear.

Rachette held up his hands. "Sorry, we got here as fast as we could. Stupid mix up. I didn't know about this until an hour ago. You all right?"

Wolf looked down at his arm hanging in the sling. "Fine," he said.

Patterson stood dutifully behind Rachette. She wore a Sluice County Sheriff's Department uniform that looked two sizes too big, with sleeves and pant legs rolled up.

Wolf nodded to her. "How you holding up? Is he showing you the ropes?"

She flicked a glance at Rachette, and then nodded her head. "Yes, sir."

Rachette turned his head a fraction, and Wolf thought he saw a hint of red in his cheeks. Rachette turned to Sheriff Greene and held out a hand.

"Sir, I'm Deputy Tom Rachette. This is Deputy Patterson."

Introductions went all around.

"How's Jack?" Rachette asked.

"He's fine. Tired. Sleeping now."

Rachette nodded. "So, when are we going up?"

Wolf excused himself from Greene and McCall, and motioned for Patterson and Rachette to follow him down the hall.

"I need you two to take Jack to Rocky Points."

Rachette stopped. "Patterson can take him back. I'm going up to the trail with you. We've gotta chase those bastards. They could still be up there."

"Listen to me," Wolf said. "It's more important that you stay with Jack. He could be in danger. When we escaped, he got a look at one of the two guys shooting at us. He says he shot one of them in the arm."

Rachette frowned. "You think they know who you guys are?"

Wolf looked toward the rotating glass doors of the front entrance. "I think it wouldn't take much to figure it out. Jack spouted off that I was a sheriff to the guy I killed at the campsite. That man relayed it on the radio to the other men that were there. They could be close now, checking us out here, for all we know. Jack is the only one who would recognize the man." He looked at Rachette, then at Patterson. "I need you two to stay with Jack."

They nodded.

"And Sarah?" Rachette asked.

Wolf stretched his neck and exhaled. "She's on her way now, probably not far behind you."

...

Not more than ten minutes later, Sarah burst through the doors of the hospital, spotted Wolf, and ran toward him.

Her sky-blue eyes were wide and her eyebrows were pulled together in concern. She wore a maroon sweat suit and padded across the floor on slippered feet.

"What's going on? Is Jack all right?" she asked with shaking lips.

"He's fine, Sarah. He's just down the hall, sleeping in a room."

She looked past him and started walking. "Where?"

Wolf followed her. "Sarah, wait. I'll take you." Wolf walked to the door and cracked it open.

Sarah blew past him inside. Jack twisted in the bed and looked up at her with half-closed eyes. "Mom?"

Wolf slipped inside and waited patiently as Sarah hugged and kissed her son, running through a long list of questions making sure Jack was okay.

She stood up and turned to Wolf. "What the hell

happened?" There was an accusatory note in the way she asked it, but then her face softened. "I'm sorry, I ... what happened?"

"Some men were shooting at us on the mountain. We don't know why."

"Dad killed one of them, and I shot one in the arm." Jack looked up with wide eyes.

Sarah's face turned white, and she looked down at Jack. Then she sat down on the bed. She gripped her face for a second, and then looked up at Wolf.

"Did you ... so what—"

"I want Jack to stay with Deputies Rachette and Patterson until I can figure out what happened up there, okay?" Wolf said.

Sarah looked at Jack and rubbed his face with both hands, as if feeling him for cracks. Then she looked back up at Wolf.

"Do you think they're coming after Jack? What are you saying? Is that what you're saying?"

Wolf hesitated. "I don't know, Sarah. But I don't want to take any chances."

"So where are you going? What are you doing?"

"I have to go find them. Investigate." Wolf sat down next to her and reached across his injured shoulder to caress her arm. "Sarah, please. You can be with Jack as much as you want, but I want cops—with guns—with you two, all right?"

Sarah nodded and wiped her eyes. "What happened to you?" She looked at Wolf's shoulder.

"I was shot by one of them."

She held a hand over her mouth. "You've gotta get these guys."

Wolf nodded and looked her in the eye. "That's the idea."

There was a soft knock on the door, and then it cracked open. A tall man Wolf recognized as Mark Wilson, Sarah's current boyfriend, poked his head inside. "Sarah?"

"Come in, Mark," she said. "Come in."

Wolf stood up and offered his hand to the man who'd claimed Sarah since her last stint in rehab—a counselor turned lover. Wolf suddenly felt out of place.

Mark gripped Wolf's hand and eyed his shoulder with genuine concern. "Are you okay?"

"I'll live," Wolf said, stepping aside.

"You doing all right, Jack?" Mark asked.

Jack nodded.

Mark looked at Wolf again. "Okay, sorry. I just wanted to check in. I'll be out in the hallway, getting some coffee." He disappeared before anyone could protest.

Wolf watched the door click shut. Every interaction Wolf had with Mark Wilson left him wanting to simultaneously like and hate the man. But Wolf failed to find it in himself to do either.

"David?"

Wolf snapped out of his thoughts and turned back to Sarah. "Yes?"

"I asked if you're coming back to town tonight."

"Yes, I'll come back. If I'm not coming, I'll call you."

She walked to Wolf and gave him a gentle hug. Wolf

wrapped his arm around Sarah and looked at Jack, and then released her when he saw their son was staring at them with something that resembled hope.

"Rachette and Patterson will follow you guys home. I'll see you later." Wolf walked out of the room.

CHAPTER 16

McCALL DROVE with expert off-road skills up the road to the Grimm Lake trail, swerving left and right, keeping a steady speed that was five miles an hour faster than Wolf had taken it the day before.

Wolf gripped the ceiling bar as hard as he could, trying to keep the movement of his upper body to a minimum. Each bump and sway of the SUV sent a throb of pain into his arm, but he insisted that McCall continue at the impressive pace.

Two Garfield County Sheriff's Department Ford Explorer SUVs waited in the lot at the top, and there was a deputy milling around, focusing on the ground near the trailhead.

Wolf and McCall parked and got out into the thin air. There was a flicker of a breeze that was cool on the skin, counteracting the midday sun blazing in a cloudless sky.

They approached the uniformed man. "This is Deputy Allison," McCall said.

Wolf shook his hand. "You finding anything?"

Deputy Allison was a strong-looking man with a mustache that curled downward at the edges of his mouth. "I saw some shell casings in the parking lot." He gestured to Wolf. "I'm assuming they were discharged from your weapon. Four casings, nine-millimeter."

Wolf nodded. "And here?"

They were standing in the spot that could have been where Jack had shot one of the men.

"Our dog detected blood scent here." He pointed at the rocky ground. "Just taking final samples. We've got a bunch of samples from the trail, too. Probably drops of blood from your arm, from what I heard about your wound. But we'll see after testing."

McCall nodded. "Okay, I'll sign off on those samples when we're done." He pointed up the trail. "Who's up there?"

"Greibel and Bishop."

McCall gestured Wolf ahead and they walked up the trail.

...

An hour later they reached the high meadow where Wolf and Jack had seen the tattooed man on the trail.

Wolf stopped and turned to McCall. "You ever been up here?"

"I can't remember being here before." He twisted and studied the surrounding peaks.

Wolf nodded. "We saw the guy with the overloaded

backpack and the tattoo right here. I asked him why we hadn't seen his car. He said he'd taken a different route to get here, but I've been coming here for years, and I've never seen another trail merging with this one."

McCall continued to survey the area, breathing through bared teeth. He took off his backpack and took a long swig from his canteen. Standing with his hands on his hips, he closed his eyes toward the sun. "I'd have to look at a map," he said finally. "Meantime, let's keep an eye out." The man looked as exhausted as Wolf felt.

They trudged ahead for another hour, all the way up to Grimm Lake. There they found two deputies wearing rubber gloves, kneeling on the ground, putting dirt in plastic containers, taking pictures, and rummaging in bags.

A bear-sized German shepherd sat with stoic stillness, eyeing them as they approached.

"Bishop, Greibel, this is Sheriff Wolf," McCall announced.

The two men greeted Wolf and gave empathetic nods toward his injured arm.

Wolf frowned and looked around the campsite. His orange Kelty pack and Jack's black North Face were still leaning against the rock where they'd left them. Wolf's camping stove sat knocked over, and Wolf could see Jack's hotdog roasting stick lying at the edge of the fire pit.

He walked to his tent and put his hands on his hips, studying the empty ground where he'd shot and killed the man the night before.

"No body?" he asked.

"Nope," Deputy Bishop said. "Nothin'. But Sheila

went crazy right here. Blood scent everywhere, right here." He pointed at the ground. "And you can see that the dirt has been pretty well disturbed. It looks like someone came and moved the guy you shot, and then tried to hide the blood evidence by kicking it over with dirt."

Deputy Greibel held up a plastic container. "We'll see what the soil samples say." He knelt down and put the container back in his bag.

Wolf turned away and looked up the mountain at the western ridgeline.

He lifted his arm an inch to relieve the stress from the sling, and since it already throbbed with each beat of his heart, the movement sent a cascade of pain from his bicep to fingertips and back again.

McCall walked up next to him and looked up. "That where they shot from?"

Wolf nodded.

McCall looked up at Wolf with raised eyebrows.

Wolf sighed and started walking toward the slope. McCall followed close behind.

CHAPTER 17

FORTY-FIVE MINUTES later they stood atop the mountain, nearest as Wolf could estimate to the spot where he'd seen the red dot of the infrared illuminator the night before.

This time they both huffed through clenched teeth and breathed in steady sighs. They sat down on the loose rock, and Wolf's arm pulsed with more pain than ever. At least it took his mind off his aching calf muscles, hamstrings, and lungs.

After five minutes of catching their breath in the rarified air, they ate a snack bar and chugged water, and only then stood up.

A frigid wind blew steadily from the west at the top of the mountain, and it made conversation difficult.

They decided to split up, Wolf going north along the ridge and McCall south.

Wolf tucked his chin under the neck of his jacket and walked carefully over the rocky terrain near the edge that overlooked the area below. He studied the ground, looking for anything out of the ordinary.

He reached a point where he knew he was too far, and turned around. The wind pressed the right half of his clothing against his body.

In the distance McCall bent down and fished a finger in the rocks.

"You got something?" Wolf yelled over the howling wind.

McCall ignored him. He was too far, Wolf realized. He continued toward the deputy, stepping on rocks that teetered and scraped beneath his boots.

McCall turned, and then raised something in his hand.

Wolf upturned a hand in a questioning gesture.

McCall nodded and held up a spent rifle shell glinting gold in the sun.

When Wolf finally reached him McCall said, "Got a case. .308 Winchester." He dropped it in a zip-lock bag and handed it to Wolf.

Wolf looked at the brass casing in the fluttering bag. The .308 was the most popular hunting cartridge in the world and was also used by snipers, police and military. In other words, it told him nothing in itself. "Any others?"

McCall shook his head. "I can't see any. Maybe they cleaned up, because there aren't any others. Must have forgotten one. We'll check it for prints."

Wolf nodded and gave it back to McCall.

He looked down at his watch. It was 2:38 p.m., and he was feeling the effects of the chase last night, getting just a few hours of sleep, and two long hikes in the span of twenty-four hours. He looked down at the cirque valley below, longing to be back down.

A single figure was walking in from the open end of the valley, toward the two men at the campsite.

"Head down?" McCall yelled over the wind.

Wolf nodded gratefully.

As they stepped over the edge, the air went still and quiet. Warmth from the overhead sun radiated from the loose scree under their feet—a welcome contrast to the elements on the ridge.

As they descended, Wolf only took risks with his footing on his right side, putting his right hand down when he needed to keep his balance. In between spots that required his concentration, he stole glances at the approaching person below.

It was a woman with a shiny head of brown hair, pulled back in a ponytail. She wore dark pants and a black jacket with FBI in yellow on the back, both fitting snug against her athletic-looking figure. She walked briskly with sure feet and jumped over obstacles without breaking stride.

Wolf watched her for a few moments, and waved when she turned to look up at them through sunglasses. She gave a quick wave back and continued toward the campsite.

Wolf watched the men stand at attention, greet her, and begin showing her what they'd found.

He reached the meadow at the bottom of the slope a few seconds behind McCall and followed him to the camp.

Wolf watched the agent and McCall shake hands as he approached. His earlier assessment was correct. She had a slender and athletic body, but what he hadn't seen from such a distance earlier was how good-looking she was.

She approached Wolf with an outstretched hand. "Sheriff Wolf?"

Her hand was slim and warm with a strong grip.

She pulled up her sunglasses, revealing cinnamon eyes that were slightly upturned. She blinked, and her long lashes brushed the top of her cheeks, reminding Wolf of the plumage of a tropical bird.

"Yes," he said.

"I'm Special Agent Kristen Luke, Glenwood Springs field office." She turned back to McCall. "You were the one who called this morning?"

"Yes, ma'am," McCall said.

Special Agent Luke took center stage, and all eight of the men's eyes surrounding her were glued.

"Did you two find anything up there?" She looked at Wolf and nodded toward the peak.

Wolf nodded to McCall.

"A single shell casing," McCall said. "A .308 Winchester."

She creased her eyebrows and studied the bag McCall held up. Her forehead skin crinkled with the smooth elasticity of a sixteen-year-old, but her demeanor was that of a much older woman with a lot of experience. She nodded, and then unzipped her jacket and wafted it open, revealing a tight black T-shirt that accentuated her small breasts.

The men fell quiet.

Wolf left them and walked to his tent. He bent down

and yanked a rain-fly stake and threw it on the ground, then moved to the next one.

"What are you doing?" Luke asked behind him.

Wolf wadded the rain fly in his hand and flipped it over the tent to the other side. "I'm packing up my stuff."

She turned to Bishop and Greibel. "You guys good with that?"

They looked at each other and shrugged.

"I don't think they came back and took a nap in our tents after they chased us down the mountain. They had a lot of work to do, and it looks like they got it done." Wolf walked around and pulled out the remaining stakes. "You'll find blood, hair, and plenty of other fluids with DNA in them in the soil sample they took over there. And we'll find blood in the soil Deputy Allison picked up at the trailhead."

Luke tilted her head and shrugged, then grabbed the rain fly off the ground and wrapped it in a ball.

The other three men got started on Jack's tent, and before long they had the entire camp pulled down and packed in the two backpacks he and Jack had left.

A few minutes later, Bishop and Greibel were done packing their bags with the numerous samples and camera equipment, and they were ready to go.

Wolf insisted on carrying his Kelty pack on his good shoulder, and let McCall take Jack's North Face.

"Let me take that," Luke said to Wolf ten minutes into the hike.

The Kelty pack teetered on Wolf's one shoulder, and

Wolf had to walk at an angle to keep it from slipping, which it still did every ten steps.

"This is stupid. You're hurt. I'm strong. Give me the pack," she said.

"I got it, thanks," said Wolf.

A few steps later the pack lightened, and was pulled off his shoulder. He twisted to grab at it, but she'd already yanked it out of his reach.

Before he could protest, Luke had it on both of her shoulders and was jerking down the straps.

He watched her get situated under the heavy load and then smile up at him, revealing a perfect set of white teeth.

"Thanks," he said.

"You're welcome. You can take your daypack." She nodded at the ground.

He picked it up, put the five-pound weight on his good shoulder, and began walking.

Thirty minutes later they had navigated down the steep switchbacks at the top of the hike and were walking along the flat valley.

"So can you tell me more about this guy you saw on the trail?" Luke asked from a few steps behind Wolf.

"Yeah," he said. "Like what?"

"Well, I heard about the tattoo, and I heard you said it was in the shape of the EOD badge."

"I said it *was* the EOD badge," Wolf said.

She walked quietly for a second. "And you have experience with Explosives Ordnance Disposal units enough to know that for sure?"

Wolf took a few more steps. "Yes."

"Okay, so the tat was EOD. What about the guy? Like, how was he acting?"

"Like he was running from something. But when I asked if something was wrong, he completely ignored us. Like we weren't there. He was spooked, and since I was with my son, it spooked me." Wolf looked down the trail. McCall and the other two men were well ahead and out of sight.

"Yeah? And?"

"So I pulled my gun, and stopped him."

She whistled. "Really?"

"Yeah, well. Something was way off. And I was right, wasn't I?"

They were in a dense patch of forest now and a woodpecker knocked somewhere nearby. A breeze followed them down the path, bringing a whiff of Special Agent Luke to Wolf's nostrils. She smelled like shampoo.

"Yeah, I guess you were," she said. "So you let the guy go, saw his tattoo ... and then you heard shots later?"

"Yeah. My son and I were setting up camp, right at sundown, and we heard two rifle shots."

"You sure they were rifle shots? Not shotgun? Pistol?"

"Yeah, they were rifle shots. Supersonic rounds."

Another silence from Luke.

"I guess a ranger would know the difference," she said.

"Or any hunter," Wolf said, ignoring the hint that she'd not only been looking into his story, but he himself before coming up this trail.

"Okay," she said, "and the guy at the fire. Tell me about him."

"He had a Steyr scout rifle with a white-phosphorous night-vision scope attached. The whole getup—the gun, his outfit, everything—seemed brand new. He had Cabela's boots on, Carhartt pants, and a Carhartt jacket. All black."

"Okay." She walked a few steps in silence. "So what do you think that means?"

Wolf thought about his struggle with the man. The man had been sloppy. He'd landed a lucky punch, but other than that he'd been a strong guy who didn't know how to leverage his strength against an opponent. "He wasn't military."

She said nothing for a few moments. "What else? Anything else about his appearance? Hair color?"

"I think red hair," Wolf said.

"Red?" She sounded almost skeptical.

Wolf turned and looked at her. She kept her eyes on the ground.

"Yeah," Wolf said, "or light blond. He had pale skin with three moles under his mouth. I remember the moles."

She didn't respond. Her questions had apparently run out, so Wolf concentrated on the hypnotic thump of his steps, thinking about a hot meal and a few hours of sleep in a soft bed.

For the next twenty minutes they walked without speaking, descending the mountain, all the while Wolf periodically catching the scent of Luke on the trailing breeze.

They finally reached the parking lot, where the three deputies were waiting in a huddle. Their two vehicles were all packed up and running, and McCall walked to his hatchback and pulled it up.

Wolf walked straight to it and set his daypack next to Jack's backpack, which was already inside lying next to a plastic bin full of evidence bags and containers.

"How about I give you a ride," said Luke. She nodded at McCall. "Do you mind?"

McCall shrugged and looked at Wolf.

"It's just that I need to ask you a few more questions," she said. "It's important."

"Okay." He shrugged. "Fine with me."

CHAPTER 18

WOLF AND McCALL followed her to her black Chevy Tahoe with tinted windows.

She clicked a button in her pocket and the lights blinked, and then she swung up the rear door. With ease she lifted Wolf's heavy pack off her shoulders and laid it gently in the back, took Jack's pack from McCall and did the same, threw Wolf's daypack inside, and shut the door. Her movements were elegant, like a dancer's, and showed her body to be flexible and strong.

"What?" she asked, and only then did Wolf realize they were staring dumbly at her every move.

They said goodbye to McCall, Bishop, and Greibel and climbed in the hulking SUV.

It must have been the latest model because the dashboard had more glass than knobs, and it still had that new-car smell inside. He brought the seatbelt across his chest and buckled it underneath his slung forearm—a move that was surprisingly painless.

He'd noticed that he felt his wound less and less as he moved more and more, but he knew the real healing was starting, and the pain would come back. It would probably return by the end of the car ride, and by tomorrow morning it would be a bitch.

"Jesus," she said.

Wolf looked at her.

She was staring at his shoulder. "You've gotta clean and redress that thing."

He looked down. There was a shiny pancake-sized blood spot seeping through the black sleeve of his jacket. He looked inside and saw that the bandage was sopping. "Oh, yeah."

She fired up the engine and the inside of the SUV exploded in a deep rumble of bass with a funk drum beat over it. She pressed the button on the radio with lightning speed, sending the cab back into silence.

Wolf twisted a finger in his ear and looked at her.

She blushed and backed up the SUV.

She drove cautiously down the road at a steady pace, and with a look of such intense concentration that Wolf opted not to speak for the thirty-five minutes it took to reach the highway. They headed north toward Rocky Points, through a wide treeless valley surrounded by towering white-veined mountains on either side.

She stepped on the gas and got up to a quick seventy miles an hour, then swerved to the oncoming lane and passed a gas truck.

"So, what do you think?" Wolf finally asked. "Where we at on this?"

"What do you mean?"

Wolf watched her check her rearview mirror, and then fumble with the side-mirror setting for a second.

"I mean we've just collected some evidence," he said. "But how about the database? You think we can get somewhere with this tattooed guy? EOD? Tattoo on his neck? Can't be too many men with that combination."

"Yeah," she looked at Wolf and raised her eyebrows. "Great minds."

"What?"

She shook her head and pointed through the windshield. "Look, I'm really hungry. Do you want to stop and eat? We can talk there."

"Yes," he said. "God, yes."

...

They pulled into a low one-story log building with a wooden sign that said *Merritt's* in yellow letters.

Wolf stepped out onto the gravel parking lot and into a stiff wind. It was late afternoon on a cloudless early June day and the air had a cool bite to it.

He shut the door and waited as Luke got out, opened the rear door on her side, and then disappeared for a moment.

A few seconds later, she stood up, shut the door, and walked around the bumper with a manila folder in her hand.

A string of bells clanked as they entered the almost empty restaurant. A waitress held up a finger in their direction as she finished pouring a glass of water for an old man wearing a flannel jacket.

"Go ahead and seat yourself. I'll be right there," she said.

The old man stared at Luke, and so did the cook from the kitchen window.

Then Wolf stared at Luke as she led the way to a corner booth and sat down.

Wolf slid in opposite her, finding himself facing the wall.

Horseshoes, spurs, old farming equipment hammered from iron, black-and-white photos, and other western knickknacks that hung in ninety percent of other small restaurants in the mountains of Colorado hung everywhere.

The waitress came over, holding two plastic cups with her fingers inside each of the vessels. She dropped them at the edge of the table and sloshed some ice water inside, then grabbed two menus from her apron and tossed them in the center of the table.

"Can I get you a drink?" She looked at Luke.

"Coke, please."

"Coke," Wolf said.

The waitress left without a response.

Luke's eyes narrowed. "She seems happy."

Wolf took his glass of water and drank the whole thing in one breath.

Luke looked at him with wide eyes and pushed her glass in front of him.

Wolf pushed it back. "No thanks. I'll wait for her to come back around. You take it."

She pushed it toward him. "No, please. Take it. I can't stop thinking about what was on those fingers of hers anyway, and apparently you have no problem with it."

Wolf pulled the cup toward him. "What makes you think the Coke is going to be any cleaner?"

"You ever dropped a penny in Coke? I'll take my chances."

The waitress returned with their cokes and Wolf ordered two bacon cheeseburgers and fries while Luke ordered a club sandwich.

They waited for their food in silence, listening to Willie Nelson songs rattle out of an old jukebox and the sound of sizzling food coming out of the kitchen, all the while ignoring the manila folder on the table.

When the food came, Wolf finished his two bacon cheeseburgers with a speed just shy of a competition eater and then worked on his fries, feeling stronger and in a better mood as the nourishment coursed through his exhausted body.

Luke ate half of her club sandwich and appraised his plate with an amused smile.

A few minutes later, the waitress returned to take the plates away. When she was gone Wolf gestured toward the manila folder. "Okay, what's inside?"

Special Agent Luke took a deep breath and sighed it out, then scooted the folder in front of Wolf and flipped it open.

Inside was a color photo of the tattooed man he'd seen on the trail.

Wolf narrowed his eyes and looked at Luke.

"I take it that's the man you saw on the trail."

Wolf pushed the folder across the table and sat back. "What the hell? You ... knew about the guy on the trail? That whole time? Before you even came to meet us?"

She held up a hand. "No. I didn't know for sure, until just now. You just confirmed my suspicions."

"Okay." Wolf glared at her. "Well, speak up. Who is this guy? How did you know about him?"

She scooped the picture back into the folder and slid sideways out of the booth.

Wolf sat still as she picked up the check and walked to the cash register.

She paid and then stopped at the door, looking toward Wolf with raised eyebrows.

Wolf stood up reluctantly, stared at Luke and made his way to the door. "See ya, Jennifer," he said.

"Later, David," the waitress replied without looking up from her stack of receipts.

Luke squinted at their interaction, and then moved out the door.

CHAPTER 19

Sergeant McCall drove in front of Deputies Bishop and Greibel in his SUV for thirty miles before he picked up his cell phone.

"Hello?" Greibel yelled into the phone. McCall could barely understand him over the classic rock blaring in the background.

"I'm going to stop and get gas, I'll see you—"

"Just a second." The shitty song finally quieted. "What was that, sir?"

"I'm stopping to get gas." McCall kept his urge to scream into the phone at bay. "I'll see you guys back at the station."

"That's all right—we'll stop, too."

"Nah, don't worry about it. I gotta take a dump."

"Ah." Greibel paused like an idiot, and then laughed like one. "Okay, I get it. We'll see you back there."

The Conoco station came up fast, and McCall stepped on the brakes and swerved off the road. For an instant, he watched in the rearview mirror as Bishop turned with him. Then Bishop straightened and accelerated onward down the highway.

With an exhale of relief, McCall waved as the two deputies sped past. He pulled in and parked next to a gas pump, put in twenty bucks' worth, and walked inside.

He nodded to the clerk behind the glass enclosure. "Box of Rain," a Grateful Dead cut that was deep enough to suggest the clerk's hippyness, vibrated out of the boom box on the counter. If that wasn't enough proof that the kid was high on marijuana, then his dreadlocks, the beads around his neck, and his bloodshot eyes sealed the deal.

He stared at the clerk for a beat, hitched his duty belt, and then walked along the coolers to the furthest aisle.

The volume of the music lowered to barely audible, and McCall smiled to himself. He reached the island where the station sold hotdogs and pulled six napkins out of the dispenser. He held them in a wad in one hand and rested his other hand on his holster near his gun. He walked to the next aisle over, taking his time with each step.

He eyed the corn nuts, the candy bars, the chips, never altering his slow stride. Then he walked down the next aisle. And up the next. And down the next. And then he came to the first row of shelves he'd encountered when he'd walked in.

He stopped, bent down to pick up a small can of lighter fluid, and stood. Locking eyes with the clerk, he walked to counter.

"How you doing today, Officer?" The clerk's stench of

natural oils and body odor spilled out of the glass pod he sat in.

McCall plucked a pink lighter out of a Bic display and set it down without moving his face or breaking eye contact.

The clerk lowered his gaze and scratched his poor excuse for a beard, and then grabbed the can of lighter fluid from the counter with a shaky hand. He almost dropped it, and fumbled with it against his chest.

McCall tilted his head a little and scowled—like the clerk's movement had somehow told him something.

The clerk scanned the lighter fluid with a beep, and then scanned the lighter. "Do you need a bag?" he asked, avoiding eye contact.

McCall dropped a five on the counter and waited for the kid to give him change. The clerk did so with haste, then held out his palm with a few coins. When McCall stood unmoving, the clerk put the change on the counter.

He picked up his items and change with controlled slowness, and walked out without saying a word.

He got in the SUV, pulled out, and accelerated to cruising speed up the highway. Then he chuckled with a smile and shook his head. He sucked in a breath and felt his face redden as shame washed through him.

He had just acted like his father in that gas station. Although his father probably would have taken it all the way and beat the kid with a can of soda until he admitted he was high and promised he'd never do it again. Then his father would have gotten hammered at the bar, and come home to his kids and his wife in an even darker mood.

McCall's face dropped as he reflected on that.

He vowed then and there that he'd take a portion of his money and open a center in Glenwood, or maybe in Carbondale. So all those kids fucked up on drugs with terrible parents could come talk with someone who would listen. To help them.

He continued north on Highway 82 until he reached the outskirts of Aspen. Shit, who was he kidding, he could afford to open a center in the heart of *Aspen*. He really needed to learn how to think bigger. Especially now. As he cruised down Main Street, spying the clean buildings, the huge houses in the surrounding hills, the best that money could buy all around him, he allowed himself to do just that—to think bigger.

A couple miles out of town the traffic thinned and he took a left on Juniper Hills Road. He made his way into and up the low plateau hills of orange, gray, and brown earth. There were multi-million-dollar houses on either side of the road, and juniper trees, sage brush, and blue-green grasses carpeted the hillsides. Even with the windows closed the scent of the surrounding foliage came strong through the vents of his SUV.

After a few miles of driving, he slowed and turned onto a dirt road. His truck vibrated and kicked up a plume of dust behind him as he drove for another half-mile, up and over a rise. He meandered down to a point where the road passed through a dry gulch, and there he parked and got out.

The low hills on either side of the gulch blocked the wind, which whipped against the junipers higher up the slopes. The sun was warming, but it would drop behind the hills in a matter of minutes. Insects buzzed everywhere and he heard the cry of a hawk flying stationary in the rushing air above.

He walked around the Explorer and opened the rear door; then he put on a set of rubber gloves. He carefully chose six plastic canisters and put them in his pocket. Then he shoved a black marker and the zip-lock bag into his jacket and closed the door. He grabbed the lighter fluid and napkins out of the front seat and went down the gulch for fifty yards, away from the view of the dirt road.

Kneeling down, he opened the zip-lock bag, set the bullet casing on the outside of the plastic, and opened the lighter fluid. He doused the casing with the pungent liquid and scrubbed it hard and thoroughly. Then he set it down to dry on a flat rock.

He opened each of the full canisters and threw the dirt into a pile, dug out a small pit, and set them, now empty, inside it. He took out of his pocket the three empties and scooped the pebbly dirt next to him into each. After screwing the lids on tight, he took out his marker, copied the labeling, and sealed them all.

The casing went back in the bag, and the new containers went in his pocket. Everything else went up in flames, lit by a hot-pink Bic lighter. He stepped back to watch the fireball, and threw the lighter in. It exploded with a dull thud and the flames spattered out of the hole, dissipating harmlessly on the sand.

CHAPTER 20

"So who's the guy?" Wolf asked.

Luke looked left and right and pulled back onto the highway.

"I asked you something."

"I know, I know. Listen, the guy is part of an investigation that we've had ongoing, and you just broke it open for us. It's something that I can't talk about." She kept her eyes on the road, and reached down to turn on her headlights.

"This is part of my ongoing investigation now." He stared at her. "My son was shot at more than ten times by these men, and I was hit. My son is currently in danger because of these men. He shot one of them. He can identify one of them."

She shook her head. "Listen, so can I. And I know that these men are going to be long gone by now."

Wolf frowned. "What the hell does that mean?"

"It means they're going to be on the run. There's a one

hundred percent chance of that. And we'll pick up the chase. And you can go about your business."

Wolf glared at her, and she squirmed in her seat, flicking sideways glances at him.

They passed an old pickup truck and then she looked back at Wolf with a pleading expression.

"Look, I can't tell you about it," she said. "I'm sorry, but if I want to keep my job, I can't tell you. It's a national-security matter. Just know that you've flushed them out. They were in hiding, and you've exposed them, and we'll take it from here."

Wolf turned away and shook his head. Rather than explode in a fit of cussing, which he felt like doing, he stared out the window at the passing landscape. The valley was now cast in shadow and the eastern peaks blazed bright in the early-evening sun. They passed a sign that read *Rocky Points 13 miles*. Pine trees grew denser, swishing by the window as they climbed in altitude up Williams Pass.

"How?" he asked, keeping his eyes out the window. "How are you going to chase them?"

"Don't worry about it," she answered quickly.

Wolf let the rush of anger evaporate, and ran through options in his mind as they summited Williams Pass and then dropped down the other side and into the southern end of Rocky Points. He had connections he could check with. None in the FBI, but others he could call on. Maybe he could track down the guy in the picture himself. But it was little to go on with just a neck tattoo and a burn.

A *burn*. The burn was fresh, and the guy wasn't burnt

in the picture Luke had sitting in her manila folder. That had to be a clue. Maybe he'd been hurt in an explosion or a fire recently. In a recent EOD training exercise on a nearby base? Fort Carson, in Colorado Springs?

As they pulled into Rocky Points and down Main Street, the sky was orange, and only the tips of the eastern peaks were still illuminated by the sinking sun.

The SUV crunched and wobbled as they pulled into the SCSD station lot, and the pain in Wolf's arm had returned with a vengeance, just as he'd predicted.

Luke parked and looked at Wolf. "I'll be in touch."

Wolf ignored her remark and got out, walked to the rear door of the Tahoe and pulled it open. He grabbed his orange pack and slung it over his shoulder, walked a few steps and tossed it toward the base of the wall next to the frosted-glass garage door.

Luke followed silently with the remaining two packs and set them down gingerly.

Wolf inserted his key in the side door, walked in, and shut it behind him.

CHAPTER 21

KRISTEN LUKE SPED out of Rocky Points in contemplative silence. Her pulse raced as she thought about what had happened to Wolf, and to his son. A tear spilled down her cheek and she wiped it with the back of her hand so quickly that it failed to reach her chin.

"Fucking fuck," she said through clenched teeth.

She took a deep breath, then a few more, and after a few minutes she had composed herself. Only then did she pick up her phone and dial.

"What d'ya got?" Michael Vance, her special agent in charge, never had liked greetings.

"Not much," Luke said. She could hear men talking in the background, and since the dashboard clock said it was after five o'clock, that meant he was probably at the bar.

"Really? It's not our guy? EOD tattoo? Colorado? Are you kidding me?"

She huffed into the phone. "Yeah. Believe me, you know I want it to be, but I don't think it's our guy. I don't think it was an EOD tattoo he saw. After I grilled him on it, he didn't seem too sure, then I showed him the picture—"

Luke squinted and looked into the rearview mirror. There were headlights approaching so fast it was like she was standing still. She looked down at her speedometer. She was going sixty-five miles per hour.

"Jesus," she said.

"What?"

"Nothing, just a second ..." She shook her head as the headlights got brighter and brighter, closer and closer. But they never passed. They just sucked up against her back bumper, now so close they were out of sight behind her tailgate.

"What the fuck? I'll call you back." She hung up and dropped the phone on the passenger seat, and then gripped the wheel with two hands. Her body hummed with electricity. She breathed deeply to control her movements, and relaxed her face to calm her thoughts, just like she'd learned from her sensei in college.

Was that what was going on? For a split instant, she was back at the University of Colorado—with hands groping her and slapping her face—and she strangled the life out of the steering wheel. Was this another psycho? Was this it? She'd spent the past ten years of her life preparing for another moment like this. Preparing to never, ever, be caught off guard again. Since then she'd trained in self-defense for thousands of hours. She was a second-degree black belt, an expert in Krav Maga. Quantico had elevated her shooting to the next level.

She tapped the brakes, and then pressed them continuously, slowing down a good twenty miles per hour.

The lights stayed glued behind her.

She eyed the road ahead and saw a shoulder pullout on the next turn. If this asshole wanted some, he could have some. She and her SIG Sauer P220 would be able to settle this just fine.

She reached into her coat and thumbed back the hammer, then put both hands on the wheel and slammed the brakes as hard as she could without locking the wheels. At the final instant, she pulled over and stopped on the shoulder turnoff.

The lights followed her every move, staying just behind her, as if the driver shared her every thought.

She jammed the car in park, whipped off her seatbelt, and opened the door. As she twisted out of the Tahoe, she reached back into her jacket and pulled the SIG. When her feet hit the pavement, she was aimed.

There was a figure already out of the door of the vehicle behind her, and the cab light illuminated a man with one hand up, and the other looking like it was tucked inside his waist.

"Freeze! Freeze!" she yelled, tensing her finger on the trigger. When the figure didn't move, she almost shot, almost put a bullet in the tall man's chest. But her peripheral vision took in the shape of the vehicle behind her and she comprehended who it was at the last instant. There were dark turret lights on top of the vehicle, and the man wasn't reaching into his waist—his arm was in a sling.

She dropped her aim. "What the hell are you doing? Are you kidding me?"

Wolf lowered his hand and slammed the door of his vehicle shut. She squinted against the bright headlamps, unable to see his face as his silhouetted figure crunched toward her with fast strides.

She raised the gun again. "Just stop! What are you doing?"

He continued, and now she noticed he was holding up a small square of paper in his free hand.

She stepped once to meet him halfway. Before she knew it she felt her pistol wrenched from her hand. There was a loud clank on the top of the Tahoe, and she realized Wolf had lobbed it up there.

Without an instant's hesitation, she launched into a flurry of punches. She glanced one jab off his cheek, but he easily blocked the next three quick shots. Suddenly the square piece of paper was shoved in her face, and that was all she could see.

"Look at this!" he yelled.

She was too shocked not to. It was a picture of a child, maybe ten years old. A boy kneeling next to a soccer ball, smiling with a hole where a front tooth used to be, with a long mess of black hair.

"Take a good look," he said, making sure his headlights shone on the picture. He continued in a softer voice. "Those men shot at my son. Were inches from killing him. Over and over, they shot at him. And I had to watch it, and hope to God they missed every time. I couldn't help him."

She shook her head and clenched her eyes. "I'm so—"

"Tell me!" he screamed so loud it hurt her ears. "Tell me about that man with the tattoo."

A pair of headlights illuminated them, and a car drove by slowly.

They stood staring at each other until the car disappeared into the distance.

Luke lifted her chin. "The man you saw on the trail has been assumed dead for seven months."

Wolf waited for her to continue.

"He went MIA in the mountains of Afghanistan. Seven months ago. And now you just saw him yesterday."

Wolf narrowed his eyes. "And he's back here in the US?"

Luke nodded. "Apparently."

"But there were four of them last night. Him, two shooting at us, and the guy I shot at the fire."

"His whole team went MIA. There was an explosion inside a cave, and they were believed to be inside."

"How many team members?" Wolf asked.

"Four. Him and three others."

Wolf stepped away and looked into the darkness.

"So I ask you, what do you think they're going to do? Come after you and your son? Why? Because you know they're alive, and you can identify them? If they do that they're going to run into a shitload of FBI agents. Because we're on their asses now. They're going to run. They were coming after you last night because you saw them. But it's too late now and they know it."

Wolf turned back toward her, but kept his eyes on the ground.

"And we're going to catch them," she said. "So you can go about your business as usual, and not worry about it. You have plenty of things on your plate. What, a music festival in two days?" She softened her voice. "I understand where you're coming from. You're worried about your son. But please don't worry. We're on it."

Wolf looked her in the eye.

Her chest tightened under his intense glare, feeling like she'd just been hit with twin spotlights. His eyes were like knotted dark wood, glowing in the headlights of his SUV. His body was tall and strong. His hair was a thick chestnut-colored mess. He had a handsome face covered with a two-day beard that was thick and perfectly symmetrical. *Dangerous as hell.*

Then there was the way he'd taken her gun. One-handed. Or, if he'd used his other hand, she didn't know how he'd done it. Suddenly, this small county sheriff from small-town, nowhere, Colorado, was a much larger presence to her.

She looked away, realizing her thoughts had to have been showing on her face. "All right," she said, standing on her toes to look at the roof. "Now, get me my gun."

Wolf walked to the rear and stepped on the back bumper, sagging the Tahoe down, and pulled it off.

He handed it to her without saying a word, got back in his SUV, backed up, turned around, and drove away.

She watched his taillights recede and then disappear behind the pines, and listened to his revving engine fade into nothing.

"Goddamn it," she said, and got back in the Tahoe.

CHAPTER 22

WOLF LOOKED at the ticking football-clock on the wall, and at the phone sitting on his office desk. He contemplated making the call, and wondered whether or not the man on the other end would be at his desk. It was just after eight o'clock p.m. Colorado time, seven o'clock Pacific. And General Haines was the type of man to get to work early and stay late.

Wolf dialed the phone, and a few seconds later a woman's voice answered. "General Haines's office."

"General Haines, please."

"He's currently not available, sir. Can I take a message?"

"Tell him David Wolf is calling."

"I'll tell him you called."

"I'd prefer if you told him I'm calling. You know, put me on hold and tell him."

She chuckled softly. "I'll tell him you called. Can I take your number?"

Wolf gave it to her and hung up. He'd run out of ideas already. There were a couple of other people he could call, but they'd probably be off killing people in a foreign country at the moment.

He sat staring at the puddle of light on his desk, and the phone rang, splitting the silence.

"Sheriff Wolf," he answered.

"Are you the one crank-calling my secretary?"

Wolf smiled. "Hello, General. How are you?"

"I'm doing well. You caught me just in time. I was about out the door for a drink."

Wolf looked at the ceiling. "Let's see. Wednesday night. That's Popeye's, isn't it?"

"You remembered."

Haines broke into a loud laugh that made Wolf smile as wide as he could. It was a laugh that had probably helped hoist the man up the ranks over the years, from a lowly first lieutenant when Wolf had met him to the lieutenant general he was now.

"What the hell are you up to, son? I hear you're still working law enforcement. Still in your home town? Rocky Flats? Or what was it?"

Wolf smiled. "Rocky Points." Haines had a mind like a steel trap, and wouldn't have mistaken the name of Wolf's town for the now defunct nuclear-weapons production facility in between Boulder and Denver without a tongue in his cheek. "I'm actually sheriff now."

Haines whistled. "Wow. You're not even forty years old yet, by my calculations. That's gotta be a pretty big deal."

Wolf didn't answer.

"Then again, you were always a pretty big deal."

"Thank you, General."

There was a long pregnant silence. He hadn't spoken to the LTG in years, and the last time they'd spoken was in person—in a bar near Ft. Lewis, south of Tacoma, Washington, where Haines had spilled his guts to Wolf about how he'd always thought Wolf was one of the good ones. One of the best ones he'd wished he could have held on to.

"So what do you want?"

Haines had never been one for rehashing old memories.

"I need to know the identity of a few missing soldiers. Army EOD. Four total. They went missing in Afghanistan, supposedly seven months ago."

Haines sighed. "Oh. My drink is going to have to wait, huh?"

"It would only take you a few minutes to log into the database and check, right?"

There was another pause. Wolf knew the man was computer inept.

"Just a second," he said, and there was the rustle of a hand being pressed over the phone, and muffled conversation. "I've got Angie checking it out. It should take less than a few minutes. She's incredible with these computers."

Wolf smiled again and leaned back in his chair. The blood moved in his shoulder and his wound throbbed.

"Brian Richter. EOD team leader. Chad Hartley ..."

Wolf scrambled for his pen and paper and started writing.

"... Wade Jeffries. Marcus Quinn. There's your four. Went MIA October 30th, last year in an explosion in Tora Bora."

"You're kidding," Wolf said.

Tora Bora was a cave system in the White Mountains of Afghanistan that Wolf knew well. Though the rangers had not been present at the battle, Wolf and his company had kept up with the news, waiting on orders to assist that ultimately never came from the brass.

Back then, Tora Bora had been described by the Western media as an impregnable fortress, rumored to have over two thousand troops housed in an elaborate tunnel system, with underground roads large enough to drive tanks through, a fully operating hospital, ventilation systems, ammunition stores, even a hotel. And, of course, Osama bin Laden.

What allied forces had found was completely different. Though they knew bin Laden had been there, in the end he'd slipped away, and the infrastructure they found was less than earlier described by the media. Rather than an elaborate feat of engineering, they'd found a system of limestone caves naturally carved out by water over the millennia, a couple of hundred cold and hungry troops, and a few haphazard piles of ammunition.

"What were those guys doing in Tora Bora? Weren't we completely withdrawn from that area years ago, after the battle?" Wolf asked.

General Haines didn't answer for a beat. "Yeah, I

admit that these men being there is ... strange."

Wolf let the silence hang for a beat, then asked, "Can you send me the files of these men?"

"And leave a paper trail leaking out of my office to a no-good deputy in the middle of nowhere, Colorado? I think not, Sergeant."

"Technically, it would be a digital trail. And that's sheriff now, sir."

"Not to me," Haines answered.

Wolf doodled on the corner of his paper. "Okay. How about just where these guys are from, and I'll do my own dirty work from there."

There was another muffling of the phone, and a minute later Haines came back.

"Jeffries was from Delta, Colorado. Hartley from Boise, Idaho. Quinn, Reno. Richter, Glenwood Springs, Colorado."

"Glenwood Springs," Wolf said as he wrote.

"That close to you?"

"It is." Wolf set down his pen. "I appreciate your help, sir."

"Anytime, Sergeant. You know I'm here for you anytime. I was sorry to hear about your brother last year."

"Thank you, General. When you retire you'll have to come over to Colorado. I'll take you fishing."

"Sounds like a damn good plan."

They hung up and Wolf looked at his notes. He stood and opened his office door and stepped out. The squad-room windows were darkened, but the room itself was ablaze with fluorescent lights humming overhead.

Deputies Rachette, Patterson, and Wilson were sitting on the edges of desks laughing at Jack, who was standing in the middle of them and telling a story.

"Jack," Wolf said. "Let my deputies work."

They all stopped and looked at Wolf.

"Rachette, how're the festival grounds looking?"

"Good. Everything's getting set up. We've got the parking lot cordoned off, entrances and exits as planned. Perimeter lighting is set, which we're going to check out tonight. We worked with Jen Beasley all day, and she's saying everything is looking good."

"All right. Otherwise, all quiet?" Wolf gave a quick glance toward Jack.

Rachette caught Wolf's meaning. "Yeah, all quiet. Nothing suspicious as far as we could tell. Jack helped us out all day ... well, he helped Patterson out all day. I think Jack has a new girlfriend."

Jack turned red and glared at Rachette. "Tsss," he said in retaliation.

They all smiled as Jack shrunk away to look at a piece of paper on Wilson's desk.

"You going home?" Rachette asked.

"I don't know." Wolf had been thinking about that. Ever since half his house had gone up in a ball of flame last fall, it had transformed from a disaster site, buttoned up under plastic through the cold months, to a slowly progressing construction site. He had a small section of the house he'd been using as a sort of indoor camping spot, and to bring Jack in there was borderline child abuse. Even if that weren't the case, Wolf's house wouldn't do for safety. Not until any and all danger was eliminated.

That meant Sarah's parents' house, where Jack had been staying exclusively for the past few months, was not a good option either. Wolf wasn't prepared to spread the potential vulnerability to other family members.

Wolf reached down and plucked the sketch the Glenwood Springs artist had done with Jack off the top of Wilson's desk.

"Sorry I couldn't do better, Dad," Jack said, watching Wolf.

Wolf looked at the sketch. Nothing stood out. The hair was covered by a winter cap, the eyebrows neither dark nor light, thick nor thin. The face was square with colorless almond-shaped eyes, with flat lines for lips. It was a plain, nondescript representation of a Caucasian male.

Wolf set it down and shrugged. "Like the Garfield County sheriff said, you were firing a pistol at the guy, in a high-stress situation, at night. I doubt an experienced police officer could do any better."

Jack looked down at the carpet. "I still bet I would recognize him if I saw him, though."

And that was the problem, Wolf thought. He looked at Jack and sighed. "How do you feel about doing another night of camping?"

"Where?"

"Here."

Jack shrugged and smiled. "Sure? What do you mean?"

"We'll sleep in my office," Wolf said.

"What? No, you guys can stay with me," Rachette said.

"In the butt-hut?" Wolf asked. "No thanks."

Rachette's face turned crimson.

Patterson eyed Rachette and cracked a smile. "The butt-hut?"

Wilson rocked back in his chair and howled with laughter.

"But I appreciate it," Wolf said. "We'll be comfortable here. We've got showers, and we have all our camping gear. Rachette, you'll be in charge of the volunteer orientation tomorrow."

Rachette glared at Wilson for a beat and stood up straight. "You got it. There's eight of them coming, total, right?"

Wolf nodded. "Three from Vail, three from the Summit, and two from Glenwood."

Wilson looked at Patterson. "That's three from Vail PD, three from Summit County SD, and two from Glenwood Springs PD."

"Got it," Patterson pulled a stray strand of hair behind her ear. "Thanks."

"She's from Aspen, dude," Rachette said. "She knows what we're talking about." He ignored Wilson's glare and turned to Wolf. "Aren't you going to be there tomorrow?"

"No, I'll be gone in the morning. And I'd like it if you guys took Jack again."

Rachette shifted and glanced back at Patterson. "Wilson and Baine are going to be there, too. Right?"

Wolf looked at Rachette. "Not tomorrow, not for setup. You'll have thirteen deputies and officers at the festival grounds for a time tomorrow. No sense stacking it anymore. We've gotta have a patrol in town, too, until Friday night."

Rachette nodded, unable to hide the disappointment in his eyes that he was stuck with the rookie once again, and, by the looks of it, Patterson read his expression easily enough.

Wolf took a deep breath and looked at Patterson. "Patterson, your father."

She raised her eyebrows. "Yeah?"

"He's an entertainment lawyer, right?"

She nodded. "Yes."

"Kind of a big deal, right? He's worked with some celebrities in his time?"

She hesitated. "Yeah, I guess so."

"So you've met some of those celebrities, right?" he asked.

Rachette sat back on the edge of Wilson's desk and watched Patterson.

"Ye-es?" Patterson tilted her head.

"So like, Kevin Costner, he's up there in Aspen sometimes?"

She nodded, and Rachette raised his eyebrows.

"Tom Cruise?" Wolf asked.

Patterson nodded again.

"TC?" Rachette shifted, knocking over the cup of pens on Wilson's desk. "Shit, sorry. You've met TC?"

She eyed Rachette. "TC? Yeah, I've met Tom Cruise. I didn't know he went by ..."

Wolf walked with Jack to his office and shut the door. His work was done for the day.

CHAPTER 23

"SOUTH, CHECK."

"West, check," Wolf responds.

"North, check."

"East, check."

Wolf is sweating even harder now. There is a pull on his left shoulder, and a dull ache. It must be that an insect bit him inside his ACU.

He ignores the pain and turns to the right. There is movement outside the jungle wall, and he walks toward it.

"I've got movement on the west jungle wall. It's a kid," Wolf says into his throat mike.

Wolf fights to wade through the long grass, like the blades are wrapping his legs. Like he's wading through tar.

He sees that the kid is carrying an orange backpack, about half his size, and he has something in his hand.

Wolf realizes what he must do, and he raises his rifle.

The kid looks straight at Wolf, and Wolf can see him clearly behind the crosshairs in his scope lens.

It's Jack.

...

Wolf sucked in a breath and sat up, and then rolled onto his right elbow, clenching his teeth to fight the throbbing in his left arm. His entire upper body was drenched in sweat, and the nylon sleeping bag underneath him was cold and wet.

Jack stirred next to him, rolling away from the racket Wolf was causing.

A thin sliver of dim light peeked from under the closed wooden blinds of his office, and a bird was calling incessantly somewhere outside.

He checked his watch—5:20 a.m. He climbed out of his sleeping bag, put on jeans, gray T-shirt and Carhartt hooded sweatshirt, and padded down to the locker room.

The bandage on his arm was soaked in blood, so he unwrapped it and carefully peeled off the final stretch of sticking gauze. Underneath were thirty-six crosshatches of dark-blue stitches, with pieces of stiff thread jutting out in places. The skin surrounding the wound was such a dark blue it was almost black, and it faded outward to a sickly yellow, and finally to his normal olivine skin color.

He cleaned the wound vigorously with soap and warm water, and re-wrapped it, then took a shower, being careful to keep it relatively dry. In the shower he winced as he stretched his arm out in front of him, then to the side and down, and then up again, and decided he wouldn't use the sling for the day but would take it along just in case.

When he was washed and ready, he quietly packed his sleeping bag, letting Jack sleep off his exhaustion from the previous days' events, and walked out into the squad room.

It smelled like fresh doughnuts, undoubtedly brought by Tammy, and coffee. He gratefully took some of each and headed out to his Explorer. There he checked in with Rachette, who was pulling into the lot, and then drove out of town to the south.

He climbed Williams Pass, avoiding deer milling alongside the highway on the Rocky Points side and a herd of elk that wandered across the road on the other side. He crossed to the west on County Road 31, and then started north on Highway 82.

He drove through the posh town of Aspen, through Basalt, and north through Carbondale. Finally, an hour and fifteen minutes after he'd left Rocky Points, he entered the city of Glenwood Springs.

The red sandstone hills surrounding the town were verdant with junipers, low shrubs and grasses.

Wolf continued onward to the north edge of town and passed over I-70, where steam billowed onto the roaring interstate from the hot-springs pools that made the town famous. He turned onto a frontage road, and entered the parking lot of the Glenwood Springs FBI field office.

It was a nondescript building, looking like any modern commercial office building one might see in any part of the US. There was no sign for the FBI on the Plexiglas box sign on the front lawn, only what looked to be some law firms and an insurance company.

He walked in, went up the stairs, down the carpeted

hall, and through the glass doors of the FBI suite. A large half-moon desk waited inside, and a receptionist in a red dress looked at him over her eyeglasses, and then continued to pound her keyboard. Her phone rang and she turned away from Wolf to answer it.

Wolf waited patiently, and watched men and women walk past an open doorway, into what seemed to be their equivalent of the SCSD's squad room. They were all dressed in slacks and button-up shirts, wearing paddle holsters with SIG Sauers or Glocks. Some carried coffee, and a few laughed and conversed loudly.

Then he saw Luke. She was walking straight toward the doorway, looking in an empty coffee travel mug. She swerved between desks with swaying hips, walking with a spring in her step. Her straight brown hair was down, looking more auburn today than he remembered. She wore black slacks that fit her perfectly, and a slim-fitting suit jacket that was splayed open, showcasing a white blouse that cracked open to show tan skin beneath.

She stopped abruptly when she saw him, sending her hair tumbling across her face. There was a flash of surprise in her eyes, and then they narrowed.

"Can I help you, sir?" the receptionist asked.

Wolf turned to the receptionist, who was scrutinizing Wolf with a critical eye. Wolf was dressed casually, probably too casually, with his old jeans, gray T-shirt, and hooded sweatshirt, and he didn't blame the woman for being suspicious of his intentions.

"I'm Sheriff David Wolf, of Sluice County."

"Sheriff Wolf," Luke walked fast out of the doorway.

"No sling today? You're a fast healer." She held out her hand and Wolf shook it.

"Thanks, Gwen. I'll ... talk to the sheriff." Luke held a hand toward the door he'd just entered from and began walking.

Wolf watched her. "Don't you want to go inside?"

She shook her head and opened the door, then waved out to the hall and looked at him.

Wolf walked past her, catching her familiar scent.

She walked next to him, keeping her eyes on the gray carpet ahead. "What are you doing here?" she asked.

"I was just stopping by to let you know how my investigation was going, and to see if you wanted in."

She gave him a look like he'd just belched. "Really? And how's your investigation going?"

"I found out who the four missing men were in Tora Bora. I'm just stopping by on my way to Brian Richter's family's house, and then I'm off to Delta to talk to Jeffries's family."

She stopped and closed her long eyelashes, then tilted her head to the asbestos tiles of the ceiling. "Let me get my stuff. I'll meet you outside." She turned and walked quickly down the hall.

Wolf walked to the stairs and went outside. He stood by his SCSD Explorer and took in the sun. There were some approaching clouds in the west. The wind that had kicked up so fierce the day before must have brought in a cold front, but for the time being it was gorgeous.

She came out and walked straight to Wolf, then looked past him into his driver's side window.

"I'm not going in that," she said, and then walked away down the parking lot.

Wolf looked through his window at the passenger seat. It had a few wadded-up napkins on it and some multi-colored sprinkles from the doughnut he'd eaten earlier. The two cup-holders had four coffee cups stacked one within another. He didn't need to look at the floorboards to know she had a point.

He locked his SUV and walked after her, then hopped in her already-running Tahoe. She backed up and they headed out onto the frontage road.

Wolf sat quietly with growing interest as she drove through town and took three turns without consulting notes or a map.

"You know where Richter grew up?"

"I grew up here," she shrugged. "And I looked up the house on Google Maps earlier today."

Wolf nodded. "All right. So you were planning to see his mother today?"

"That was the idea," she said.

"I found out that Richter had a sister, too. Lives in Chicago."

She nodded like it was old news.

"And Richter's brother?" Wolf asked.

She looked at Wolf and narrowed her eyes. "What about him?"

"He's Garfield County Sheriff's Department. Were you going to talk to him?" Wolf asked.

She looked at him like he'd just spoken a foreign language.

"What?" Wolf asked.

"We can't talk to him."

"And why is that?"

"I checked in on him this morning, and he's in Rocky Points today, helping out the Sluice County Sheriff's Office with their music festival."

"Oh," Wolf said.

CHAPTER 24

SERGEANT MCCALL PULLED into the parking lot of the Mountain Goat Bar and Grill, and parked facing Grand Avenue, the main thoroughfare through the old part of Glenwood Springs.

He sat watching out his window as citizens drove by, and then jammed their brakes with wide eyeballs as they noticed him in his Sheriff's Department SUV. After a few minutes of the entertainment, he stepped out into the cool air. The clouds had rolled in, and it was going to get chilly. Even colder up in the mountains.

He looked at the Mountain Goat, a squat, red-brick building with tastefully carved wood trim, and felt a surge of pride.

The Mountain Goat Bar and Grill had been Sergeant McCall's establishment for thirteen years now, ever since he'd sold his controlling share of his drug-trafficking business for a quarter-million to a man he simply knew as Dragon.

On paper, he had nothing to do with the place. It was owned by a corporation, whose sole member was his kid brother, and he was a silent partner. McCall's name didn't show up anywhere, but there was no dispute between him and his brother about who owned the place.

There were never any disputes between him and his brother. Their bond was forged by blood and was unbreakable.

Forged by blood. McCall thought about what was happening now, and how far he'd come. How far *they'd* come. And how close they were to a better life.

It had been thirteen years ago, when he was twenty-three, when he'd made his money with drugs and decided to become a cop to hedge his various interests. But ten years before that, at only thirteen years old, he'd been forced to become the man he was now—a man who did what it took to survive.

His father, a respected officer on the Carbondale police force, had been the one who'd made sure of that. Six days a week, his father would come home after dark, too much liquor in his system, and step into the house, enraged by something real or imagined and itching to make someone pay. It had taken every ounce of his and his brother's wit and strength they had to survive.

Night after night after night the rotation was predictable. First, his mother would take the beatings. And then his father would come after him, and then his little brother. If that didn't satisfy the old man, he would give the furniture or the walls a once-over. Then, if they were lucky, he would go to sleep.

Tuesdays were the worst, because Monday had been his father's day of rest. On Mondays, his father would break down crying, apologizing for being such a terrible father. Monday was the day he'd make promises, and give out hugs instead of forearm swings. But Tuesday ... that was the dangerous day, because he'd shown his remorse the day before, and let you see his true feelings and his pain, and *you were laughing at him now. Weren't you?*

And then they got it.

Well, McCall thought as he inserted the key into the back door of the Mountain Goat, he'd given it to his father in the end. He'd flattened his head with a baseball bat, and they didn't have to worry about him anymore. The past couldn't be changed, and he needed to let it lie, just like his father's body lay under a pile of rocks near the Snowmass quarry.

McCall shook his head and knew there was no way that was going to happen. He would never let it lie—just forget it and move on. Because his past was who he was. Drove everything he did. Was the reason he'd become a deputy, and was the reason he still had his finger on the pulse of the drug trade through this valley to this day. He survived. He did whatever it took to survive, and he wasn't going to forget it. And they were going to survive this little fiasco too.

"About fucking time," his brother Tyler said, making no move to get up from his lying position on the couch.

McCall appraised him as he stepped inside the office at the back of the bar and closed the door.

His brother looked bad. He was still lying on the tweed

office couch looking at McCall with pinpoint pupils. His skin was pale and slick with moisture, and his brown hair was dark and shiny from sweat.

McCall dug in his pocket and passed him a bottle of pills. It bounced with a rattle and rested on his stomach.

"Percocet. Take a couple."

Tyler sat up and put the bottle between his kneecaps, then tried to unscrew the cap with his good arm.

"Here, sorry." McCall grabbed the bottle, unscrewed it, and gave him two pills. "Just a second." He walked back out into the lifeless bar, filled a glass of water behind the horseshoe counter, and went back into the office.

Tyler threw two pills onto his tongue and sucked down the entire glass of water.

McCall went and refilled the glass, picked up the bag of first-aid supplies, and then sat next to his little brother and redressed the wound on his shoulder.

It looked clean. The doctor they'd used yesterday morning knew what he was doing. For three thousand cash, he'd better had. The through-and-through bullet wound wasn't deep, but it was deep enough if you were the one with a hole in the arm. He felt for him.

"You want a beer or something?" McCall asked.

Tyler broke a smile. "What is it, nine a.m.? No, thanks."

McCall looked at the cardboard box on the floor. It was a laser printer, top of the line. He got up and picked up the packet of plastic sheets, the kind you put on an overhead projector.

"Wood glue?" McCall asked.

"Yep. In the plastic bag on the desk."

McCall sifted through the bag and saw that he'd gotten another packet of plastic sheets as well. He twirled the mouse on the computer, and watched as the screen flicked on. Then he took the USB drive out of his pocket and put it in the port on the side of the monitor.

He opened the finder window and double-clicked the file. A multi-celled window appeared, with a man's picture, vital statistics, and digital pictures of his fingerprints.

"Here you go," McCall said, and got out of the desk chair.

Tyler closed his eyes and nodded, then took a deep breath and stood up.

"No time for healing, I'm afraid," McCall said.

"I know. I'm not bitchin' about it."

"I know you're not." He watched his brother collapse down behind the computer and grab the mouse.

"So you went back up with them yesterday?" Tyler asked.

"Yep."

"And did they figure out where he came from?"

"No, not yet, but they will. So I need to head up there ASAP."

"Who's *they*?" Tyler asked.

"So far, *they* are the FBI agent, Luke, and Wolf."

Tyler stared at the wall for a second, like he was re-calculating the outcome of their plan. "All right, set that thing up, and I'll start printing."

McCall bent down and cut open the box with a key.

"After this, then what?" Tyler asked.

"Then we have two more people to get rid of."

"How? Where?"

McCall pulled out the laser printer, and began explaining the plan.

CHAPTER 25

THEY STOPPED on the side of the road in front of Brian Richter's house, and Wolf stepped out of Luke's truck and followed her lead to the front door.

Brian Richter's house, or rather the house Brian Richter grew up in, was an early 1900s design on the outskirts of town, now occupied by his mother, Bernadette Richter. According to Wolf's research into public records, Richter's father had quitclaimed the house to Bernadette fifteen years ago. Wolf assumed that meant the father was out of the picture.

Perhaps somehow that fatherly absence contributed to Brian Richter's motivation to join one of the most dangerous divisions in the army, playing with explosives day in and day out.

The house was a square with an A-frame roof, and a set of stairs in the dead center of the property that ran up to the wrap-around covered wooden porch. There were a few flowerpots sprouting green plants, a wind chime made of brass tubes, and a porch swing held up by chains red with rust. The trim was blood red, and the house was painted white.

Luke rang the bell, and a minute later they heard faint footsteps and the clicking of locks from within.

An old lady peeked out—one eye, then two—then she slowly pulled open the door, revealing a happy smile that was bright with enthusiasm. She wore a flowery nightgown and slippers.

"Hello," she said. "It's you again."

"H-hi," Luke said, and held up her ID card. "I am Special Agent Luke, of the FBI, ma'am."

"Oh, the FBI," Bernadette Richter said with awe.

"And this is Sheriff Wolf of the Sluice County Sheriff's Department."

Wolf nodded. "Hello ma'am."

"We'd like to ask you a few questions about your son, if you don't mind."

Mrs. Richter looked at Luke like she was waiting for her to say something more.

"Do you mind if we come in and ask you some questions?" Wolf tried.

"Ah. Yes, come in." Mrs. Richter stepped aside and opened the door.

There was a stairway that led upstairs on the right, a family room on the left, and a kitchen straight ahead that was bright and airy. The old wood floors shone in the morning light that streamed in from the kitchen ahead, and it smelled like pine cleaner.

The place was immaculately clean, except for a lone

bowl full of what looked to be soggy cornflakes on the kitchen table. There were small piles of the cereal surrounding it, and an open gallon of milk. The box lay on its side on the otherwise immaculately clean kitchen counter a few feet away.

"Come in. I was just having some breakfast. Do you need some?"

Luke and Wolf looked at each other.

"No. No, thank you," said Luke.

Mrs. Richter continued into the kitchen and stared at the table, then looked back at them and flinched, as if they were strangers who'd just snuck up on her.

"Uh, do you mind if we sit down here, and talk about your son, Mrs. Richter?" Luke asked quickly.

Mrs. Richter's face relaxed and she led them to the family room.

Wolf took a look around. There were old paintings of mountains, and black-and-white photos of long-gone relatives. There was crochet art on the walls with various flower patterns of green, brown, yellow, and red, but no recent photographs of the immediate family.

He stopped and ran his finger along the wall at a spot that was discolored. It looked like a painting had hung there for years, but had recently been moved, and a square of dirt still remained.

Luke sat down next to Mrs. Richter and looked up at Wolf.

Wolf took a seat in a wood-framed chair with a cloth cushion near the front window. There were lacy drapes clouding an otherwise great view of the red mountains in the distance.

"Have you talked to your son lately, Mrs. Richter?" Luke asked.

She smiled. "Oh, yes. I talk to him all the time."

Luke looked at Wolf. "I'm talking about Brian. Your son, Brian? Have you seen him?"

She nodded and didn't blink. "I saw him today. He came over, and he mowed the lawn."

Wolf pulled the drapes open with a finger, and saw that the lawn was freshly mowed, probably within the last day.

"And I saw you, too." She nodded her head at Luke with wide eyes so filled with wonder that she reminded Wolf of a little girl. Then she looked over at Wolf and scrunched her face in confusion. "Did I see you? You were here, right?"

Wolf shook his head. "No, I wasn't here."

They sat in silence for a moment, and Wolf racked his brain for something he could ask a senile woman that might help their investigation.

"How about your husband?" he asked. "Is he nearby?"

"He'll be back when the war is through," she said with a serious expression.

Wolf nodded. "Is he in the Middle East?"

She frowned. "Vietnam."

Wolf stood and took her hand. "Thank you. Do you mind if I look upstairs?"

She smiled. "Go ahead." She looked over at Luke. "You can go see her room."

Luke blushed. "Thank you, Mrs. Richter. I think I'll go up with him and see that."

Wolf walked upstairs and Luke followed closely.

When they reached the top, Luke sighed. "Jesus. She doesn't know where or when she is. Or who apparently."

The wood squeaked underneath Wolf's work boots as he walked down the hall, and Luke padded lightly behind.

There were three doors in the main hallway upstairs, all wide open. They went to the first on the right and walked in. The walls were pink, and on one of them hung a mirror and an impressionist painting of a meadow full of flowers. There was a single bed in the corner, made up with sheets and a comforter.

The dresser was empty and had nothing on top of it.

They moved to the next room—there were two single beds within, but the room was just as barren in terms of décor.

The third room had a queen-sized bed, and a standing-length mirror on a swivel stand. Again, there were no pictures in sight.

"It doesn't make any sense," Wolf said.

"What?"

"The house. It's so well maintained, so clean. But it's like it's cleaned out, too. No pictures. Nothing personal."

She frowned and nodded. "Yeah. There aren't many family portraits."

"There aren't any family portraits. None."

"Yeah ..." Luke let her voice trail off and she went to the window and looked out. "The lawn is freshly mown.

Probably her son, the deputy in the Sheriff's Department, comes and mows it."

"You know the brother in the department?"

"Dan Richter. I've heard of him, and his picture looked familiar. I think I've met him before on an investigation, maybe when I was at the Sheriff's Department headquarters in town. But I never knew him growing up or anything."

She turned and looked at Wolf with raised eyebrows. "Well? Ready for a drive to Delta?"

Wolf looked around the barren room one more time, and nodded.

Wolf and Luke said goodbye to the old woman and got back in the Tahoe. As they drove away, Bernadette Richter waved with a bright smile.

They both waved and didn't speak for the next few miles.

CHAPTER 26

THEY STOPPED at a gas station and Luke gassed up the Tahoe, got some sodas, and headed out west on I-70.

She drove cautiously at a consistent five miles per hour over the speed limit, which put them at a steady eighty miles per hour.

Wolf watched her fiddle with the dial of her radio and smiled.

"What?" she asked.

"I was just thinking about the first time I got in this vehicle. And how my ears are still ringing."

She laughed and then shrugged. "I like my funk."

"Loud," he added.

"Yes. Loud."

They drove in silence. It was a tense silence, and it seemed that all the moments had been between them since they'd met. She was reluctant to work with him, and, as Wolf figured it, that could only mean one thing—that she was hiding something. So until she wanted to open up, the tense silence could stay. And he needed to remember that his job—to make sure his son was out of danger—was much more important than camaraderie with a beautiful FBI agent.

That's what the dream had told him, wasn't it? He could sense it. Jack was in danger. Wolf took a deep breath. *The dream.* Wolf couldn't remember having had that dream in at least ten years, and now he'd had it twice. It was a dream he'd moved on from. A memory. One that'd driven him away from serving his country and pushed him home to Rocky Points. To serve his son, Jack, and his wife, Sarah. And to serve his hometown, rather than some larger ideal that meant he killed little boys for a living.

Of course, life with Sarah hadn't worked out, had it? He'd failed there. Didn't have Sarah to call his wife anymore. She was off loving another man, one who apparently understood her pain better than Wolf ever could. That was a loss he didn't like—not one bit—but it was something he could live with. Could move on from, no matter how difficult.

But Jack? He still had Jack.

"You okay?" Luke asked.

Wolf turned and relaxed his jaw, not realizing he'd been clenching his molars. "Yeah."

He turned to look back out the window.

"So." She took a sip of her Coke and set it back in the center console. "Army ranger, huh? Why didn't you stay in the army?"

Wolf gave her an ironic smile and didn't answer.

"Ah. Okay, how about ..." She let her question fade.

"How about you tell me what you're hiding?" Wolf asked. "Until then, let's just forget the small talk."

She swallowed. "What are you talking about?"

Wolf nodded and kept his gaze on the passing sedimentary layers of the mountains.

"I'm hiding your involvement in our case from my boss. That's what I'm hiding," she said quietly.

Wolf didn't reply.

"I could be out of a job for bringing in un-approved outside consultants on this," she said.

Wolf stayed silent for a moment. "How about the other two guys that went MIA? Quinn and Hartley? Hartley is from Boise, and Quinn is from Reno. Have you looked into them?"

Luke nodded. "I've got calls in to the nearest field offices, and boots are on the ground, going to talk to the families."

"Right now? Today?"

She nodded.

"So how long have you guys been on this case?" Wolf asked.

Luke hesitated. "Why?"

"I'm just wondering why all this is happening now. Haven't you already talked to Jeffries's family in Delta? Haven't you already talked to our friend Mrs. Richter? She was right in Glenwood Springs; all you had to do was go down the street to talk to her." Wolf looked at her. "So? Had you already been to her house? Have you already been to Delta to talk to the Jeffrieses?"

"Why do you think we would have already talked to

them?" she asked.

"You had a picture of Jeffries with you yesterday." Wolf took a sip of his soda and watched Luke. She kept her eyes on the road. "I've just been assuming my description raised a flag with you guys," he said, "like it was an ongoing investigation."

Luke's eyes narrowed, and she took a breath before answering. "It was, but we didn't know these guys were back. We knew they were missing in Afghanistan, and your description tipped us off that it was one of them, and that they're now in the country."

"From my description"—Wolf looked at her—"you figured out it was one of the four missing men? Not one of the other hundreds of thousands of soldiers either enlisted, or on leave, or once enlisted?"

She nodded. "Well, there was the neck tattoo."

"But that's not enough to single the guy out, is it? There's gotta be thousands of guys with neck tattoos. It's only recently they've starting cracking down on that in the military."

She held up a hand. "Fewer than you think, and it's a little more complicated than that. Your description raised our flags because of some ... recent developments I can't talk about."

"So, like I said, let's cut the small talk until you want to explain. Until then, I have an investigation I'm working here, and you're just inking it up for me with your bullshit."

She looked back to the road, he to the passing hills, and the tense silence returned.

CHAPTER 27

RACHETTE LOOKED up the grassy ski slope and cringed at the speed of a mountain biker rolling down the dirt trail above. Nothing was more gut wrenching to Rachette than to see a person disregard his own safety like the maniac kid flying down the narrow path. It was why he stuck to enjoying the mountains on his two feet, rather than on bicycles, or skis, or a snowboard. He'd even seen a kid strap his feet into an off-road skateboard, with four thick rubber wheels, and no brakes. Maybe it was the lack of oxygen that caused such moronic behavior in the population of the mountains. Maybe they needed a few days on a farm in Nebraska.

An instant later, the biker flipped over his handlebars, and rolled to a motionless stop. Rachette sucked in a breath and brought his radio to his lips, and then watched with hawk eyes as a group of bikers on the trail went over to assess the damage. The kid got up from the ground, dusted himself off, and smiled at his friends.

Rachette shook his head and turned around to survey the festival grounds below. Restaurants with tall windows glared in the morning sun. Two ski-lift terminals turned, and people—hikers and morons alike—swung gently on the chairs on their way up.

In between the two lifts, the stage for the first annual Rocky Points Music Festival looked completely set up, but a swarm of men still hammered and screwed boards, rods, and screws into place. Some of the men were high on the rafters, hanging lights, and others were on the ground, pulling cable; others pretended to look busy, and still others just stood around looking like a waste of taxpayers' money.

Rachette sighed when he saw Patterson, fitting her into the latter group of people he'd been observing. She was talking to a man who had a hammer in his hand, and she had Jack and the man enthralled by a story. She was laughing and talking, and Jack was laughing and talking, and then the guy was laughing and talking.

This new girl was throwing a big wrench in the cogs of the machine that was the Sluice County Sheriff's Department. He couldn't put his finger on it, but he was just put off by her. *She was too ...* He couldn't figure out what her problem was quite yet. Too proper? Too comfortable? Too cocky? *Too cute?*

A cruiser came into view in the far distance off to the right, followed by another, and another. Rachette stepped toward the parking lot. One of them was unmistakably a Vail PD cruiser— a jet-black, shiny new Saab with the Vail PD logo on it. Another was a Ford SUV with the Garfield

Sheriff's Department logo, and the last vehicle was a Chevy SUV from Summit County.

Patterson, despite her distance away, clearly saw the commotion and ran with Jack toward him.

"Finally showing up?" Patterson said breathlessly, meeting him halfway to the parking lot.

Rachette didn't bother answering the rhetorical, and flawed, question. First of all, they weren't *finally* showing up, they were showing up exactly on time. Since they had all been staying at the Edelweiss the night before, and would be for the next two nights, it looked like they'd followed each other here in train-like fashion.

Patterson made a face at Jack that Rachette couldn't see, but Jack smiled wide and then looked at Rachette.

"I was joking," Patterson said. "Looks like they're raring to go, showing up right on time."

Rachette felt his face warm, and shook his head. He was going to earn all of his measly salary today, babysitting these two. He just hoped these eight men and women were going to be less mentally taxing.

It was eight men, Rachette realized as he watched them all pour out of their vehicles, looking well rested and sharp in their uniforms. They chuckled with one another, donned their hats, and looked around at the bustling activity.

When they saw Rachette approaching, they straightened and walked over.

For a ridiculous amount of time, they stood in a circle and shook hands and introduced one another. Each and every one of them looked at Patterson with varying degrees of too much interest. Her smile was engaging, and all the men seemed to be enthralled by her.

Rachette suddenly wished he'd requested some female officers to counter the imbalance. Patterson's presence was already distracting.

"And this is Jack," he said, pulling Jack in front of him. "This is the sheriff's son."

Jack gave a quick wave, blushed a little, and then left the circle.

"Don't go too far," Rachette said.

Jack pretended not to hear as he stood looking up at the mountain bikers.

Rachette turned back to the men, and caught a tall officer from the Vail PD raking Patterson's body with his eyes.

"On behalf of Sheriff Wolf," Rachette said in a hearty tone, "and the whole Sluice County Sheriff's Department, I thank you for coming to Rocky Points to help us this weekend."

"Where's the sheriff?" one of the Garfield deputies asked. "Still dealing with that shooting?"

Rachette looked at the big man. The name stripe said *Richter*, and Rachette pegged him at least six-four, two hundred thirty pounds, in his early forties. With closely cropped brown hair and a bushy brown mustache, he was clearly a man's man, and had probably been a force to be reckoned with on the football field back in his day.

"Yes, he is, Deputy Richter," Rachette said. "I didn't see you at the hospital yesterday morning."

"That's because I wasn't there," said Richter. "We had

a lot of things to take care of because we were coming here."

"Yes," Rachette said, eyeing the tall man, wondering how he was supposed to read that last statement.

Richter's neutral expression let nothing on.

Patterson cleared her throat. "We realize you're all leaving pressing situations at home," she said, "and taking time away from your families isn't any fun, either. But, like Deputy Rachette said, we really appreciate it. Hopefully we can accommodate you gentlemen adequately, and, well, hopefully we can all have a fun time working with one another in the process."

Richter and the other seven men broke into a smile and nodded at one another, as if the first lady herself had just bestowed compliments on all of them.

Patterson looked up at Rachette with raised eyebrows, and Rachette forced himself to smile and nod. "We'll be helping with general security today, and a little bit of setup, and then tomorrow the first acts will be coming on at around sundown. Patterson, why don't you lead everyone to the area in front of the stage, and we'll continue our orientation. I'll be right there." The men scattered and began following Patterson, and Jack turned and joined them. "Deputy Richter," Rachette called, "could I talk to you a moment?"

"Yes?" Richter turned around and looked down at Rachette.

"I just wanted to know how the investigation was going," Rachette said. "I was kind of wishing I was involved in that investigation as well. That's my sheriff that was shot the other night, after all."

Richter nodded.

"So? Any news?"

"I don't know," Richter said. "You'll have to ask your sheriff. I've probably heard just what you have. I think they got a bullet casing, and some soil samples, but when I talked to the station this morning on the phone, they said they weren't getting any hits on AFIS or CODIS."

Rachette frowned. "Shit."

Richter looked over Rachette's head, like he was itching to leave.

Rachette nodded and waved him by. "Go ahead. I'll catch up in a few minutes."

Watching the big man leave, Rachette pulled out his phone and dialed Wolf.

"Hello?" Wolf's voice was choppy.

"Hey, it's me. How's it going?"

There was a pause a second too long.

"Do you hear—" Rachette said.

"Hey, not bad," Wolf said. "Listen, I'm glad you called. I need to talk to Patterson."

Rachette rolled his eyes and looked at the group walking away. Richter had jogged to catch up and was talking to Jack.

"She's not here, I'll go get her."

"No," Wolf said, "don't worry about it. Just have her call me as soon as possible."

"Okay, will do."

"Later," Wolf said, and the phone went silent.

"Hello?"

Rachette checked the screen of his phone and saw that the call had been disconnected. He shook his head and shoved it in his pocket, then trudged after the group of men, and one very annoying woman.

CHAPTER 28

WOLF AND LUKE drove west on I-70 for forty minutes, along the meandering Colorado River, and then headed south on Highway 50, along the portion of Colorado known as the Western Slope of the Rocky Mountains, or simply, the Western Slope.

Long, sweeping valley floors rose to flat-topped plateaus as far as the eye could see, or as far as the shape of the earth allowed if one had perfect eyesight on a clear day. Today, however, the clouds had rolled in and ahead of Luke's Tahoe showers dumped out of the clouds like shower heads spraying white plumes against the landscape.

Wind buffeted the vehicle side to side, and the vastness of the land outside, along with the elements, made Wolf wonder how those early settlers, after just trudging their way through the unforgiving Rockies, had ever looked beyond and decided to keep going.

As they approached Delta the dry landscape became

greener, if not only because of human intervention. Fields of various crops lined both sides of the highway, with apple and peach orchards interspersed.

Delta, and the rest of the Western Slope, was known for growing produce. Orchards, and even wine vineyards, thrived in this portion of the country, and that's apparently exactly what had brought Wade Jeffries's family here however long ago, because they were approaching a house that was on a small hill, smack dab in the middle of an orchard of peach trees.

The house was a newer looking one-story building. There was a bright coat of navy-blue paint on the house, and it looked like the back yard was still in the middle of being landscaped. A small earthmover sat idle in the back yard, and a pile of bricks near the rear door of the house were stacked near a new brick patio that was half-finished.

"Nice place," Luke said. It was the first thing either of them had said in over forty-five minutes.

"This is the house Jeffries grew up in?" Wolf asked.

"Yep. The file says he was born in town, raised right here. Father was killed in some sort of agricultural accident eleven years ago. And Jeffries went into the army shortly thereafter."

"Is this their orchard?" Wolf asked.

"Yeah, it is."

"And who took care of the family business when he was off disarming bombs in the Middle East?"

"Good question," Luke said. "I guess it had to have been his sister and mother. Julie and Wanda Jeffries. Julie's the sister."

Wolf nodded and eyed the house as they drove up the final stretch of the dirt driveway. "It looks like the orchard is doing well. This house looks completely renovated, and then some."

Luke nodded. "Yeah."

They parked in the driveway next to a Nissan X-Terra that had a temporary plate taped in the rear window.

"New truck," Wolf said as they got out.

The air was cool and shifty, and the breeze carried a few droplets of moisture from the shapeless clouds that blanketed the sky.

Wolf zipped up his hooded sweatshirt, wishing he'd pulled his jacket out of his SUV before they'd left the field-office parking lot.

The windows were covered with heavy drapes that hung still—no one peeking outside to see what uninvited guests just pulled into the driveway. The house was quiet, and so was the surrounding land, with nobody in sight in the orchard below.

The garage door was open to their right, revealing a riding lawnmower inside, and an old Toyota Land Cruiser taking up the bulk of the space.

Something caught Wolf's attention, and he pulled up his sweatshirt and drew his gun.

"What?" Luke stepped next to him with her gun drawn, following his gaze into the garage.

"Look at that door."

The door in the garage to the interior of the house was open a crack, and it looked to have been forced because the doorknob was hanging by a screw. Wolf looked closer and saw that the knob was mangled and had a hole through it. The door itself was splintered.

Wolf and Luke crouched and aimed their guns ahead as they entered the garage. Wolf aimed with his right hand, letting his now throbbing left arm hang limp by his side.

Luke stopped and backed herself against the rear of the Land Cruiser, and Wolf continued past her.

"Hey," she hissed.

Wolf toed open the door and aimed his pistol inside. A dim hallway stretched for a few feet, ending at an equally dim kitchen, where a stainless-steel refrigerator sat humming on a tile floor.

Wolf waved his injured arm for Luke to follow him, ignoring the punch of pain in his bicep, and stalked inside. The smell was pungent, and it was unmistakable that they were going to see some kind of grisly death in the next few steps, probably to the right, judging by the blood-spatter pattern on the refrigerator and the brightening light in that direction, suggesting that the space opened up.

Wolf flipped a switch on the wall. The hallway lit up, and the spattering on the refrigerator brightened to a dark maroon. He stepped soundlessly, keeping his pistol aimed, and watched a puddle of dried blood come into view on the black-and-white tiled floor. And then he saw a head of gray hair, and the motionless body of a woman in a pink nightgown.

"Careful," Luke whispered behind him.

Wolf was being careful, but knew they had most likely missed the window of danger. No one shot a woman in a kitchen, stuck around long enough for the smell to kick in, and hung around to really breathe it in and invite further trouble.

Luke darted into the next room gun-first, and Wolf followed behind her. There was only darkness for an instant, and then Luke clicked on a wall switch, bathing a family room in yellow light. She swept her gun across the space and then strode fast across thick carpet, her feet swishing with every step, to a narrow hallway beyond. Wolf followed right on her heels, gun at the ready.

Luke stopped at a T-junction in the hall and looked at Wolf. She pointed to the right and disappeared to the left.

Wolf took the right, and walked down the dark hall toward two closed doors. The one on the right had a faint sliver of natural light shining beneath it. The one on the left was pitch black.

He twisted the knob on the right and flung open the door, ready to fire. It was a small bedroom with a queen-sized bed, an open closet, and an open door to a bathroom.

He swept the room, checking the closet, under the bed, and the bathroom, then peeked out. The quick-moving shadow of Luke crossed into another room down the hall.

He reached for the next door and opened it. He couldn't see a thing in the pitch-blackness, but a stench punched him in the nose, even worse than the smell they'd encountered in the kitchen.

"Oh," Wolf said involuntarily, calming his gag reflex through sheer willpower.

Wolf raked the back of his hand across the wall inside the door, sliding it across sticky patches until he found the light switch. He flipped it on and saw an unmistakably dead person tied to a chair.

The first thing that Wolf noticed was the hair. The head was slumped forward, exposing the top of the person's head. The hair was cut in a boyish style; matted with blood, with only a wisp of the true-color blonde showing through.

Wolf studied the rest of the corpse, and saw it was a woman in her twenties. Two exposed breasts, grayish-white with dark black nipples, protruded from underneath strands of blood-soaked rope. The rest of the body was naked, covered in downward streams of dried blood.

"Clear!" Luke said from somewhere behind him.

"In here!" Wolf responded.

Luke ran down the hall and flew into the room with gun raised.

"Jesus." She stopped on a dime and turned around with a hand over her mouth. "Jesus."

Wolf bent down and looked up at the face. It was heavily damaged and disfigured, the nose and jaw unnaturally bent.

"Julie Jeffries," Wolf said. "Looks beaten to death."

"No shit. Oh God."

Wolf went to the window and pulled open the heavy drape. It squeaked open, letting in a few photons of natural light. The sound of rain pattered on the window in a steady rhythm. Wolf noticed blood on the glass underneath the drapes. It looked like someone had closed it up after the deed was done.

"Good God." Luke studied the corpse. "What the hell?"

The room looked to have been used by the Jeffrieses as a home office. A desk stood against the north wall, and there were two file cabinets tucked in the corner. The woman was tied to a wooden swivel chair, and it was in the center of the room, directly underneath the overhead light on the ceiling.

Wolf walked around the rear of the corpse and studied the knots on her hands. They were crude. Double knots, tripled, then quadrupled on themselves.

"It looks like she was being interrogated," Wolf said.

Luke nodded. "Yeah."

Dollops of blood, mixed with skin and hair, had stuck to a wooden desk behind the corpse. A framed picture stood on the corner of the desktop. Underneath the blood-streaked glass was a picture of two teenaged children smiling on a much sunnier day in the past. The kids both had the same eyes and the same facial bone structure. Boy and girl, and the boy Wolf recognized as Wade Jeffries, minus the neck tattoo and burned ear.

"Why kill them?" Wolf asked aloud. "And who?"

"The other EOD guys?" Luke asked.

"But why? They're all supposedly in hiding with Wade."

"Shit." Luke pulled out her phone and dialed a number.

Wolf watched her as she stared at the ceiling with impatience, her phone pressed to her ear.

"Hawes. This is Luke. I need you to go to 392 Dahlia

Lane, in Glenwood. You know it?" She listened for a second. "Right. Just west of Main. I need you to check on the occupant of the house, and call me the second you confirm that the woman is okay. What? No, now. And call me the second you find out."

She hung up and looked at Wolf.

"You think Bernadette Richter is next?" Wolf asked.

"Let's hope not."

Wolf's phone buzzed in his pocket and he pulled it out. It was a phone number he didn't recognize. Probably Patterson, giving him that call he was waiting for. He forwarded it to voice mail. It was hardly the time.

Luke and Wolf left the gore in the home office and walked back through the house to the kitchen—to the first display of death they had encountered.

Standing on the tile floor, they studied the old woman on the ground. She had a neat hole in her forehead and a bigger exit wound in the back of her head, exposing the insides of the skull.

"They must have broken in from the garage, but they had to have stepped around her, and then shot her," Luke said. "The spatter is toward the refrigerator, or basically toward where they came in from."

"Which means what?" Wolf asked.

"I don't know. I'm just talking. I'd rather talk than just sit here staring at her."

"Let's call the locals," Wolf said.

She nodded, but didn't reach for her phone, so Wolf took his out and dialed the Delta PD. After a brief conversation he hung up.

"How about we head back into the—"

Luke's phone rang in her pocket and she pulled it out.

"Yeah." She glared at the wall of the kitchen as she listened.

"Good. Stay there until I get there, which will be"—she looked at her watch—"in about two hours, give or take." She listened for a few more seconds, then held up a finger to Wolf and walked into the other room.

Wolf watched her go around the corner, and her voice dropped in volume so he couldn't hear. She spoke quickly, in a flurry of mumbling.

After a few seconds, Wolf walked after her, his curiosity piqued. When he rounded the corner she was all the way across the room, shoulders rounded, finishing a terse whisper into the phone.

"Then get Shaw to come do it," she said loudly, and then turned around and rolled her eyes at Wolf as if he could empathize with the stupidity on the other end of the line. "But I don't want that woman left alone for a second. I have reason to believe she's in danger. I'll be there soon."

Luke hung up the phone without waiting for a response and looked at Wolf.

"What's up?" she asked.

"Mrs. Richter is all right?"

Luke nodded.

Wolf turned back to the kitchen. "What do you say we step outside to wait for these guys?"

"Haven't heard a better idea all year," she said and walked past him, through the kitchen, and out the garage.

CHAPTER 29

THE DELTA POLICE DEPARTMENT ended up storming in with five vehicles blaring their sirens. Wolf and Luke greeted them, told their stories, describing their actions and what exactly they'd touched, and then stood outside in the drizzle, talking to the local chief named Bradley Van Wyke.

"And why were you here?" Van Wyke asked Wolf.

Van Wyke was a tall, heavy man, as many men who played offensive line in college were during, and after, their football years. Closely cropped hair poked out under his cowboy hat. With a flash Wolf remembered the last time he'd seen him—just over two years ago at a law-enforcement conference in Durango. Van Wyke was the same now as before, with a brown handlebar mustache that looked to be kept for weekends riding a Harley-Davidson. His eyes were wide and locked open with tiny dots for pupils. Coupled with his jerky movements, it looked like the chief was hopped up on adrenaline after seeing the dead bodies inside, and probably would be for the next few days.

"I'm afraid we can't talk about why we were here, sir," Luke said, answering before Wolf had a chance.

Van Wyke scowled down at Luke. "Oh, really?" He shook his head and looked over at her shiny black Tahoe. "I suppose it's a matter of national security."

"Something like that." Luke didn't blink.

"Bullshit." Van Wyke turned to Wolf. "Come on, Wolf. You gonna play me like that?"

Wolf sighed and slid a look to Luke. "I was involved in a shooting the other night. We suspected Wade Jeffries might have had something to do with it. We were just checking in with his family, and we found them like this." He shrugged. "End of story."

Van Wyke tilted his head and glared at Wolf, then at Luke.

"Wade Jeffries has been MIA in Afghanistan for a year, hasn't he?" asked Van Wyke. "It was big news around town last year."

Wolf nodded. "That's the interesting part."

"Huh." He frowned at Luke, then at Wolf. "So, what the fuck?"

"We'll keep in touch," Luke said.

Van Wyke ignored Luke and locked eyes with Wolf.

Wolf looked down at Luke and then back to Van Wyke. "Thanks, Brad. Keep us in the loop, eh?"

"You leavin' already?" Van Wyke didn't wait for an answer. "Yeah, fine. I'll keep you informed. Not for this suit"—he kept eye contact with Wolf and thumbed in the direction of Luke—"but for the best quarterback I ever sacked. Twice." Now Van Wyke looked at Luke and bounced his eyebrows. "In one game. Yeah, I'll keep you informed." He tipped his hat, "Ma'am," and then walked away.

...

They drove the whole hour and twenty minutes back to Glenwood Springs like they had most of the way to Delta—in silence.

Wolf took advantage of the lull to listen to his voice-mail—a message from Patterson calling as per his request—and then typed out a message to Rachette and Patterson that said, *Rachette, as you were. Patterson, I need you at the station in thirty minutes.*

A few seconds later they responded with their own texts and Wolf sat back and zoned out on the passing rapids of the Colorado River.

"You want me to drop you off at your car first?" she asked just before they reached town.

"No, I'd rather stick with you, if you don't mind," Wolf said.

She shrugged, showing no sign of annoyance, and exited a different ramp at Glenwood Springs. She headed south through back streets and then, for the second time of the day, they were parked in front of Bernadette Richter's house.

"I'll just stay here, if you don't mind," Wolf said preemptively.

She looked over and creased her forehead. "You don't want to come back in?"

"Nah, I'll leave the FBI work to you. Besides, our partnership is supposed to be secret, right?"

She nodded and exhaled. "Thanks. I'll be a few minutes."

Wolf nodded, and watched her through the streaming droplets of water on the windshield.

She hopped the tiny picket-fence gate, walked with a quick stride up through the yard, and then skipped two steps at a time up the wooden stairs to the front porch. She moved like a ballet dancer with a gun, Wolf thought.

Wolf took out his phone and hit the number.

"Hello?"

"Hey. How's it going over there?"

"Good," Patterson said in a chipper voice. "How are things going with you? Any progress?"

"Getting there. On that note, are you back at the station?"

"Yes, sir."

"Get on a free computer."

Wolf heard her soft breathing and then the squeak of a chair.

"Okay," Patterson said. "Just a second, booting up."

"Great." Wolf looked up at the house. Luke was inside the open front door, shadowed against the brightly lit interior of the house. He could see Mrs. Richter smiling up at her, and then the door closed slowly, swallowing them both inside.

Wolf looked at the perfectly manicured lawn, now

soaked in the rain, and at the trimmed rose bushes, the clean soil of the garden on the side of the house, the mailbox with the flag up, and the fresh outside paint job.

"Okay," Patterson said. "I'm on."

"I need you to check on someone," Wolf said.

CHAPTER 30

WOLF WAS STILL on the phone when Luke left the house a few minutes later. She shut the door behind her, trotted down the wooden steps, jogged the path, and jumped the small gate again.

"Ah, it's getting cold out there," she said as she slid up into the driver's seat. "Oh, sorry."

Wolf held up his phone. "No problem. I'm on hold."

"What?" Patterson said into his ear.

"Yeah," Wolf said into the phone. "Just let me know, I'll wait."

"Ah, okay, just a second," Patterson said.

Luke drove down the street toward the commercial center of Glenwood Springs, and Wolf listened intently as Patterson rattled off the information she'd gathered.

Wolf listened in silence for a few minutes, only grunting to spur Patterson on. When he was satisfied, he said goodbye, hung up, and put the phone in his pocket.

Luke turned onto Grand Avenue, and headed north toward the FBI field office.

"Hey," he said looking out the window like he'd just seen something. "Can you pull over? Behind those buildings, in the back alley?"

"What?" She frowned. "Why?"

"Trust me. I think I saw something." Wolf sat back and gripped the ceiling bar.

Luke shook her head and hit the brakes. "We gonna bust a drunk?"

Wolf kept his intent glare out the window.

She took the next right and then turned in the alley behind the retail shops that lined the main street in town.

"Right here." Wolf pointed out the windshield toward the back door of a building.

She stopped. "Here?"

Wolf got out, and Luke shut off the engine. There was no traffic in the secluded back alley. Tall old oak trees blocked the road from most of the rain. There was a low hum from a heating unit on the back of the building, which had a blue-painted door that read *Monty's Leatherworks* in white stenciling.

Wolf crouched and put his hand on his pistol, then shuffled toward the door.

Luke came up next to him, and pulled her pistol. "What's going on?" She kept her eyes on the door, and then double took at the sight of Wolf aiming at the side of her face.

"Drop your gun," Wolf said in a calm voice.

She turned a fraction, and Wolf pushed his barrel closer. "I said drop your gun, now."

"What the fuck ..." She crouched down slowly and set her gun on the cracked asphalt.

"Stand up and put your hands on the hood."

She stood straight and faced him. "No."

"Do as I say, or I'll shoot, and then I'll tell the whole story to your special agent in charge, *Ms. Richter*."

Luke's skin flushed and she swallowed.

"I know everything," Wolf said. "Now, please, don't make me shoot you in the leg, and get up against the hood."

She shook her head and clenched her teeth, then walked to the hood and assumed the position. "Go ahead, have at it."

Wolf lifted his left arm out in a stretch, and the bruise pulsed. Thanks to the information gleaned from Patterson, he now knew Luke was a second-degree black belt and trained in other martial arts. She was clearly no pushover, and he needed to be careful.

She had been watching him over her shoulder, a sly smirk playing on her face.

"Don't try it," he said. "I've got a hair-trigger setting on this thing."

He held the pistol in his right hand and placed his left hand on the inner thigh of her right leg, working his way down to her ankle. Her muscles were firm, the fabric of her pants warm. He moved to the left leg, feeling it tense under his fingers.

She kicked across and back with her right foot, connecting squarely against the inside of his left bicep.

Wolf jumped back, and her fist breezed past his face less than an inch away. Pain seared through his arm to the point where his vision blurred. He could feel a warm trickle of blood running from his stitches down his arm.

Wolf stood still and aimed at her head, feeling the warmth under his bandage grow. "Last warning," he said. "Next time I shoot."

Her face was impassive. She didn't blink or make a sound. Just turned around and spread her legs again.

Wolf walked up fast and pressed the barrel of his gun against the back of her right thigh, and checked her left leg from top to bottom. Then he checked her waist, and up underneath her breasts.

"Turn around," he said, stepping back.

She did, and he wasn't prepared for the hate in her eyes. She glared, like he had just violated her on the deepest level.

He didn't care.

"Take off your jacket," he said.

"I'm not—"

"Take off your jacket." Wolf returned her glare.

She unzipped her parka and opened it, then pulled it off her shoulders and let it fall to the ground. Underneath she wore a white long-sleeved button-up blouse that was somewhat see-through.

Wolf studied her skin under the shirt. He could see the brighter white line of her bra against the fabric, but the sleeve was loose, and the material and dull light kept her arm hidden underneath.

She followed his eyes, and in a quick move ripped open

her shirt. "There, you get a good look?" A button bounced off Wolf's arm and onto the ground at his feet. He was now looking at her breasts, which were covered with a thin white bra, and her taut abdomen, which was smooth and muscular.

"Take off the left sleeve," he said.

She looked down at her arm and pulled her eyebrows together. "What?" A moment later she widened her eyes. "You think I was there? Shooting at your son?"

Wolf nodded to her arm.

She pulled the sleeve and revealed her thin, muscled arm, and displayed it for Wolf in a twisting motion. There was no bandage, no wound.

Wolf turned around and walked to her SIG and picked it up, holstering his own gun. When he turned around, he found her unmoved, her upper body still exposed to the chilly air.

"You can put your shirt back on now," Wolf said.

She didn't move, but her defiant glare lowered and melted into a distant look. "I'm not involved in this," she said quietly.

"I know. But you think your brother is," Wolf said.

Luke slipped on the sleeve of her blouse and bent to pick up her FBI parka.

"Is it you who takes care of her?" Wolf walked slowly back to Luke. "Mows the lawn, trims the bushes, cleans her house, takes care of the mail?"

She nodded, slipping her jacket on. "Yeah. My brother doesn't do shit. I'm the one who takes care of her. She's completely gone, completely helpless, and my brother just ignores her."

Wolf stopped in front of her. "She remembers you."

"That's about all she can do, nowadays. It's so strange," she said in a quiet voice, "that she remembers me."

Wolf flipped her pistol around and held it out handle-first.

Luke looked at it, then up at Wolf, and took it.

"We need to talk," Wolf said.

She nodded, holstering her pistol.

"I'm hungry." Wolf stepped to the passenger door and got in.

Wolf watched through the mirrors as Luke moved slowly around the rear of the SUV with the enthusiasm of a death-row inmate's last walk. She finally rounded the Tahoe and climbed in without saying anything, fired it up, and drove.

CHAPTER 31

SPECIAL AGENT KRISTEN LUKE had been hurt three times by men in her life. Her father had made the first emotional cut, leaving when she was in high school to join the Bozeman PD in Montana. She'd never gotten a reason from him for leaving his wife, daughter, and two sons. And she'd never gotten an explanation from her mother. And as far as an apology from her father in the eleven years since he'd left? She'd never gotten that either.

Her father had hurt her first, and probably the deepest. At least that's what she thought nowadays, now that she was in her mid-thirties and had had plenty of time to sulk about it. But at the time, immediately following his disappearing act, she'd pretended like she didn't care. She'd pretended to others and to herself. Which led to a phase in her life that she commonly referred to—to herself rather than out loud to anyone else other than her best friend, Linda—as *the slut period*.

In her first year in college at Boulder, she'd found herself more than willing to allow the young men in the dorms into her pants. She figured that if they had the guts to ask, or make a move, she was obliged to "give it up." Though it repulsed her to think about it now, she remembered feeling secure when a drunk guy had groped her with his warm hands. It had made her feel wanted. Classic daddy-doesn't-love-me syndrome.

In the end, it wasn't one of the drunken hormone bags in the dorms who had hurt her, who had been the second man in her life to shake her to the core. It had been an honest-to-God madman on campus. The kind of thing you hear about on the news that makes you say "holy shit", blink, and then flip the channel, because it's just too bad to think about any more than that.

She'd been on her way home from the library late one night, when a man with a red ski mask had jumped out of the bushes and attacked her on the lawn of the Geology building. For thirty of the worst seconds of her life, she'd kicked and screamed, and was overtaken and beaten into a quiet haze she could scarcely remember then or now. Luckily, two tennis-racket-wielding seniors were walking by after a late match and saw it happening. When the blur of evil was off her and gone, and she woke up in the hospital the next day, she found out that the guy hadn't raped her. At least that had been something. But he had stripped her naked, and pulped her face to the point she couldn't see out of one of her eyes for two weeks. That was something, too.

That something, her second mental torment, triggered the beginning of what she referred to as the *lesbian period* of her life. She knew it was a misnomer. Sure, it was a drastic change of lifestyle that she'd undergone after the attack, but not so far that she actually made out with other women. In truth, that image repulsed her now, as it had then. Instead, she'd just dressed the part, wearing baggy flannel and corduroy, cut her hair butch, and done anything and everything to repel members of the opposite sex.

For the remainder of her college career she kept a stiff-arm against males. And for the remainder of her college career, she built a strong fortress around her brittle, shattered inner self. Starting with martial-arts training four nights a week in her sophomore year, she gradually became stronger inside, as well as out, and by the time she was done with college, she was a brown belt in karate, had majored in law enforcement, and felt the most self-assured she had been since her father left those few short years ago.

For the third, and final blow, from a man, she'd finally dropped her lesbian façade and opened herself up to love. Brendon had been a different sort of guy, charming and funny, and showed his abrasive side only to the worst of people who deserved it. A real looker. The whole package.

She'd turned him down for months at Quantico, where they'd met, and when they found themselves stationed together in Chicago, she decided she couldn't fight him anymore. She decided she didn't want to. After two years of dating, they'd built what she considered at the time a solid relationship, and despite the entirely unique pressures of them having the same high-stress, high-pressure job of being FBI special agents, they'd gotten married.

Nowadays, she was disgusted by the thought of her "first love." Because she'd been the one who'd let the man in. It wasn't her father leaving, or an attack out of the blue, it was she who had done it to herself. She'd invited Brendon into her life, despite her instinct telling her not to, and watched as he screwed around on her, humiliating her in front of her entire field office in Chicago. It was disgusting to think about—her naiveté in thinking a man could be a source of joy in her life.

Luke thought of these three men at various times in life. It was her past, and was what had shaped her into the special agent she was now, and every once in a while these three men would loom big in her mind.

But since she'd met David Wolf, these three men seemed to flash in her brain every minute. It was her instinct talking to her, and she was listening. Wolf was big trouble. Not in the truest sense of the word—*trouble*. Not like he was into holding up people at the ATM and doing drugs kind of trouble. He was just ... trouble.

But she also knew her troubled past wasn't doomed to repeat itself, and she was finding Wolf to be a man she wanted to confide in. She was at the end of her rope, and the truth was getting too big for her to handle alone. Someone else had to know, and there was something about Wolf. Sure, he was trouble, but it sure seemed like he could help, too.

As they sat in the Mountain Goat Bar and Grill, eating their late lunches, she watched Wolf shovel food into his mouth in silence. After completely humiliating her in the alley a few minutes before, calling her out, her literally exposing herself to him mentally and anatomically, now he sat with seemingly infinite patience. He wasn't pushing her, not asking a single thing. He was letting her start.

So she did.

"My dad left us when I was in high school. I was the only one who kept his last name—Luke." She shrugged. "I don't know why. I guess I had ideas back then. My two brothers changed their names, but I ..."

She let the sentence die and felt her face flush.

"Why'd you come to Glenwood Springs from Chicago?" Wolf asked, gratefully skipping past the subject.

"I wanted to keep an eye on my mother, and Wade Jeffries's sister and mother."

Wolf narrowed his eyes. "So you had met Jeffries's mother and sister before."

"Yeah. Seven months ago, when my brother died, or ... went missing. I came home for my brother's memorial service after he disappeared. Then after that I went back to Chicago, and I started doing some digging into my brother's death, talking to a few contacts I have in the CIA. They said he'd been in Tora Bora, the caves where they were looking for Osama bin Laden when the war in Afghanistan started all those years ago."

Wolf nodded.

"You know the area?" Luke asked.

"Yeah."

"Then you know. That was the battle of Tora Bora, what, over a decade ago? And my brother's up there with his team still blasting tunnels a decade later? Why? Didn't you guys get all that done back then?"

Wolf shrugged. "In theory. It doesn't make sense he was there. But I'm not privy to military intelligence."

"Well, my contacts said the same thing: The whole team shouldn't have been there." She shoved her plate to the edge of the table. "Anyway, I came back home to Glenwood for vacation a few months after my brother's service, and went to go talk to Wade Jeffries's sister. I don't know what I was looking for, other than just someone to talk to about it, I guess. Our brothers were both missing in Afghanistan and she was a short car ride away. I didn't know if maybe she had some knowledge about the whole thing. Maybe she had contacted her brother before he'd disappeared, or whatever.

"And what I found was his sister was acting strange. Like, real strange. She was hiding something, no doubt. I asked her if she'd heard anything from her brother before he went missing, and she said no. But she was lying, plain as day. Her mother was even worse when I asked her. These two were acting like they were covering for Wade. Like he was hiding behind the door the whole time when we were talking, or something."

Wolf raised his eyebrows and took a drink of his Coke.

Luke played with the straw in her own drink, thinking about the way Julie and Wanda Jeffries had broken out in a sweat when she'd asked them about him.

"And?" Wolf asked, showing his first sign of any impatience.

"I left." Luke shrugged. "And then hacked into their emails."

Wolf raised an eyebrow.

"And I found an email buried in Julie Jeffries's deleted folder that caught my attention. It said, *Don't worry, I'm still alive. I'll see you soon.* No signature, no nothing."

"And the email address?"

"It was from a throw-away Gmail account created two days after Jeffries and the rest of my brother's team went missing, created from an IP address in Kabul, Afghanistan."

Wolf nodded. "So, it stood to reason, if Wade Jeffries was still alive, which looked to be the case, your brother was still alive."

"My brother was the EOD team leader. He was in charge of where these guys went, what they did." Luke's eyes gushed without warning. She realized she hadn't told a single soul what she'd been thinking for over four months, not even her older brother, and now that she'd shared her secret, her burden, a flood of emotion surged through her.

"So, yeah, he's gotta be alive." She wiped her tears. "Gotta be one of these men. And shooting at sheriffs and their little boys. And killing people. Innocent women." She shook her head. "Goddammit. I can't believe he would ..." She clenched her eyes shut. "That's what I've been trying to hide. I knew my brother had to be involved in this, and I just ..."

When she opened her eyes, Wolf stared back at her with a relaxed gaze. It was an unreadable expression that made her uneasy.

"I don't know," she continued. "I thought I could buy some time, and find him, and get him to stop whatever the hell he's doing. My little brother always listened to me. I was the reason why he was in Afghanistan in the first place. I pushed him to go, and he did. I know you probably hate me, and want to just about kill me right now."

Wolf sighed and looked past her.

"I'm sorry," Luke said.

Wolf put his elbows on the table, and looked vacantly at the walls. "I guess I see where you were coming from. I had a brother, and I would have done anything for him. And I probably would have been itching to kick his ass, alone, if it looked like he was going around killing people."

Luke sniffed in response, unsure of what to say.

"There's only one thing. Something that doesn't add up."

Luke tilted her head. "Yeah?"

"The guy I killed at the fire. That wasn't your brother, or any of the other men on his EOD team who disappeared that day in Afghanistan."

Luke frowned, and remembered the description Wolf had given on the trail that day they'd met. Wolf had said that the man he'd killed had had red hair, or really light blond, with a mouth full of moles. It had startled her to hear that then, as none of the men on the EOD team could have possibly been mistaken for looking like that. They all had dark hair, brown, or darker, dark eyebrows, and most definitely did not have moles on their faces.

"Are you sure?" she asked. "The guy didn't just have some scabs on his chin, or his lips?"

"No. The guy had moles. I was only inches away, and I saw them clearly. No mistake. And I remember faces, especially the ones I shot with a .357 in front of my son. And none of those four faces was the guy I killed at the fire. And ..." Wolf stopped talking.

"What?"

"I just don't get why they'd fake their own deaths, and come home. What's in it for them? A life of dodging civilization? A life of dodging any of the people you used to know? And I keep thinking about Wade Jeffries on that trail. He had some serious equipment in his backpack, like bomb material ... or something. What was he carrying? Why was he running?"

Luke turned around in her seat and waved her hand at the bartender for the check.

The man behind the bar was sweaty and pale, like he wasn't feeling well at all, but he immediately responded with a nod and walked their way.

"Thanks," she said when he dropped it off. Then she turned to Wolf. "I think I may have the answers to those questions."

Wolf wiped his hands on his napkin. "Oh? And what are those?"

She scooted out of the booth and put on her jacket. "I need to show you."

"Show me what?"

"Something that came to my house a few days ago."

Wolf looked like he wanted answers, but once again he kept quiet, stood up and followed her out the door. That patience of his was becoming irresistible to Luke. And now she was bringing him home. *Trouble,* she thought one final time as they left the Mountain Goat and walked into the cool drizzle.

CHAPTER 32

RACHETTE STOOD in the doorway of a large merchandising tent at the base of the mountain and looked outside at the steady rain. It wasn't raining hard, but it was relentless, going for two hours now.

He sipped on a styrofoam cup of coffee and looked out at Patterson, who had just returned from her secret errand for Wolf, and was now walking with Jack and the big guy from Garfield County, Richter, toward the stage. Jack and Richter were enthralled by a story Patterson was telling, and then they were laughing. She was probably telling a story about how Jack Nicholson had once come to dinner at her family's house and pissed in the houseplant.

"Deputy Rachette," said a nasally voice, snapping him out of his daydream. Rachette turned to find Charlie Ash.

"Hello, sir. How are you doing today?" Rachette held out his hand, trying to contain the surprise in his voice and movements. He'd spoken to Ash once before in his life, and was sure he'd made zero impression on the new chairman of the county council at the time. Now Ash was coming up behind him and using his name, like they were actual acquaintances.

Ash ignored Rachette's hand, or he needed a new set of glasses. Rachette suspected it was the former.

Ash was the same height as Rachette, which was to say he was shorter than average. Ash's neck had a stoop, reminding him of a vulture, and the older man wore a red Rocky Points Music Festival baseball cap over his bald scalp. He thought the chairman's eyes looked calculating. Intelligent. Almost the exact color of the gray sky above. The gold-framed eyeglasses were expensive.

"Where's Mr. Wolf this afternoon?" Ash asked, still yet to make eye contact with him.

"I'm not sure where the sheriff is at the moment, sir." His instincts were telling him to lie, which would somehow protect Wolf.

Ash locked eyes with him, catching him in the middle of his scrutinizing glare, then swiveled and looked out toward Patterson, Jack, and Richter. "I didn't know the Sheriff's Office offered babysitting as a service. That's a new development I'll have to discuss with the council. May be a new revenue stream. We could put out an advertisement."

Rachette took a sip of his coffee in response.

"What do you think about the new recruit, Deputy Rachette?"

Rachette raised his eyebrows and nodded. "She's good. Sharp." Rachette knew full well that Ash's son had been thrown out on his ass after his interview, and Ash would have to be pretty bent out of shape about it.

"Well, she's signed the contract, but it still needs final approval." Ash sniffed and sipped his own cup of coffee.

He frowned and flicked a glance at Ash. "I thought you needed her to be hired to get grant money from the state."

Ash nodded. "Yes, I admit." Then he tilted his head. "Or, we could have promoted another deputy up to sergeant. We would have gotten the same grant money that way. Ratio of lower and higher ranks within the department"—he waved a hand—"or some bureaucratic stipulation I can't remember exactly. But we left that decision up to Sheriff Wolf. And he chose to go with the new hire, instead of"—Ash looked over at Rachette and slapped his shoulder—"pulling those up the ladder who lifted him there."

Rachette frowned and looked outside at Patterson, and then back at Ash. He felt his face getting hot, his chest tightening as his lungs took shallow breaths, and wondered just what the hell Ash thought he was doing, driving a wedge in between him and Wolf in such an unsubtle way. It was ridiculous and childish. And, yet, the sliver of doubt was inserted into Rachette's mind, and was already working its way deeper. If what Ash was saying was true, why wouldn't Wolf promote Rachette? Hadn't Rachette proved himself over the past two and a half years in the department? Maybe not. Maybe Rachette was expecting too much in such a short amount of time.

"Well," Rachette said, "I'm sure Sheriff Wolf knows what he's doing."

Ash blew out of his nose and brought the coffee cup back to his lips. "That's one way to put it." Ash took a loud sip, slapped him on the shoulder again, turned around and walked back toward the racks of clothing and volunteers setting up tables of merchandise. "I'll see you around."

Rachette stood silent. *Prick.*

He turned and walked outside, and the drizzle cooled his hot cheeks. Patterson turned and waved at him, and he gave a little nod in return, wondering just what she had been doing for Wolf, and why he couldn't have been the one doing it.

He shook his head and poured the rest of his coffee out. It hissed and exploded into a small cloud of steam.

Prick.

CHAPTER 33

WOLF CHECKED his wound underneath his hooded sweatshirt as Luke drove them south through town on Grand Avenue. The bandage had a large patch of maroon underneath where he felt his cut, and he hoped it was still stitched together. Now, when he moved his arm, there was a short stab of pain followed by a long, echoing ache to the bone.

"Sorry about that," Luke said, keeping her eyes on the road.

Wolf swore there was a hint of a smirk on her face.

"I have some first-aid stuff at home," she added. "We'll check it out, and redress it."

He nodded and zipped up his sweatshirt. "We need to talk to the Garfield County Sheriff's Department, see what they found on the casing and soil samples."

"Here." She passed him her phone. "You can use mine. Look up GCSD."

Wolf navigated through the menus, found the number, and dialed it up.

It rang twice and a woman's voice answered. "Garfield County Sheriff's Office, Glenwood Springs Headquarters. How can I help you?"

"Could I speak to Sergeant McCall, please?"

"One moment."

The phone clicked and soft music played for a few seconds, then clicked again, and the woman came back on. "I'm sorry. Sergeant McCall isn't answering. Can I transfer you to somebody else?"

"Could I talk to someone in forensics, please?" Wolf asked.

"And who's calling?"

"This is Sheriff Wolf of Sluice County. I was with Sergeant McCall at a crime scene yesterday, at Grimm Lake, and we gathered some evidence that you guys were testing. I'd like to discuss the results with someone."

"Hold," she said, and the soft music returned.

The music cut out and a male voice answered. "Michaelson, here."

"Hello, this is Sheriff Wolf of Sluice County, I was with Sergeant—"

"I know who you are. What can I help you with, sir?"

"I was wondering if you guys picked up any finger-prints on that cartridge brought in yesterday, and if there was any news yet on the soil samples."

"No fingerprints on the cartridge," he said quickly, "and as far as the soil samples go, we need a few more hours. We've got the top-of-the-line equipment here, but even that can leave ya impatient." He laughed for a beat.

"Okay." Wolf shook his head at Luke. "Not even any partials on the cartridge, huh?"

"Nope. Nothing. Clean as a whistle." The phone rattled for a few seconds, like he'd just dropped it. "Can I take a number and I'll call you about the soil samples when the tests are through?"

Wolf gave his number and hung up.

"Nothing?" Luke asked.

"No."

As they drove south out of town, the valley opened a little wider, and the red earth that saturated the surrounding hills became swirled with browns and grays. They passed a golf course on the right that edged its way up to the rippling waters of Roaring Fork River, filled with people with less pressing problems.

A few miles past it, just when Wolf wondered whether Luke lived in the next town of Carbondale, she slowed and turned left on a dirt road. The road passed through a flat farm field, and then meandered up into the hills.

There were houses along either side of the road, but there was plenty of nature in between each of them. Wolf could smell the wet junipers and sage through the open vents of Luke's car.

A few minutes later they were driving well above the valley below, and Luke slowed at a driveway and turned.

Her house was modest, a smallish one-story, but Wolf suspected that the back of the house, which faced the valley below, and west, toward the setting sun every night, would have some views that made up for any lack of living space.

The Tahoe crunched down the driveway toward her garage door, which rose after she pushed a button on her visor. She came to a stop and shut off the engine, and Wolf soon realized why she hadn't parked inside. The garage was full of boxes of all shapes and sizes, and there were two mountain bikes leaning up against the wall, two kayaks hanging from the ceiling, and a 250 cc dual-sport motor-cycle propped on a kickstand.

Wolf got out and whistled. "I see you like the outdoors."

Luke walked past him and into the garage.

Wolf followed. The space was cold and smelled of the nylon, rubber, plastic and the other synthetic materials her toys were made of. She unlocked the door to the house and walked in.

Inside was open and light, and thankfully warm after a long day of being perpetually damp. They entered a spot-less kitchen with shiny hardwood floors and granite coun-ters. A few dishes were piled in the sink, but that one untidy blemish in the otherwise clean space was easily overlooked, as a wide kitchen window yawned, framing the valley below.

"Grab a beer in the fridge if you want," Luke said as she walked through the eating area and creaked out of sight around the corner.

Wolf opened the stainless-steel refrigerator and heard the faint rattle of bottles. The shelves were empty save a plastic box of baby spinach, a few sacks of vegetables, a package of tortillas, and a twelve pack of Stella Artois. He dug in the box and pulled one out.

"I'll take one, too," Luke said as she entered the kitchen again. She'd lost the FBI jacket and her shoes. She took the two beers, produced a bottle opener from a drawer and opened them.

Wolf took the beer back and gazed out the windows. "Nice view you've got here."

"I wish it was mine. I'm renting."

"Well, still. Nice view."

The backyard was a flat twenty or so yards of lawn that ended at the natural shrubs and vegetation of the surrounding land. The hill swept down out of sight, and the next piece of visible land was at the bottom of the green valley. There was a small grove of aspen trees flanking the side of the house on the right, a sage-covered hillside climbed up to the left.

"I like it," she said. "There're no neighbors in sight from the back, and it's modern inside. I got lucky. It's a family friend's place."

She walked out of the kitchen, and returned a few seconds later with a wadded-up paper bag held in her palm. Something inside it knocked against the granite countertop as she set it down. Removing the bag with a magician-like flourish, the contents, two bars of gold, were now on display.

Wolf pulled his beer away from his lips and popped his eyes open. "Wow."

Luke picked up the top piece and held it up for Wolf to inspect.

Wolf held out his palm and she put the bar in it. It was the shape of a credit card, but between two and three centimeters thick. It felt heavy for the size; a sensation only gold could create. He ran his thumb across it, turned it in his hand, feeling small pits on three sides. The second bar was identical or, rather, probably poured and pulled from the same mold, as it had the same pits on the three sides as the first bar.

"These came to my house two days ago," she said.

"Who from?"

"There was a note." She put a yellow piece of paper on the counter.

The note read, *You deserve some of this, too. I'm sorry,* written in black ink, in shaky handwriting.

"Did you check these for prints?" Wolf held the gold bar away from him, suddenly aware of how much he was fondling it.

"Yeah. Nothing. I checked the note, too. They were both clean."

"What about the handwriting?" Wolf asked.

"Nothing definitive. I checked it against my brother's high-school yearbook. It's close, but," she shook her head, "I don't think it's his handwriting. But it's shaky. Could have been him if he was ... on drugs, or ..." she stopped talking.

"What about Jeffries? Have you checked it against his handwriting?"

She blinked, looking like she snapped out of some deep thoughts. "No, not yet."

He twisted the bar for another minute, thinking, and

then set it down. It rang out as he set it on the granite counter. Then he walked to the window again, this time seeing nothing of the view outside.

He thought of Wade Jeffries on the trail, with a backpack loaded so full it had almost split at the seams, with material that clanked with every step. *With gold.* He thought of the load he must have been carrying. It was heavy enough to compact a disc in his back at the least.

"What are those, pound bars?" Wolf asked, turning to look out the window.

Luke shook her head. "Kilogram bars. Kilo bars."

"That's worth at least ... I have no idea how much that's worth."

"A kilo bar is about thirty-two troy ounces. I haven't checked the price of gold today, but the other day I calculated one of these to be just over thirty-eight thousand dollars."

Wolf pictured Jeffries's eyes, with the look of fear that his handkerchief and his baseball cap couldn't hide. "They were after the gold in his backpack."

"Wade Jeffries?"

Wolf didn't hear her. He was over seven thousand miles away, thinking about Tora Bora, Afghanistan. "Bactrian gold?" he asked to no one.

Luke jumped up and sat on the counter next to him. "What?"

"The caves of Tora Bora." Wolf blinked and turned toward Luke. "They were a Taliban stronghold right around the time of 9/11. That is, until allied forces went in. I had a buddy in special forces who went in after the initial bombing runs, and he talked about how it was a real possibility they'd find some sort of stash, either of money, or gold, or jewels. That was part of the financial life-blood of the Taliban."

"So what did you say? Bacteria something?" she asked.

"Bactrian gold," Wolf said.

"What is that, a legend?"

"No, not a legend. It was the real deal. A stash of gold that's the national pride of Afghanistan." He looked at Luke. "I heard the story while I was over there. We all did. It was a local hot topic before 9/11. And then after 9/11, when the Taliban was after the gold, it was even hotter.

"In the seventies, the Soviets uncovered some ancient graves in northern Afghanistan, in an area that used to be known as Bactria two thousand plus years ago. There was something like twenty thousand pieces of gold and jewelry found inside. Then the Soviets invaded, and the country went into civil war, and the gold disappeared.

"Twenty years later, in the late eighties, it showed back up, in Afghanistan. The president was flaunting it, making it known it hadn't been looted by the Russians all those years ago, and it was still a national treasure they'd kept in their homeland. But then it disappeared again.

"Well, it didn't disappear; it was moved to the vault of the central bank in Kabul. Moved by a few select members of the government who chose to keep the treasure intact, rather than melt it down for however many millions it was worth. But when I was over there, the location of it was still a mystery. There were rumors it was in the central bank, but it wasn't known if it was in the vault or not, and nobody was telling. And right after 9/11, the Taliban wanted to find out once and for all, so they raided the bank, put guns to the heads of the bank officials, and made them open it up."

"Did they find it?" Luke asked.

"No. They made off with a bunch of money and bullion, but not the Bactrian gold. Or, at least, that's how the story went."

"So it wasn't in the vault all along?" she asked.

Wolf shook his head. "A couple of years after 9/11, I remember hearing that they found it *was* in the vault. They had somehow tricked the Taliban. Hidden the boxes under paintings or something like that."

"Or," Luke said, "the Taliban could have gotten away with some of it after all, you're saying, and the story was wrong."

Wolf shrugged and took a sip of beer. "That's really just the tip of the iceberg when it comes to treasure gone missing in the past thirty years in Afghanistan. This gold could be the Bactrian stuff melted down into bars, or this could be some of the bullion the Taliban made off with that day, melted down from the larger bars to a more manageable, or sellable, size. Or it could be some of the national treasure that was never accounted for. We were briefed that seventy percent of the treasure was looted from the Afghanistan National Museum during the civil war, and most of it still hasn't been found.

"Obviously, I can't exactly say what gold this is." Wolf pointed at the bars. "But whatever it is, your brother's EOD team got it, brought it home, and ... whoever came after me and Jack was after Jeffries because he had this. A whole lot of this. And whoever got Jeffries has a new net worth with a long line of digits."

Luke set down her beer and paced, staring at the ground. "So how did they do it? Let's say my brother and his team find a bunch of gold, whether it's the Bactrian stuff, or national treasure bullion, or whatever, then what?"

Wolf shrugged. "Then they get the gold out. Out of the hole, and into a Humvee, and blow up the cave, and disappear into the mountains, or a pay a local to stay hidden, and go MIA. It would be difficult for engineers to come in with the necessary equipment to excavate the collapsed cave, to look for your brother and his team. The terrain, and the overall atmosphere, isn't suited for it."

"That's what my CIA contact told me after my brother's memorial. He told me that the official word from the army was that it was next to impossible to pull them out of the rubble. But he said the real reason was that it wasn't high priority. Like it was obvious my brother and his team had been somewhere they weren't supposed to be, and they'd got what they'd had coming to them."

They stood in silence for a few moments.

"How many other people were on the EOD team, besides your brother and the other missing men?"

"Four more," Luke said.

Wolf frowned. "So eight total? And what did the other four say happened?"

Luke shook her head. "They said they were under orders to be there. Not in the caves, but the valley a few miles away. It was apparently a two-day convoy, and they were on their way through to Kabul, and then onward to Bagram Air Base."

"And your brother and the other three men broke off?" Wolf asked. "What was their explanation to the rest of the team?"

"There was no explanation. One of the soldiers said Hartley, Jeffries, and Quinn disappeared with a Humvee one night, and my brother woke up the next morning and went after them, alone."

"Alone?" Wolf pulled the corners of his mouth down. "That's a strange decision."

Luke nodded. "You're telling me."

"They have GPS transponders on those Humvees," Wolf said. "Your brother could have easily gone after them and tracked them down."

Luke nodded. "Or maybe he was in on the whole scheme and that's why he went by himself. Maybe there was a rendezvous point they'd set up beforehand."

Wolf stared at the floor. "Maybe your brother wasn't part of this. Maybe he was sucked in somehow."

Luke looked at him. Her eyes started shimmering and she lowered her gaze to the gold. "So then why would he drop this on my doorstep with a note that says, *Some of this is yours, too. I'm sorry?*"

Wolf shrugged. "That's not exactly an admission of guilt from your brother. It could have been one of the other three EOD team guys. You said it yourself, it didn't look exactly like his handwriting."

Luke sighed and took a sip of her beer.

"Let's talk about how they got out of the country,"

Wolf said. "Four men and a hoard of gold? How does that go down?"

She stopped and dug another beer out of the refrigerator. Handing it to Wolf, she bent down to get another. "They'd have to have had outside help, right?"

Wolf nodded. "Yeah, they would. They'd need to fly out of Afghanistan, or drive their Humvee into Iran or Pakistan, and then get home, which seems less likely to me. It would have been difficult to go, by road, undetected with a Humvee full of American soldiers and gold. They would have been stopped. Searched. It would have caused some sort of incident that would have gotten around, and into the ears of your contacts at the CIA." Wolf stared at the unopened beer, lost in thought.

"Well, however they did it," Luke said, "it worked. Just take a look at the Jeffrieses' peach orchard and house. Maybe that was the gold money at work there. Maybe you and your son walked into Wade Jeffries being punished. You know, for going outside the circle, the pact, and giving his family money? When you saw him on the trail, they'd probably just killed his family for knowing too much. You saw Julie Jeffries. She'd been interrogated before she was killed. They must have been asking her what she knew."

Wolf looked at Luke, and then to the gold bars on the counter.

She followed his eyes, and took a deep breath. "If that theory is correct, then I'm next." Luke shook her head. Her eyes narrowed to dangerous slits, and her lips moved soundlessly.

Wolf knew what she was thinking: It was bad enough

that innocent people were being killed, but it was a whole new level of bad that her brother was involved.

"How did you and your brother get along?" Wolf asked.

"Like, would my brother be willing to come kill me?"

Wolf shrugged. "It doesn't make sense that he would give you some of the gold, then come after you to kill you. Unless ... you two really didn't get along."

"No, we were close. He was my younger bro, and I was his big sis," she said, and then she picked at the label of her beer. "I guess it's more complicated than that."

"Try me. I'm used to complicated," Wolf said.

She smiled meekly, and then looked at Wolf. "My dad left us. When we were kids. I was graduating high school, and he was a couple of years younger. And we both went through some tough times after that. My older brother, he didn't seem to care as much, but me and Brian ... I went to college, and went through my changes and struggles and whatever, and he stayed here and started doing meth and coke. I snapped out of my funk, but he just kept on digging deeper into his. That went on for years, the drugs, and stealing, and ... and finally, right before I went to Quantico, I told him he had to shape up. And I told him I'd come back and bust his ass and throw him in jail as many times as it would take for him to stop being a coward, and to start living."

She stared at the wall in deep thought.

"So you pushed him to join the military?" Wolf asked quietly.

"Yeah. And he did. And according to him, he loved it. I

lost track of how many tours in the Middle East he volunteered for. But for eight years he just kept coming and going, happy as ever. I actually wondered if he'd gone suicidal and wanted to die over there. Even asked him that once. But he told me I'd saved his life and not to worry about him over there. He said he loved it and owed me everything." Her eyes glistened. "Now I wonder if he meant that or was just somehow playing me."

Wolf turned around and scanned the property outside the window. The bushes swayed in the wind. The grass bent in waves. The rain had stopped and the clouds were breaking up. Shafts of sunlight lanced out of the sky onto the valley below.

"I missed something," Wolf said finally, turning back to Luke.

She wiped her eyes and looked up with a hard expression, as if trying to hide the dark place she'd just allowed herself to go. "What do you mean? Where?"

"On the mountain."

Luke frowned. "Okay, can you be more specific?"

"We're talking about four men that went missing in Afghanistan, and I killed someone at our campsite that wasn't any of those men. I'd bet my life on it."

Luke narrowed her eyes. "Okay."

Wolf nodded. "The math doesn't add up. There're four guys missing from Afghanistan, including your brother, but we're talking about five different men now."

"The outside man," Luke whispered, "who helped them into the country."

Wolf nodded. "I've been racking my brain, and I swear

there weren't any more vehicles in the parking lot that night. There weren't any when Jack and I parked there earlier in the day, either. So where did all these guys come from? And then where did they go? We have to go back up."

"Well, it's going to be dark in an hour, and it's probably still raining up there. We can't go now."

Wolf sighed and took a sip of his beer. "You'll have to be careful, tonight, that's for sure. You know about the gold now, and it fits that that's the reason why Jeffries's sister and mother were killed. Meanwhile, I need to go back into town."

"Why?"

"I need to call my deputies and see how they're doing with my son. Then I need to find a motel, get freshened, and get some sleep if we're heading back up to the trail tomorrow."

Luke rolled her eyes. "Shut up, you're staying here. I have an extra room with a bed in it."

Wolf looked around. He realized he felt the warmest he'd been in over a day, and didn't have any desire to argue the point.

"Thanks," he said.

CHAPTER 34

SERGEANT MCCALL SAT on a barstool in the Mountain Goat sipping a Guinness. He looked at the television and sighed. He could think of a dozen better ways to kill time than watching the Colorado Rockies get tromped by the Reds, but none were available, and he was flat tired from the hiking and driving he'd done all day.

He heard the muffled thumps of car doors shutting outside and turned, squinting into the evening sun that streamed through the west windows. The first wave of cops was showing up for dinner and to belt a few before heading home to their families. *Just like Daddy used to do,* he couldn't stop himself from thinking.

If only these cops and FBI agents knew the truth about the building they were walking into every night of the week. That it was Sergeant McCall who owned this place free and clear, and sucked four grand a month, and that was just his cut, out of the local law-enforcement paychecks to help fund his more lucrative deals. Deals that went down behind the backs of the local police, sheriff's deputies, and the local FBI. Not that it took a genius to outsmart the bunch of assholes that carried badges and IDs in this valley. McCall had met them all, and none of these guys could solve their way out of a shitter.

Sheriff Greene waddled in with Sergeant Willis and one of the many suck-up deputies of the department, Michaelson, trailing behind. McCall smiled and gave a high wave. They waved back, unsurprised to see him. He was sitting in his favorite stool, visiting his brother, like he did most nights of the week after clocking out at the station, or so he led them to believe.

McCall watched them sit down. Sergeant Willis popped back up to fetch a menu for Sheriff Greene from a neighboring table, and Michaelson was laughing at something the sheriff had said that he probably hadn't intended to be funny.

"You need another one?" Dirk, their hired-on manager, asked from behind the bar.

McCall shook his head. "Nah, thanks."

Dirk turned and tended to another patron sitting on the other side of the horseshoe bar. Dirk was a competent, strong man who could hold his own in a fight. And he could have run the place for a month without any input from Tyler or McCall. And if they'd given him access to the money, he'd be able to run it for years.

McCall saw him as the keystone for the Mountain Goat, and paid him accordingly to keep him happy and loyal. Without him, the bar wouldn't collapse, but any outside activities McCall and his brother partook in would have to be put on hold. Tyler would be chained to this place, taking orders, placing orders with vendors, cleaning glasses, and counting money. There wouldn't be any cocaine wholesale operation, no weed distribution chain they had a hand in, and sure as hell not the opportunity, the goldmine, they were sitting on right now.

He smiled a little, picked up his Guinness, and walked over to Sheriff Greene's table.

"Sheriff," McCall nodded.

"McCall," Greene said, keeping his eyes on the menu. "What's your brother got for specials tonight?"

Sergeant Willis smirked.

"Not sure. You'll have to check with Dirk."

Greene looked past McCall to the bar. "Can you get him?"

McCall blinked, noticing Willis was having trouble containing his full-fledged smile now.

"Sure," McCall said. "I wanted to ask you something first."

"Shoot," Greene said, studying the menu again.

"I just wanted to say I'd be happy to volunteer for the Rocky Points Music Festival that's happening this weekend. I know you already have Richter and Jones out there, but if they need anyone else, I wanted to make sure you know I'm interested. I could use a change of scenery."

Greene nodded and flipped a page. "All right. But I don't think they need it." Then he looked up and past McCall again. "Can you get Dirk over here? I'm famished."

McCall nodded and turned to the bar.

"Hey," Greene said. "What's with your brother? I saw him last night and he looked like death. Is he all right?"

McCall turned back. "He's not feeling well. Some sort of bug, I guess. In fact, I was going to check on him now. I'll get Dirk." He walked away from them.

"Can you tell Dirk to bring us a pitcher?" Willis called after him. "Budweiser."

McCall gritted his teeth and walked on. He passed the bar without looking at or saying anything to Dirk, knowing Dirk didn't need reminding of anything about doing his job efficiently, and entered the dark wood door to the back office.

Tyler looked up at him from behind the desk. "Hey."

"Hey." McCall shut the door behind him.

Tyler's cheeks had a red hue and he sat straight in the chair.

"You're looking better," McCall said.

Tyler nodded and the chair squeaked as he leaned toward the computer. "The doctor did me up pretty good today. Gave me some sort of vitamin concoction, and stuck me with some needles, right into the frickin' stitches."

McCall sat down on the couch and sighed. "Well, I've been freezing my ass off all day up there, but everything's set."

Tyler studied his brother. "So what's the plan for tonight?"

McCall leaned on his side, and the leather of the couch groaned under his weight. He wanted to just lie there for an hour or five, but there'd be the rest of his life to lounge around and do nothing if he chose to. If they passed over this last speed bump without incident. *Then* he could rest.

He dug his hand in his pocket and pulled out the crisp-edged metal key. He sat up, leaned forward, and slapped it on the desk.

Tyler picked it up and looked at it. "That's to her house?"

McCall nodded and sat back. The air in the cushion deflated slowly, and he was sucked into a deep comfort.

"How the hell did you get that?" Tyler asked, clearly impressed.

"Dragon's got a locksmith, and we employed him today."

Tyler narrowed his eyes and nodded. "That helps."

"Yes, it does."

CHAPTER 35

WOLF AND LUKE sat in silence on Luke's back deck, watching the last rays of sun as they disappeared behind the mountains across the valley. The few remaining clouds in the sky glowed bright orange, fading like cooling embers in a fire pit.

The tension between them had diminished greatly since their talk. Wolf mused that Luke had become a completely different person, easy-going and someone that he found easy to talk to. But as they sat conversing and enjoying another round of beers, Wolf still had a nagging feeling in his gut.

He wondered whether Luke's involvement was going to help or hinder them. He wondered what would happen if Luke was faced with the choice of taking her brother down, or hesitating. Wolf had seen hesitation kill many soldiers on the battlefield, and something told him he was edging closer to yet another battle.

"I'm heading in," she said, scooting back her plastic

chair. "Gonna take a shower. You can go after me, then we'll fix up that wound of yours. It probably looks like shit."

Wolf watched her walk to the sliding glass door.

"Make yourself at home," she said, unzipping her sweatshirt and getting started on the top of her blouse. "We can make some pasta when we're done."

Wolf nodded and averted his eyes to the exquisite view underneath her blouse. He'd already stolen a look at that earlier, and figured it didn't give him the right to take another. He felt himself blush a bit, and realized there was still plenty of tension between them, though it had morphed into a different kind.

After a few minutes, he stepped inside and walked into the cozy living room. It was just around the corner from the kitchen, and had windows that looked out onto the front property of the house. There was a bookshelf with a stack of pictures and personal papers, and lots of other things besides books.

Facing east, the space would be sunny and warm during the morning hours. Probably a room Luke never got the chance to sit and enjoy while the rays of sun streamed in. Not with her job, and with her apparent love of the outdoors. She was probably out biking a trail, or paddling a river, or riding a few miles on the motorcycle during her time off, rather than sitting down with a good book.

She had no television, and Wolf couldn't tell whether it was her décor on the walls or not. Maybe it wasn't even her furniture. Could have been a fully furnished rental, which would have explained the stack of boxes in the garage. Maybe there was no room for her personal stuff in the house.

He looked back at the stack of photos in hard frames, and then bent down and pulled out four of them. The first was a washed-out picture of her and her family framed in dark wood. She was little, probably ten years old, and just as cute then as she was now. Her little brother stood leaning against her, shorter and younger. Her older brother was tall and gangly looking, in his awkward teen years, and keeping his distance from the rest of them. Her father's smile was partially hidden by a bushy mustache. Her mother was pretty and young, wearing a heavily sprayed hairdo and a smile with eyes that looked more intelligent and aware than the Bernadette Richter of today. They all wore clothing that was way too tight for this day and age. The thing that really held Wolf's attention was Luke holding her father's hand.

Wolf furrowed his brow at the second photo. It was Luke alone on a mountainside, looking in her college years. It was taken on the Flatirons of Boulder, the jutting sandstone geological formations that loomed over the college town. She was dressed in a huge, baggy, yellow-and-black flannel shirt. She had green combat boots on, with baggy pants tucked into the top of them. She had a short boyish haircut that would have still looked cute on her if it weren't for the scowl on her face. She glared at the camera, like she despised the act of getting her picture taken.

"That was when I was a lesbian."

Wolf turned his head to see that Luke had snuck up on him.

She studied Wolf's surprised expression and laughed.

He blushed, startled by what she had just said, and how he'd been caught glancing down the length of her body, seeing that she was only wearing a T-shirt and what looked like nothing else.

Luke held a towel in her hand and pressed it against her wet hair, which was combed against her scalp and draping onto her shirt. She padded forward on her bare feet and stepped close, looking at the photo. She smelled like lotion and that great shampoo again, or whatever it was.

"I'm better now, though," she said.

She took the towel in both hands and scrubbed her hair as she walked away and around the corner, giving Wolf a fleeting glimpse of her white panties, which gently hugged her perfect butt.

He took a deep breath and looked back down at the photos.

"I took those out of my mom's house," she said from the kitchen.

"Why? To hide that you were related to your brother?"

There was no answer from the other room.

He looked down at the next photo, which was a picture of a young man in an army combat uniform with a name patch that said *Richter*. He had shaggy blond hair, disheveled by wind and dirtied by sand. He was standing in front of a tent with his helmet in hand, smiling wide.

"There's my brother," she said quietly. She was leaning against the wall with her legs crossed.

Wolf nodded, and set down the pictures on the shelf. "Sorry for snooping."

"That's all right. I have nothing to hide."

"Now," Wolf said with raised eyebrows, then looked past her down the hallway. "Do you mind?"

She walked back out of sight. "There's a towel on the counter in the bathroom. Have at it. I'll start making the food."

Wolf walked to the hallway, and looked to his right. Luke was bent over slightly in front of a lamp. She had just flipped it on, backlighting an oblique profile of her naked upper body underneath her shirt. He sighed quietly and walked to the bathroom door that billowed warm steam.

CHAPTER 36

McCALL KILLED the lights to his GCSD Ford Explorer
and shut off the engine. He opened the door all the way
until it bounced on its hinges, and then pulled the booties
out of the center console and put them in his pocket. He
slipped on the leather gloves, and made a shuddering fist
with each hand, stretching out the fine material. He pocketed the black ski mask and stepped out into the cool,
damp evening. The clouds were a dim orange, and it would
be completely dark in a matter of minutes; then they would
be able to pick their moment.

McCall crunched along the wet gravel of the dirt road
to the rear, and stepped into the running black Chevy Trail
Blazer that was parked behind him.

The inside of the cab was silent, save for the low
whoosh of the warm air coming out of the vents. No radio.
No nonsense.

Tyler sat inside, dressed identically to his older
brother, with a black pair of sweatpants, still creased from

the way they'd rested on the shelf at the store, a black jacket, black leather gloves, and black boots two sizes too big—by design, just in case. He had a ski mask in his pocket, a pair of light-blue booties, a knife strapped to his leg, and a silenced, untraceable Beretta on his belt—supplied by their go-to Aspenite on the other side of the law, Dragon.

Tyler flipped the headlights on and drove up the dirt road for a half-mile. Before they rounded the final corner he flipped them off, without McCall having to remind him to do so. They'd gone over the plan, and it was clear; they had complete faith in one another's abilities, as they'd been tried and tested many times over the years.

They stopped behind a grove of aspen trees, just short of Luke's house, and turned the truck around. They parked and got out, donned their ski masks, and walked into the trees.

The ground was wet from the day of rain, and the aspen leaves dripped cascades of cold water when they bumped a branch.

The house looked to be fully lit inside, which would help their efforts of sneaking up unnoticed, McCall thought, just as they'd have suspected at this time of night. He pulled his Beretta and clicked the safety off, then racked the slide. Tyler did the same, and they walked across the lawn to the side of the house.

CHAPTER 37

WOLF HAD ENJOYED THE SHOWER. Despite the pain in the ass of having to keep his stitches from getting too wet, the water had warmed his body and relaxed his still sore muscles from the exertion on the trail two nights before.

Luke had set out some bandages and cotton, and even though she'd mentioned helping with the redressing of the wound, he figured he'd get it over and done with now. He drew a cotton ball across a warm stream of water and dabbed the stitches. The skin around the cut had turned black. Pus oozed through the softened scabs, which flared with pain as he gently scrubbed.

He took off his towel from around his waist and wiped the mirror, then went to the window and opened it wide to let the steam escape. As the cool and warm air met, a puff of cloud formed and dissipated into the dark night.

He turned to the mirror and was surprised to see the shadows of two feet underneath the lit crack of the door.

Was Luke standing just outside, wondering whether to come in?

Wolf stood, contemplating the feet for a moment, wondering what to do. He reached for the door and heard a faint noise. He stopped short of grabbing the knob, because the noise, a crisp knock of something on wood, hadn't come from the other side of the door. It had come from down the hall.

Was there someone else visiting Luke's house?

Wolf bent down and looked underneath the door, and every muscle in his body flexed tight. There were two large feet, way too large to be Luke's, covered in blue fabric. Like booties worn by doctors or cops when they didn't want to contaminate a crime scene.

Before Wolf could straighten back up, the door exploded in splinters above his head. Three shots cracked through the wood in quick succession. There was a pause. At that moment, Wolf twisted and dove into the window screen. The thin wire mesh stretched out against his head and then gave way almost instantly, and Wolf tumbled out naked after it.

He felt wood splinters sting his right buttock as the window frame popped and exploded. For a brief moment, he tumbled in complete disorientation, seeing only the bright light of the window flipping in his view. Then he landed hard on his right side, knocking the wind out of himself. The cold of the ground was so startling that he cried out and sprung to his feet as if he'd landed on a trampoline. Without thinking, he sprinted into the night. He heard the spit of a suppressed weapon behind him and saw the aspen trees in front of him flash with light. A bullet slapped one of the white trunks next to his head and it sprayed his face with bark. A piece of wood dug into his open eye, stinging so bad that he slapped himself in the face and almost fell over.

"Outside! Outside!" he heard a man's voice yell from the house. His voice was frantic, and was yelling back into the house, not out at Wolf.

The shots stopped coming, and Wolf stole a glance over his shoulder at the windows. Through his one good eye he saw no one was in the bathroom window anymore, and he couldn't see any movement behind the other lit panes of glass. *Luke.*

His gut tightened at a vision of her lying sprawled on the hardwood floor with a puddle of blood growing underneath her head.

Just then he heard the thump of boots on the back porch and he saw two figures dressed in black sprint onto the lawn. One ran strangely, with a limp arm at his side, and Wolf knew instantly that it was the man Jack had shot. They came right at him. The first was much quicker, and a flashlight flicked on in his hand.

Wolf turned and ran as fast as he could, dodging the white trunks of aspen. The ground was pitch black, and his right eye streamed with tears, making it impossible to see where he was stepping. His feet crunched down on jagged sticks and rocks, and slick decaying wood, tearing skin with each step. Despite the pain, he accelerated to full speed, and continued as fast as he could in the direction he remembered as downhill.

More spits came from behind, and the night lit up around him with each, but the bullets missed each time. Wolf saw the bouncing light of the man's flashlight on the trees, and it seemed to be gaining on him.

Wolf dodged left and right, but was immediately wary of losing speed, and opted to go straight again. In his fastest all-out sprint, he grunted in defiance of any danger, knowing he must be gaining a lead on the men behind him. A few steps later, the trees around him vanished and he was looking at points of light, blurry in his wet vision. The instant he realized it was the lights of the valley below, he was already tipping forward with his legs whiffing the ground that had dropped out underneath him.

The wind rushed in his ears. He looked down and saw nothing. His head thumped, and stars filled his vision as he connected with the ground. His naked skin raked against rocks and gravel as he rolled uncontrollably, like a fighter pilot caught in a death spiral, smacking cold bushes and thick juniper trunks, and bouncing off boulders, until finally he felt sand on his back and slid to a stop.

He lay motionless for a few seconds, sucking in deep breaths with lung-stinging exertion, watching the blanket of night stars above twist and return like a rotary phone dial.

For what seemed a few minutes, he lay in a thoughtless daze. Then, finally, he sat up. He looked up the mountainside he'd just tumbled down, and awareness came back to him in a flash, sending his heart racing.

He stopped breathing and listened, heard only the faint whoosh of cars and trucks driving on the road far below him, and the bouncing of his shivering jaw. There was no movement above, no one coming down the hill. Nothing.

Wolf walked up the slope deliberately, slowly, keeping behind the junipers and sage bushes when he could to shield himself from the aim of the gunmen above. His feet slipped almost every other step up the steep incline, and the flesh on the bottom of his feet was so raw he couldn't feel them anymore.

By the time he reached the back yard, his whole body was shaking, which felt like a jackhammer on his bad arm. But he remained otherwise motionless behind a juniper tree, surveying the windows for any movement. Then he saw her. Luke was face down on the hardwood floor of the eating area inside, and that was all Wolf needed to take the risk of running to the house.

He sprinted across the lawn, up onto the wood deck, and darted through the open sliding glass door. He slipped on his feet, slick with blood and moisture from the lawn, and ducked down next to Luke.

"Luke. Luke." He studied her close, and couldn't see any blood. There was nothing on her white T-shirt or on her gray sweatpants.

"Kristen," he tried, and pushed her over onto her back. She flopped over and her eyes were closed. He checked her pulse and it was strong. He pulled open an eyelid to check the pupil, and she twisted her head and groaned.

Relief that she was okay quickly gave way to panic that

he was seconds from getting shot in the back. He remembered his pistol, and how it sat on the bed of the spare bedroom in his holster.

He stood up and turned around. There was no one in the living room or kitchen. He pressed himself against the wall and peeked down the hallway toward the bathroom and bedrooms. There was no movement, so he stepped out, slunk down the hall, and peeked into the bedroom.

He grabbed his gun, and though he was shivering harder than ever, he felt warmed by the assurance that the weapon was now in his hand. He stalked through her bedroom, down the hall, past Luke and out into the garage. There was no one. They were gone.

When he returned to the kitchen, he saw Luke grabbing her head and leaning on her elbow. She looked up at Wolf and her jaw dropped.

"What happened to you?" she croaked.

Wolf looked down at his naked body. Bright-red blood flowed down his left arm from the wound, now ripped wide open. The entire right side of his body, from foot to shoulder, was streaked with red scrapes, blood droplets oozing from them. Everywhere in between was covered with dirt skid marks or dangling pieces of squashed plants.

He walked past her and to the front door, then opened it and looked into the night. The road at the end of the driveway was clear of cars, and at that moment he remembered seeing a black SUV when he'd gotten up off the ground below the window and headed into the trees. It'd been how he'd gotten his bearings of where downhill was.

"I think they're gone," Wolf said, turning around.

Luke was gone, and Wolf raised his gun.

Then she stepped out of the hallway and into view. She held her own gun and a blanket. She walked to Wolf with a vacant look in her eyes and handed the soft, heavy, enveloping square of warmth out to him.

CHAPTER 38

LUKE WOKE FROM A HEAVY, dreamless sleep. No, something had woken her. Something close, but how close? Was it a dog barking?

She blinked and focused on the dim room in front of her. There was a tube in her arm, and she was tilted up at an angle. A dark television mounted high in the corner of the room reflected a small rectangle of light, and above it was a ceiling lined with institutional-looking asbestos tiles.

She turned her head and squinted from the pain that throbbed inside the right side of her skull.

"Uhhhh!"

She sat up abruptly, forgetting the pain to see what had made the horrific noise next to her.

Wolf sat facing her in a chair on her left. His arms were crossed, like he was cold, and his eyes were scrunched tight. His head was tilted forward unnaturally, like he was worried about something crawling up his legs.

She realized he was sleeping. They were in the hospital. She was in a hospital bed, and he was sleeping next to her.

"Jack!" he yelled.

She fought the pain, leaned out of the bed and grabbed his leg.

"Wolf," she said.

The chair squealed as he pushed himself back and opened his eyes. Then he shook his head and looked around. For an instant he was in sheer terror, like some unseen demon was coming at him. The next, he saw Luke and relaxed his face.

"How are you doing?" he asked. His folded arms rose up and down with his heaving breaths.

"How am I?" she asked. "How are you? Are you okay? You were having a wicked dream."

Wolf blinked and gave a thousand-yard stare, then shrugged. "Yeah, I'm fine. Just a dream I've been having lately."

"You said Jack," she said quietly. "You yelled it."

There was a knock on the door, and Luke realized she was exposing her naked ass through a hospital gown to whoever was about to walk in. She sat down and felt the bowling ball shift in her skull again.

"Come in," she said testily.

It was Danny. "What the hell are you doing here?" she asked.

Her big brother rolled his eyes and stepped into the room. Wolf stood up and Danny walked over to him.

Here it goes, she thought. Danny was predictable as ever when it came to men in her life. Not that Wolf was a "man in her life." *Would he be?* But being seated so close to her hospital bed, her older brother was bound to jump to the same hot-headed conclusion he always had growing up whenever a member of the opposite sex talked to her. *You're not good enough for her. Forget it. If you have a problem with that, here's my fist.*

"Hey. Haven't seen you in a long time. How are you?" he said, as he shook Wolf's hand.

Luke scoffed. "Are you kidding? You two know each other?"

Danny was smiling and sizing up Wolf like an old friend he hadn't seen in years. "We played—"

"Football together. Yeah, yeah," Luke said. "Why the hell am I in this hospital bed?" She pointed at Wolf. "You should be in here, not me."

"They stitched me back up last night, cleaned and patched up some abrasions." Wolf shrugged and raised his eyebrows. "You, on the other hand, passed out when the cops got to your house last night, and you've been out ever since. How does your head feel?"

She put her hand on her scalp and felt a huge bump that fit inside her whole palm. "Ahhh. Jesus."

"You have a concussion," Wolf said.

Luke pressed her fingers on the bump, feeling a small scab on the peak of it underneath her hair.

"Thanks for making the call last night," Danny said to Wolf. "Deputy Rachette came to my hotel as soon as he'd heard from you, and I drove straight here. I've been waiting outside for you guys to wake up for hours." He shook his head. "What the hell happened?"

"Two men broke into your sister's house. They knocked her out and shot a few times at me, then I guess thought better of it and left."

Luke had a vague memory of Wolf standing over her naked, holding a pistol in his hand, and dismissed it for a perverted dream.

"Is that what happened?" she said. "I don't remember shit."

Wolf didn't answer, and Danny looked between them. "What the hell is going on? Are these the same guys that were shooting at you and your son the other night?"

Wolf paused for a second, then nodded. "Yes. They are. Last night, one of the guys had a limp arm from where my son shot him. It was them."

"We have to tell my brother about Brian," Luke said.

Danny frowned and looked at her. "What?"

Wolf told him to sit down, and they spent the next few minutes getting him up to speed. About Wolf and his son seeing Wade Jeffries on the trail, and how he was a part of Brian's explosives ordnance team that had gone MIA. About the gold that had showed up on Luke's doorstep, and how Brian and his team were seemingly killing—each other and innocent people—all in the effort to keep their secret safe.

When they were done with their story, Danny stood up and cracked the window shades with a finger. He stared out for a few moments, then let them snap shut and turned to Luke. There was a burning hatred in his eyes that she hadn't seen in her older brother before. Even when their father had left his eyes hadn't shown such disdain. She knew he'd always resented his little brother, for reasons she couldn't fully understand growing up, and it was like he'd been waiting for permission to finally hate Brian. *Permission granted.*

"Why didn't you tell me about this? You knew about this for, for what? Months?" Her brother glared.

"I didn't *know* anything," she said, "but I did know that if I told you anything, you'd freak out."

"But you suspected"—he pointed at Wolf—"after they shot at him and his son, you suspected, and let me leave town to, no offense Wolf, to go watch a stupid music festival? When our brother is roaming the mountains killing people?"

Danny shook his head and turned to the window again.

Luke didn't speak, and tried to steady her escalating breath. They sat in silence, listening to the electric hum of the monitor next to her and the muffled voices out in the hall.

"I always knew Brian was screwed up," Danny finally said, "but this is a whole new level for him. Murdering women? Trying to kill his own sister? For some money he can only spend if he acts like a dead man for the rest of his life? How far can the kid fall?"

Luke's stomach sank.

"He didn't try to kill your sister."

They looked at Wolf.

"They shot at me. They hit your sister in the back of the head."

Dan looked at Luke and then back to Wolf. "So, what?

He didn't try to kill his sister. Noble move. He still tried to kill a cop and his son. He's still fucked up."

Wolf sighed and looked up at the ceiling, then down at his watch. "Dan, last night I was telling your sister how that load on Jeffries's back was huge. It must have been over a hundred pounds of gold in that pack. I don't think he came from *up* the trail. It's just too steep." Wolf shook his head. "We need topo maps, and we have to go back up there."

"And we need the cavalry this time," Dan said without hesitation. "We aren't screwing around after last night. I don't care if this is my brother or not."

Wolf raised his eyebrows. "I don't object to that. I'm about done getting shot at."

Luke pulled the sheets off and slid out of the bed.

"Whoa." Wolf held up both his hands. "You need to rest with a head injury like that."

Dan smirked and turned away.

Luke gave Wolf the same glare she'd used growing up, on her brothers in the face of her wrath—the kind of wrath that left chunks of scalp on the floor when she was through.

"Get me my clothes," she said.

Wolf nodded without another word, and he and her brother left the room.

CHAPTER 39

WOLF DROVE Luke's Tahoe up Grimm Lake Road as delicately as possible.

Luke sat next to him in the passenger seat as they bounced, scraped and jolted their way up. She leaned forward and gripped the ceiling bar, her face slack and eyelids drooping, trying to keep her head still as she stared out the windshield.

Wolf knew she was fighting the jarring pain in her head that each movement must have caused, but so far she had said nothing.

There was a stream of five more SUVs behind them, four GCSD and one FBI, carrying a total of ten men with all the latest equipment and gadgets they would need.

Wolf hoped his hunch was right, and after a preliminary look at the maps chances were good that it was. The plan was simple—return to where Wolf and Jack had seen Jeffries and retrace the man's suspected path on foot. Satellite photos showed a thin off-road trail—a jeep trail that, they all agreed, would probably make the road they were on now look like a paved interstate highway.

That fact made them opt to stick to Grimm Lake Road —driving up to the lot Wolf and Jack had parked at, and go from there on foot, rather than risk traveling up an unknown route that could even be washed out from the melt waters that had flowed strong only a matter of weeks ago.

Wolf finally reached the lot and bounced to a stop. He pressed the parking brake, shut off the engine, and passed the keys to Luke. Her eyes looked dull.

She narrowed her lids, reading his thoughts. "Don't worry about me," she said.

Wolf turned away and slid out of the truck.

It was mid-morning, and the air was crisp and cool. There was no wind, which made the sun warmer on Wolf's skin. He zipped up his Carhartt, which he'd gotten, along with a change of clothing, from his SUV in the FBI field-office parking lot the previous night.

The fresh bandage on his upper arm felt tight, and the pain from each movement seemed worse than before. He figured that was probably a normal consequence of having a line of thirty stitches, then ripping them all open and sewing them back up. He took the white sling out of his pocket and draped it over his head, then tucked his arm in.

"We're quite the healthy pair," Luke said, hobbling up next to him.

They watched patiently as each vehicle lumbered into sight, parked, and their occupants stepped out and got situated.

After ten minutes of packing and gearing up, they were on the trail and heading up at a good pace.

Wolf took the lead, followed closely by the two FBI agents from Luke's field office, Special Agents Brookhart and Harris, then Deputy Richter, and the remaining train of men and women deputies with the Garfield County Sheriff's Department, with Luke somewhere in the middle.

Wolf saw that even after twenty straight minutes of a brisk pace, they had all kept up easily, and Luke was no exception despite her condition.

Just before they reached the point where Wolf and Jack had seen Jeffries and his comical dance with his heavy backpack, a soft ringing came from the pocket of Special Agent Brookhart. Wolf watched Brookhart pull out his cell, wondering just what phone company he used, and how much it was going to cost Wolf to change to that plan.

"Brookhart," he said. "Yes ... Okay, thanks."

Brookhart hung up and shoved the phone back in his pocket. "They've identified some fingerprints at Agent Luke's house."

Wolf stopped and turned around. "And?"

"Brian Richter."

Wolf's pulse jumped at the news and he looked back at Deputy Dan Richter, who was craning his neck at the mention of his last name.

"What was that?" he asked, and stepped up to join them.

"That was our lab," Brookhart said. "We found your brother's fingerprints at the scene last night. At your sister's house."

Richter shook his head and looked back at Luke, and then waved her up.

She approached quickly. "Yeah?"

"They found Brian's fingerprints at your house last night," Dan said.

Luke's face dropped.

They stood and stared dumbly at one another for a few seconds, and then Wolf turned and started walking again.

...

Ten minutes later they reached the meadow where Wolf and Jack had seen Jeffries and stopped. The lack of wind and the warm sun above was getting to Wolf. He'd broken into a full sweat, and unzipped his Carhartt to let the cool air onto his torso. The scratches covering the right side of his body were inflamed by the rubbing of his sweaty clothing, and it itched underneath his arm bandage to the point that he wanted to shoot it again with his pistol, just so he could feel anything else but the nagging irritation.

He blocked it out and surveyed the laminated topo map, Deputy Richter looming over his shoulder.

"Looks like there." Richter poked his finger on a spot on the map.

Wolf looked up and to the left. There was a valley cut in between the tall peaks and, according to the map, there would be only a gradual rise in elevation for over a mile into the valley. There were two more similar valleys well ahead of them, but this was where they'd seen Jeffries. And sure enough, this first offshoot valley ended at a point that was close to the four-wheel-drive trail—the only other vehicle-access point for over twenty square miles.

"That's gotta be it." Wolf nodded.

"What's it?" Luke asked shuffling up next to them.

"That's the valley Jeffries must have walked in from." Wolf pointed.

She followed his eyes and nodded, and Wolf saw her wince a little as she did so.

He gave her a concerned look, this time ignoring the flash of defiance in her eyes.

"Drink a lot of water," he said.

She nodded with resignation and unscrewed her canteen.

They set off again, continued up the main trail for another five minutes and stopped.

"Here?" Deputy Richter asked from behind Wolf.

They were at the mouth of the narrow valley that meandered off the left side of the trail. Faint lines forked through the dry grass, forked again, and joined countless times, worn by deer, elk, bear, mountain lions, and other native game animals of the area, and then disappeared into a dense pine forest.

They walked through the brittle grass, and buzzing insects hopped like popcorn in a pan. A grasshopper landed on Wolf's cheek and he swiped it away, ignoring the memory the tiny creature had triggered.

Just as it was heating up to unbearable, they stepped into the fragrant pines offering shade every few feet. The game trails meandered to the left toward a trickling stream. The line of men and women behind him followed, but was spreading thin, and he noticed that Luke had moved up to fourth. She now moved as quickly and gracefully as the first day he'd met her, perhaps getting a second wind on the flatter terrain.

After they continued up the valley for another twenty minutes, it gradually dawned on Wolf that a quiet had descended on them. Save the bubbling of water in the gully, the only sounds Wolf heard were the scrape and crunch of his boots and his easy breathing. There were no tittering chipmunks or squirrels, no birds whistling, no rustle of branches in the trees. Even the buzzing insects had stopped.

Then he caught the first whiff of death. He stopped and turned to Deputy Richter, who was still close behind him. He was standing straight with wide eyes, and he nodded to Wolf. He'd smelled it too.

Wolf heard one deputy mumble to another down the line, and soon there was a low grumble of voices.

Wolf pulled his pistol and racked the slide, hearing the men and women do the same thing behind him.

They followed the creek around the next bend, and then finally something besides more trees came into view. It was a small, green-roofed shack made of decaying wood, no more than fifteen by twenty by ten feet. There was a boarded-up window facing them, and a single pipe vent on the roof.

Wolf stopped and held up his hand, gun pointing to the sky. He heard the shuffling footsteps behind him halt, a few hushed whispers, then nothing.

Wolf squinted, studying the vent. There was no smoke.

Then he studied the area. There were no vehicles, and no movement of any kind. He saw another building. It was tough to see at first, almost invisible, because it was painted forest green and tucked into the trees.

And there was the smell. There was no getting around it now. Every breath was saturated with it.

He moved toward the back of the cabin, breathing through his mouth, keeping his pistol pointed forward.

Long grasses tickled the rear of the cabin, and on the side was a small stack of firewood that had been dwindled to two rows, surrounded by flakes of bark and splintered pieces of white pine. *Recently used,* he thought.

At the front of the cabin were two windows with a red tic-tac-toe pattern of wood trim in each. Both were boarded with plywood from the inside, as the glass inside the small squares was either hanging in shards or gone.

The front door was warped from years of blocking the elements. However, it blocked nothing now because it stood wide open. Inside was dark and featureless, except for two legs lying on the ground and protruding from the entryway. They wore standard-issue tan army combat boots and pants. Anything beyond was impossible to see without getting closer.

As Wolf approached he saw it was a dead body and undoubtedly the source of the smell. Getting nearer, more of the corpse came into view. It was dressed in a desert camouflage Army Combat Uniform.

There was noise here—an angry buzzing—and it was getting louder. A cloud of flies jumped and swarmed as he stepped into the doorway, revealing the gray flesh of a dead man's face. The skin was broken and gouged from where the insects had dined. None of the features of the man's face would be recognizable, even to his mother.

"Whoa," Luke said next to him.

Wolf turned. "Yeah."

"Anyone else in there?"

Wolf stepped further in, opening up the view for the others behind him.

"Nobody," he said.

There was a single bed against the far wall with a ripped-up, brown, feather mattress that was probably as old as Wolf. On it was a twisted sub-zero sleeping bag that looked much newer. There were two more identical-looking sleeping bags wadded up in their sacks and lying underneath the bed. A small wooden table with three rickety chairs stood against one of the walls, and a black heating stove was in the center of the cabin, the iron door wide open. Inside was a pile of gray ashes, and a few had spilled out onto the splintered, warped floorboards.

He stepped out quickly and put his sleeve over his mouth, then looked toward the other structure that was over near the creek. The structure was in stark contrast with the cabin—clean, a perfect rectangle, with smooth metal walls painted a fresh coat of forest green.

"It's a shipping container," Special Agent Brookhart said, banging the side of it with his hand. The metal reverberated loud.

"It's a C-H-U," Wolf said.

"A what?" Deputy Richter asked.

"NATO troops have been using these for years.

They're housing units, converted from old shipping containers. Container Housing Units. C-H-Us. They call them CHUs." Wolf pronounced it *shoos*. "They ship these things by plane and sea to bases all over. Usually using private cargo companies."

Brookhart put latex gloves on and unlatched one of the doors; then he swung it open. An instant later he stumbled back, like he was ducking from an explosion blast.

"Jesus!" he said, coughing uncontrollably.

There were two more dead bodies inside, lying on their backs, with the undersides of their combat boots pointing out. Wolf holstered his gun and covered his mouth with his sleeve, then walked to the doorway. He unlatched the second door and swung it open, illuminating the full interior.

The inside was hot and humid, and Wolf didn't dare to breathe in one molecule of the foul air inside, keeping his face tightly pressed against his sleeve.

The two men stared at the ceiling through cloudy, unseeing eyes. They were both far more recognizable than the third man in the cabin, and Wolf could see that they were both members of the missing EOD team.

Wolf pulled his sleeve away to talk. "Wade Jeffries, the guy we saw on the trail, and Marcus Quinn."

Brookhart came up next to him, holding his breath with clamped lips, and swiped through some pictures on his phone. "Yep."

"And it stands to reason that's Chad Hartley in the cabin," Wolf said, shoving his face against his sleeve again and sucking in a breath through his coat fibers.

Wolf wanted to turn around and leave, to dive out of the doorway of the stifling container, but he stepped forward instead. The dead man on the left, Marcus Quinn, had a bullet hole in the center of his forehead. It looked like he'd been executed from the front. It was too neat, too central, to be otherwise. He was dressed in the same way as the dead man in the cabin, in the combat uniform worn by thousands of troops stationed in the Middle East.

Wade Jeffries, however, had on that same green civilian Columbia jacket Wolf remembered from the trail, and the Boston Red Sox hat firmly fixed to his head. The jacket was pierced and stained red in the chest and the arm. Wolf thought back on the night he and Jack had heard the two rifle shots.

Wolf looked at Jeffries's tattoo, then at his face. He had looked somehow different that afternoon, he thought, and then he realized why. Jeffries had been wearing a handkerchief that day, and it had been obscuring the lower part of his face from Wolf most of the time. Wolf wasn't used to seeing the man's jaw line and neck so clearly.

Wolf turned and walked out of the container. Stepping quickly away from both structures, he sucked in a lungful of air. He turned around and saw Luke coming out of the container after him.

She shook her head. "Looks like Quinn was executed."

Wolf nodded. "And Jeffries was hunted. My hunch was right that night. He'd been hit by two rifle shots. Probably bled out underneath the hundred pounds of gold strapped to his back."

"They brought Jeffries here, and the gold. And they

had to chase you two, and get rid of the body next to the fire." Luke whistled. "That's one busy night. You're sure none of these other guys was the man at the fire that night?"

Wolf shook his head. "No. Jeffries in there was on the trail, but it was someone else entirely at the fire."

She eyed him and nodded after a few moments.

The forensics team began preparing their gear and suiting up, and the rest of the team cautiously examined the perimeter for clues.

Wolf stood with Luke, sucking on his water bottle. He offered her a sip and she took it. When she handed it back, he ignored her, because he was fixated on the two deputies examining the exterior of the container. One of the team members was looking up at the top edge of the roof, and calling another over to look.

"What is it?" she asked.

"Good question." Wolf walked to the two men. "What is it?" he asked.

The deputy pointed to the container with his thumb. "They painted the container recently, maybe to conceal the numbers underneath, who knows. Looks like they even did some filing"—he pointed—"right here where the serial number usually is. You can see some filings and paint chips on the ground."

"Yeah?" Wolf said, stopping next to him.

"So, a serial number is how they keep track of ship-ments, who owns what container, what's in them, where they are. All that. But these guys screwed up if they were trying to hide what container this was." The man smiled and pointed up at the top edge of the container, toward what looked like a small painted-over bolt.

"I don't see what you're pointing at," Wolf said.

"That is a radio frequency ID tag."

He nodded and looked back at the deputy. "Which ... will tell us the information about this container?"

The deputy nodded. "Where it came from, who took it, what was in it, everything."

"How do we read it?" Wolf asked.

The deputy shrugged and rubbed his chin. "Take it down to the rail yard, or a trucking company that uses active RF ID scanners, have someone scan it, then we'll get a lead."

"Bag that and give it to me," Luke said, appearing at Wolf's side. "Please," she added curtly.

CHAPTER 40

RACHETTE SAT with Jack and Patterson in the SUV, eating burgers and fries.

"What about Schwarzenegger?" Jack asked from the back seat, using his best Schwarzenegger to ask the question.

Patterson rolled her eyes. "When are you guys going to stop? Let's just say I've met everybody. All celebrities. Then we can move on with our lives. Enough with the questions."

Rachette smiled at Jack in the rearview mirror and took a sip of his Coke.

They continued eating in a comfortable silence, sitting in the festival grounds parking lot, listening to a local country-music act on KBUD radio. The activity on the grounds had already seemed to climax. The rip of a piece of tape here, a pound of a nail there, workers now milled about, making sure everything was set up so that the music could kick off without a hitch.

Tires crunched behind them, and Rachette saw it was an SUV with the green-and-black logo of the Garfield County Sheriff's Department.

"Aha, the replacement for Richter," Rachette said, watching the SUV pass behind them and down the parking lot.

Patterson looked at Rachette. "Have you talked to Sheriff Wolf today?"

Rachette shook his head as he watched the SUV's brake lights flash. It turned into a spot and rocked to a stop at the other end of the lot.

"Not since last night."

Rachette flicked a warning glare at Patterson. Patterson nodded with a knowing look. They weren't supposed to be talking in front of Jack about what'd happened the night before. There was no sense in freaking the kid out when he was already under twenty-four-hour guard.

"I was just wondering when he was coming back," she added in a happy tone. Then she turned to Jack and made a fist. "The fun starts tonight!"

Rachette wadded his wrapper and shoved it in the bag. "Yeah, T minus six hours. Yay." He opened the door, stepped out, and swiped the crumbs off his shirt. "I'll be back."

He clunked the door shut and stepped along the matted grass toward the GCSD SUV. Both doors opened. Rachette narrowed his eyes and saw that one of the men was dressed in plain clothes while the other was a GCSD deputy in uniform, which seemed a little strange.

The cop nodded in Rachette's direction and waved with a high hand.

Rachette nodded back and hooked his thumbs on his belt. It was a move he did to make him look a little more authoritative—a sheriff-walk he'd seen countless times on black-and-white TV shows growing up in Nebraska.

The plainclothes guy ignored the interaction, nodded to his cop companion, and walked away from them, toward the base facilities.

The cop strolled toward Rachette and met him halfway, tipping his GCSD baseball cap. "Deputy Rachette?"

"That's me."

"Sergeant Adam McCall," he said, holding out a hand, "at your service."

Rachette shook the man's hand. It was a firm grip, and the guy gave him a sincere look with intelligent dark-green eyes. Sergeant McCall stood a few inches taller than Rachette, and had what could only be described as a perfect beard. It was short but dense, with brown swirls of hair that made Rachette want to try growing a beard again. He'd tried once recently, but found it was blotchy and completely unsymmetrical, *like a hairy map of the Philippines pasted on your face*, as Wilson had put it.

"Thanks for coming on such late notice," Rachette sighed. "You're really helping us out."

McCall nodded. "You're welcome. No problem. I heard about what happened and, to be truthful, I kind of felt like I was being passed up when I wasn't picked to come here the first time, so believe me, it's no trouble."

"Really?" Rachette asked, surprised at the man's

enthusiasm to what was generally considered a shit job by others that had shown up.

"Yeah, I love the change of scenery." He held out his hands and looked to the surrounding mountains. "And who doesn't love Rocky Points?"

Rachette laughed, and then nodded to the man walking in the distance. "Who's that?"

"Oh, that's my brother. He wanted to come, too. So, he's going to watch the music and keep out of our hair."

"Oh, okay," Rachette said, watching the man disappear inside the visitors' center of the ski-base complex. "I didn't mean to scare him off. He's welcome to hang with us if he wants."

"Him? Oh no, don't worry. He just had to go take a leak. I'm sure we'll see plenty of him." He looked back at Rachette with that sincere grin. "But I appreciate you saying so."

Rachette nodded. "Well, if you could, introduce yourself to that group of deputies and officers there, eating near the food tent. They can get you up to speed. I'll be up shortly if you have any other questions. It's not rocket science. Pretty basic security detail for the next two nights, assuming there are no incidents, of course."

McCall nodded. "I'm fine with basic security. We don't want any incidents." He tipped his hat and began walking.

Rachette watched him go for a few steps, then walked back to his truck, thinking about beards, and how they can make a man look distinguished.

CHAPTER 41

WOLF, Luke, Deputy Richter, another GCSD deputy, and Special Agent Brookhart broke off from the group and headed back to the trucks. Luke had the radio frequency ID tag in her hip pack, and she'd made it clear to Brookhart that she and Wolf would check into it. Brookhart seemed to have the same understanding as her brother: don't disagree with a forceful request from Special Agent Luke.

As they walked down the trail, Wolf was reasonably sure they'd have enough firepower with five people should they get attacked. But, to Wolf, it looked like whoever killed the EOD team was over and done with this place.

The killer, or killers, were done. And they'd left three bodies and two mistakes. Two because along with the RF ID tag in Luke's possession, there was another piece of evidence that had been of interest at the cabin—a fingerprint. Surprisingly, there were no others found at the scene. Like it had been wiped, thoroughly. The heating stove, the doors, the inside of the CHU, the bed frames, the chairs in the cabin, the table—there were smudges, but no identifiable fingerprints.

But there was one—a thumbprint on the door of the CHU. It was so perfect, so prominent in brown mud against the green paint, that Wolf was reluctant to call it a mistake, and more inclined to say it was a calling card left for them to find.

Agent Brookhart's phone had had two bars of cell reception, so he'd snapped a photo of it with his cell, messaged it to the lab, and within one minute confirmed that it matched the print found at Special Agent Luke's house the night before. It was her kid brother's, Brian Richter's.

...

It was three in the afternoon when they finally reached the Tahoe in the parking lot, and Luke looked worse than ever. Her eyelids were half closed, and her lips were dry and parted because of her slack jaw.

The drive down the road to the highway had been hell for her, Wolf could see that, but he kept silent, and drove as fast as he could to keep her torture quick. When they reached the flat of the valley and turned onto the paved highway, Luke leaned the seat back and was asleep in two breaths.

An hour later, when they reached Glenwood Springs, Wolf nudged her awake.

"Yeah?" Her voice was sandpaper on concrete. She cleared her throat and searched the cab at her feet.

Wolf held up a bottle of water to her. "Looking for this?"

She grabbed it and sucked it down greedily. After a few seconds of rubbing her head, she looked over at Wolf.

"How long was I out?" she asked.

"A little over an hour. I would have let you sleep a little more, but with your concussion, the suspense was killing me. I had to make sure you weren't in a coma."

She nodded and took another sip of water. "So freakin' thirsty."

"So how do I get to the rail yard?"

"Screw the rail yard—it won't tell us anything. The nearest place they have a customs office and off-load anything from a rail car is in Grand Junction. I know a guy."

Wolf looked over at Luke. Her eyes were closed, and Wolf wondered whether she really was awake.

"Take a right on Fifth," she said.

Wolf cruised for another block and followed her instructions, taking a right on Fifth Street. "Now what?"

"Go to the truck yard at the end and park in the visitor lot. I'm going to rest my eyes."

Wolf saw the entrance to the truck yard.

"It's a half-block away," Wolf said.

"Mmmhmm."

A few seconds later he parked in front of a low white building and looked over at Luke.

She opened her eyes and leaned forward with a groan.

Wolf shook his head. "Stay here. I'll go inside. Then we have to get you back to the hospital."

She smiled and opened the door.

Wolf leaned over and got ready to stop her from toppling out onto the black top, but she shook her head slightly and seemed to come alive. She slid off the seat, landed, and shut the door in a quick move.

Wolf watched through the window as she stretched her arms over her head, still waiting for her to crumple unconscious to the ground. After a few seconds, and an expectant look from Luke, he got out of his own door.

The parking lot smelled like tar and truck exhaust, and the black asphalt radiated heat up the pant legs of his jeans. Semi-truck engines rumbled beyond a chain-link fence where a line of trailers were backed up to a long warehouse with gaping rollup doors.

Luke walked across the lot, pulled open the entrance door, and held it open for Wolf. They walked into a cool office space that had four messy desks with three women and a man sitting behind them. "Free Bird" came out of an old boom box that sat on top of a file cabinet against the wall. Above it was a *Hang in There* cat poster. It smelled like air freshener and grease.

A large woman with curly brown hair looked up and smiled wide. "What the hell you doin' here, darlin'?"

Luke smiled and walked up to the woman. They embraced in a long hug and then parted.

"Mel, this is ... Sheriff Wolf."

Mel eyed Wolf and then gave Luke a glance, and then Luke's face reddened.

"We're working a case together," Luke added.

"Oh, okay. I thought you two were—"

"Can I talk to Bob, please?" Luke asked, glaring at Mel.

Mel smirked and sat down. "He's in the back."

Luke walked through the office, nodding at a skinny guy with glasses who stared at her after she walked by. She opened a wood door, uncorking a cacophony of sounds, and walked through.

Wolf followed her into a warehouse that was hot and full of the reverberating beeps of forklifts and the gurgle of diesel engines, which belched fumes straight into the high interior while industrial-sized fans swiveled and attempted to blow them back out.

Luke walked straight to a glass enclosure along the back wall. Inside sat two men, both pecking on dirty desktop computers.

"Kristen! What the hell are you doing here?" one of them said, standing up from behind his desk.

"Hey, Bob. How are you?"

The man beamed and pulled up his bifocal glasses, revealing blue eyes that were bloodshot. He ran a hand over his gray Elvis hairdo, wiped it on his greasy blue overalls, then extended it to Luke.

Luke shook her head and gave him a hug. The man closed his eyes and tilted his head into her hair, putting a lot of tenderness into the embrace, and then they parted.

"Bob," she said, "this is Sheriff Wolf of Sluice County."

Wolf took the man's hand. It was slick with grease and scratchy with calluses.

"David," Luke said, "this is a good friend of the family's."

"So, how's your mother doing?" Bob asked.

"She's ... she's doing okay," Luke said. "Listen. Can you help me with this?"

Luke set the RF ID tag on his desk.

Bob pulled his glasses down off his head and looked at the wafer-like piece of plastic; then he looked up at Luke. "Help, how?"

"Can you read it?" Luke asked.

"This is a GAV active ID tag. It's battery operated, so we'll need the internal battery to be juiced in order to read it. And, of course, you need a proper scanner." He looked up at Luke and didn't blink. "And, of course, I have one."

"My hero," Luke said with a straight face.

"What's this from?" Bob asked.

"A shipping container," Luke said. "We need to know where it came from. When. Who. Etcetera."

Bob walked past them and out of the office into the warehouse. "Come," he said.

Wolf and Luke followed him across the smooth concrete floor and between five-tier metal shelves. Forklifts whirred across aisles in front of them with flashing lights, men shouted, and the same classic rock station as out in the front office blared from overhead speakers.

"Brad!" Bob yelled over the noise.

A huge guy with a hard hat and a flannel shirt looked up from a clipboard.

Bob walked up with the RF ID tag in hand and held it out to him. The big man pulled a scanner gun from his hip and scanned it, then looked down at the display on the back of the device.

Bob pulled out a pen and tiny notebook from his breast pocket, then stepped close to the other man and scribbled a note.

"Thanks." Bob walked away, and Wolf and Luke followed him all the way back to the office.

"Apparently the battery still had juice." Bob sat back down in his chair with a grunt and pulled himself against the desk. He tapped the grease-laden keyboard for a few seconds, then clicked the mouse and looked up at Luke. "You talk to him lately?" he asked, apparently waiting for the computer to react to a command.

Luke scoffed in response, and this seemed to be an expected answer for Bob, because he nodded once and looked back at the screen.

A few seconds later, Bob twisted the monitor toward them, sending a pencil onto the floor. "There we have it."

Luke bent down and looked at the green typeface on the screen. "What are we looking at here?"

Bob pointed at the screen. "There's the origin, there's the contents, there's the destination."

"Origin, Bagram Air Base," Luke said, reading the screen. "Afghanistan. Contents, *Combat Dry Goods?* Destination, Grand Junction, Colorado."

Luke and Wolf exchanged glances.

Bob pointed again. "Looks like it was air freighted out of Bagram, then shipped ocean to Tacoma, Washington.

Then railed to Grand Junction. Then ... then, that's it, I guess. No other information."

Wolf bent down and pointed at the screen. "Here. Here's what we need."

He was pointing at a single line. It said, *World Cargo Airlines, Flight Number 638.*

CHAPTER 42

WOLF AND LUKE drove to the FBI field office and parked next to Wolf's vehicle. He eyed the SUV as they got out, calculating that it had been sitting in the parking lot for two nights unattended, except for the few minutes he'd dug inside of it the previous night. There were no parking tickets and no signs of vandalism. Not that he'd expected any. As for his Toyota pickup truck, he had basically abandoned that vehicle.

"What's wrong?" Luke asked.

"Nothing," Wolf said, turning away from his SUV. "Just thinking about my truck at the Garfield County Sheriff's Department."

"Oh yeah, your truck. I think they'll take care of it. You want me to ... call someone?"

Wolf shrugged noncommittally. "I'll figure it out." Figure out something that didn't involve a few hundred bucks for a tow back to Rocky Points, he thought.

They walked to the front entrance and Luke scanned

an ID card. The door clicked open, and they walked along the terrazzo floor to the elevators, and pushed the button.

Next to the silver elevator doors was a sign listing all the tenant businesses of the building. There was an insurance company, a construction company, and a law firm.

"Kind of strange to see a field office inside here," Wolf said.

"Yeah, not exactly Chicago," she said.

They rode to the second floor, and Wolf followed Luke down the hallway to the pair of unmarked wooden doors. She walked in and approached the reception desk.

The receptionist looked up over her glasses and fixed a suspicious eye on Wolf.

"Gwen," Luke said, passing without slowing.

Wolf kept on her heels and tapped the counter on the way by. "Gwen," he said.

Luke and Wolf entered into a large common office area. A few agents sat behind desks on phones or pecked at keyboards. It looked more subdued that afternoon compared to the morning before.

"How many agents are stationed here?" he asked.

"We've got nine." She looked around; only four other agents were in the room. "This is one of those field offices that will be first on the chopping blocks if funding gets cut."

"Then it's back to Chicago for you?" Wolf asked.

Luke shook her head. "Anywhere but Chicago."

Luke stopped at her desk and sat down, and then dug into her drawer and pulled out a bottle of aspirin and took two. She produced a bottle of water from the same drawer, took a sip, and then held up both to Wolf.

Wolf raised his eyebrows and took them.

"Take a seat," she said. "I'll check out World Cargo."

Luke fired up her computer and got onto the internet; a few seconds later she pointed at the screen.

"There we go," she said, and she picked up the desk phone and dialed a number.

Wolf sat back in the chair and glanced around the office. He saw one man glare over at them, and another stare longingly at Luke, until he realized that Wolf had caught him. Wolf wondered how aware she was of these types of looks that followed her wherever she went.

The glaring guy, not the staring guy, stood up and sauntered over. "Hey, Luke. What you got shakin'?"

Luke tucked the phone against her shoulder and tapped the keyboard. "Hi, this is Special Agent Kristen Luke with the FBI, I need to ..."

"I'm Special Agent Upton." The man turned to Wolf unfazed by Luke's clear snubbing and held out a hand.

Wolf shook it. "Sheriff David Wolf, Sluice County."

Upton raised his eyebrows, pulled down the corners of his mouth, and then appraised Wolf's shoulder sling for a moment. Then he looked at Luke, who was now deep in a conversation on the phone, and turned around and walked back to his desk.

Wolf watched as the agent picked up the desk phone and looked at Luke through the corner of his eye. He mumbled something into the phone and then hung it up.

Luke picked up a pen, clearly excited about what she

was hearing. "Captain, yes, okay. Clark. And can I have his address of residence again, please? Thanks."

A few seconds later she ended the phone call and looked up at Wolf. "Captain Ryan Clark. He's our guy."

"What'd they say?"

She looked down at her notes. "World Cargo Airlines, flight 638 was a 747 400 that originated from Denver. The first officer on board was from Joplin, Missouri. The onboard mechanic, from Helena, Montana, and the captain?" She looked up at Wolf. "The captain was Ryan Clark, of Glenwood Springs, Colorado. He's been a pilot for World Cargo for eleven years."

Wolf sat back and stared into nothing. "Let's check him out."

Luke nodded and clicked the computer mouse a few times, then tapped the keyboard.

A few seconds later a voice came from behind Wolf. "Special Agent Luke."

Luke kept her eyes on the computer screen. "Sir."

Wolf turned around and saw a short man with black hair and a tan complexion glaring at Luke. He flicked a glance at Wolf but didn't offer a hand or an introduction.

"I need to talk to you," the man said.

Luke nodded, clicked a few more buttons, and then finally looked up. "Sir, we are kind of in the middle—"

"Now," he said, and he walked away down the hall at the end of the room.

Luke rolled her eyes and looked at Wolf; then she looked over at Special Agent Upton, who was now wearing a satisfied expression, staring at his own computer screen instead of them.

Luke grabbed the monitor in her hands and twisted it ninety degrees so Wolf could see it.

"There he is," she said quietly. Then she got up and walked away.

Wolf leaned forward and studied the screen, starting when he saw the picture. It was the man he'd shot in the head at the campfire. The image was unmistakable. Clark had closely cut light-blond hair with pale skin, and there were moles underneath his mouth.

Captain Ryan Clark had four addresses listed for his previous residences. The first was a Carbondale, Colorado, address, a few miles down the highway toward Aspen. The second was Delta, Colorado. *Delta.* The third was an address in Denver, and the fourth was Glenwood Springs, Colorado—the current address that Luke had just written down on her piece of paper.

The next few lines were interesting. Apparently, he had changed his name in high school, while he was in Delta, Colorado. The next line gave an explanation. His parents were deceased, both killed in an automobile accident, and he had moved to a foster home when he was twelve years old. While he was there, he'd changed his name from his original name of Jenson to Clark, taking the name of his foster parents.

Wolf stopped reading and looked up.

Special Agent Upton had stood up from his desk and was staring again in Wolf's direction.

Wolf straightened and sat back, meeting his gaze.

Upton sat back down slowly, giving Wolf a courteous nod.

Wolf was contemplating ignoring the man, going to talk to him, or waiting for Luke, when she arrived and sat back down.

"Sorry," she said and pulled her chair forward.

"No worries," Wolf said, finally peeling his eyes off Upton. "Everything okay?"

"Good as they'll ever be."

Wolf pointed at the screen. "Captain Clark. Originally from Carbondale; his parents were killed in a car crash. He went into a foster home at age twelve, in Delta, Colorado, where he changed his last name from Jenson to Clark. Moved to Denver for thirteen years, and just recently he's moved to Glenwood Springs."

Luke exhaled and clicked a few buttons. She minimized Captain Clark's window and Wade Jeffries's file, complete with picture, flashed up on the screen.

"Look here," Luke said. "Wade Jeffries and Ryan Clark went to the same high school in Delta."

Wolf nodded. "That's the connection. That's how the EOD team were helped out of Afghanistan. The EOD team gets the gold and fakes their deaths, holes up in a container, and the pilot smuggles them out."

"How could a pilot do that? He just flies the plane, right?"

"He would have had someone in on it," Wolf said. "Someone at the air base. Probably a loadmaster ... someone who would be able to put the container on, change the documents. I don't know the logistics, but this wouldn't be an impossible task. Difficult, but not impossible." Wolf stared out the windows of the big room.

"What is it?" Luke asked.

Wolf sat thinking for another few seconds.

"What?" Luke slapped him on the knee.

"I'm just trying to reconcile the math. There were four members of the EOD team that went missing—Your brother, Chad Hartley, Marcus Quinn, and Wade Jeffries. Jack and I saw Wade Jeffries on the trail and then later heard the two rifle shots that killed him. Our airline captain Ryan Clark was at our campfire, and two men were with him up on the mountain."

She frowned. "Yes. So ... it could have been the rest of the EOD team. Maybe there were three men after you. Maybe one of them dropped back before reaching the parking lot, leaving two in a shootout with your son. The math works."

Wolf said nothing.

"You would have been chased by my brother," Luke said, "Chad Hartley, and Marcus Quinn, after they already left Wade Jeffries dead on the trail." She stared into space. "Which means my brother must have killed off Hartley and Quinn later on, leaving Hartley's body inside the cabin and Quinn inside the CHU."

Wolf stared for another beat and shook his head. "But ... you saw those bodies. How long do you think they had been there?"

Luke tilted her head. "Couple days I would think. The insects had set in pretty good on Hartley's body inside that cabin. Then there was Wade's body, who looked like he'd been shot two nights ago. Quinn's body? Hard to say."

"Hard to say," Wolf said. "But certainly none of those men were killed this morning, right?"

"No," she said slowly. "I'm not sure I'm following."

"I'm thinking about the guy Jack shot, and the slack arm of the guy chasing me last night. And the faster guy with him. Your brother's fingerprints were at your house. So who was the other guy?"

She narrowed her eyes. "Yeah. You're right." She pulled out her phone and stabbed at the screen. Putting it to her ear, she said, "Hey, it's me. You guys have a preliminary time of death on those three bodies up there?"

She waited, pulling her eyebrows together as she listened. "Okay. Thanks." Hanging up and pocketing her phone, she said, "Our forensics lead is saying he's not sure the exact TOD for the three bodies up there. But he is saying it's at least forty-eight hours."

Wolf nodded. "So ... we're missing someone."

"Who?"

"That's the question," Wolf said. "Let's go to Clark's, see what we can find at our airline captain's place. We'll need a team."

They both looked in Upton's direction, then back at each other.

"I'll call Brookhart," Luke said. "And I'll see where Danny is."

CHAPTER 43

"WHAT I DON'T GET IS the way the state keeps giving money to expand the forces, but when it comes to money to improve the facilities we have in place, they don't know what the hell is going on."

Sergeant McCall took a sip of his bottled water and nodded at the idiot from the Vail Police Department's rant. Despite the steady stream of patrons coming through the gates now, the group of law-enforcement volunteers stood in the fading light of the day like they'd stood numerous times before in the past few hours—talking in a circle like a bunch of morons.

"Well, personally," Deputy Patterson said, "I'm sure glad they hired a new deputy in this county."

They all laughed, and McCall laughed with them. God he hated this; he hated these asshole cops, except for maybe the girl. She was annoying like all the rest of them, but at least she was cute.

McCall took a look at his watch. It was just after six

p.m. Sunset was still two hours away, but the sun had already gone behind the mountains. The drop in temperature of the air, and the anticipation of the night, had ramped up the electricity in McCall's body, and he was getting fidgety.

It didn't help that he kept thinking about how they'd already fucked up with Wolf, royally fucked up. But they could reverse the order of things, he was sure about it. But his confidence was draining with every second his brother didn't show, or answer his text messages. Was he passed out in the trees? Had his injury taken a turn for the worse? Was he stopped on the way up the road? Sitting in a cop car?

His phone vibrated in his pocket and he had to force himself to relax. With a slow movement, nodding again at an officer's idiotic quip, he pulled out the phone and looked at the screen for a second, then pocketed it again.

"Excuse me," McCall announced, turning and walking away before anyone could react. He looked up the grassy slope toward the thick pine trees for the hundredth time and chuffed a deep breath. *Finally*, he screamed inside his head, watching his little brother emerge from the trees. He pulled out his phone again and fired off a text. Within a few seconds he got a message back.

The festival crowd was thin, but thickening by the minute. In a couple of hours there would be so many people, with so much noise, with so much commotion, that no one was going to be able to see the abduction happen, much less hear a gunshot from a mile away. It would be mayhem with the law enforcement, and McCall would steer it in the direction of his choosing.

McCall strode through aromas of barbecue food and marijuana smoke, past people tossing Frisbees, around excited dogs, through the bustling merchandise tent, out past the complex of portable restrooms, and into the main visitors' center building.

His brother stood leaning against the wall, chugging the last ounce of a bottle of water.

"Everything set?" McCall asked. "You look like shit. Again."

"I just walked over six miles; I need more water."

"Is everything set?" McCall asked once more, this time with an edge to his voice.

His brother eyed him. "Yes."

"I'll send you a text when it's happening. Same spot as we said. I'll get him there and run interference. It's gotta be done quick."

Tyler nodded and walked away into the white-tiled restroom.

McCall turned around and took a slow walk. He looked out the windows of the visitors' center ahead, and up at the ski runs that were cut out of the green forest above. They were still lit brightly by the sun, and a few mountain bikers tracked back and forth on the trails.

"Care to rent a bike, sir?"

McCall turned to see a teenage kid behind a counter looking at him. He was bright-eyed with a facetious smile.

"Ha-ha, yeah, right," McCall said.

"It's only twenty bucks a day. That'll get you the lift ticket and rental. Can't beat that deal."

McCall shook his head, keeping an easy smile on his lips.

"All right. Well, when you're done keeping all these hoodlums in line, and are looking for a good time, you know where to come. It's beautiful up there on top, and it's a good workout." The kid raised his eyebrows, looking down at McCall's stomach, like it could stand to drop a few pounds.

McCall pulled his eyebrows together and looked at the kid. He walked to the counter and picked up a brochure, and then pretended to read it. After a second, he flipped it back on the stack.

"Does it come with a helmet?" he asked, leaning on his elbow.

"Sure does," the kid said. "Also comes—"

"You should be wearing a helmet," he said, looking the kid in the eye. "Right now. Just in case someone comes up, tries to bash you over the head."

The kid's face dropped.

He stared until the kid swallowed. "Now shut the fuck up and leave me alone. I'm trying to do my job here, got that?"

The kid nodded.

McCall turned and walked away, and straight into Deputy Patterson.

"Whoa, sorry." McCall's cheeks flushed hot as he looked down and noticed Patterson's wide-eyed look of horror. "I didn't see you there. Going to use the good bath-rooms too?"

Patterson nodded dumbly, and then glanced at the kid behind the counter.

Shit. Clearly she had heard the entire exchange, or at least the punchline.

"Anyway thanks, I'll think about it," McCall said, giving the kid a cool look. Then he slapped the counter and walked away. "I'll see you back there, Deputy Patterson."

Shit.

CHAPTER 44

WOLF, Luke, Brookhart, and Deputy Richter met a block away from Clark's property and checked their weapons in front of Luke's Tahoe. Richter nodded at a woman across the street, and she quickly swept her children inside and disappeared behind a slammed door.

It was early evening, and the sun was just dipping past the mountains to the west. Families, visible through brightly lit windows all around, sat watching television or eating around kitchen tables.

The windows of Clark's house, however, were covered and dark, blocking any view into the house. Wolf knew Clark wasn't coming home again—he'd made sure of that—but that didn't mean there wasn't danger inside.

The home was a modest size in a neighborhood just south of where Bernadette Richter lived. The properties in the area looked brand new, and Clark's house was no exception. The trees were young, the landscaping incomplete, concrete intact without chips or cracks, and the paint on the exterior looked fresh. Which also meant there was nowhere to hide when approaching, so speed was even more essential.

Wolf and Luke sprinted to the front door, and Brookhart and Richter went to the back of the property. Wolf checked the knob; it was locked. He walked down the porch and checked the windows. One of them was clearly unlocked with the latches flipped up. Wolf pulled the screen out, palmed the glass and pushed with his good arm, not budging it. Luke joined him and used both her hands to help; it pushed up with a smooth whoosh.

Wolf reached in and pulled up the wood blind, exposing the interior of the house. The family room inside had a beige carpet, and was furnished with dark wood furniture, leather couches, and a flat-screen television mounted on the wall.

Wolf straddled the windowsill and climbed inside. His feet creaked on the floorboards underneath the carpet. It smelled like leather and spray cleaner.

Luke climbed in after him and aimed her SIG and flashlight around the room. There was no one. She stepped past Wolf and into a dark kitchen. She flipped the light, revealing a modern space with white marble countertops and stainless-steel appliances. There was a sliding glass door to the back yard on the other side of a bar counter.

"I'm opening the back door," Luke said into her radio.

"Copy that," a voice came through the radio.

She stepped to the door and opened it.

Wolf walked the rest of the house, checking the two bedrooms, confirming they were clear.

"All clear," he said.

They convened in the kitchen, all donned latex gloves, and split in teams of two to search the house—Wolf with Luke, Richter with Brookhart.

Clark's bedroom was furnished like the rest of the house, with expensive, top-of-the-line electronics, and heavy furniture. Stylized photographs of planes, flying and grounded, hung on the walls in brushed nickel frames. An antique National Geographic map was above his king-sized bed, and there were some pictures of him and some male friends on the beach.

Wolf searched his closet and found a metal box underneath a flight cap. In it was a silver Zippo lighter, an old-looking Polaroid picture of a man and woman, and another few pictures underneath that.

"Take a look," Wolf said.

Luke walked into the closet and bent down.

Wolf held up a red-hued Polaroid with a brown stain on the front of it. It was of three kids. Two of the three looked to be about Jack's age, around twelve years old. They stood in a line in front of a patch of forest, all of them wearing serious expressions.

One of them was clearly Clark, as the kid in the picture had frosting-white hair with a cluster of moles under his mouth, but the other two kids were a mystery. One of them had a hard look in his eye. He was probably fourteen, Wolf guessed. The third kid was younger than Clark and Fourteen-Year-Old. Clark seemed the odd man out, because the other two had identically shaped eyes.

Wolf looked at Clark's likeness as a child, and then at

the others; he felt like he'd seen them before. He tried to put the adolescent faces on grown-up bodies but failed to come up with anyone.

"This must have been right around when he went into a foster home," Wolf said.

Luke pointed at the picture. "It looks like these two kids are brothers, right? They look alike."

Wolf nodded. "Yeah."

Wolf pocketed the picture and rummaged down further into the box. There was another picture, this time when Clark was slightly older, which would have put him around his high school years. He stood smiling, next to three other smiling kids who were starkly different from the previous photo. They all had dark hair and looked nothing like Clark. Two adults bookended the line of boys with the same dark hair and same big smile. The entire group was lined up in front of a brick house with white columns on either side of them.

"Foster family," Wolf said.

Luke nodded. "The Jensons."

Wolf pocketed that photo as well, and they walked out into the kitchen, where Brookhart and Richter were standing with their hands on their hips.

"Anything?" Wolf asked Brookhart.

"No, nothing. No gold, at least," Brookhart said. "No safe, no nothing. Checked the garage, basement, all the rooms, drawers, boxes."

Wolf took a deep breath and shook his head. "We're still missing something."

They stood in silence for a few moments.

"You guys swear you've never seen Clark in your lives?" Wolf asked.

Luke and her older brother shook their heads.

"Then I don't get the connection. I mean, I guess your brother could have met Clark on an air base in Afghanistan. But ... how long did World Cargo say he flew for them? Eleven years?"

Luke nodded. "That's what they said."

Wolf frowned. "I have a buddy from the military who flies cargo. Last time I saw him, we were giving him flack for having such an easy job. Basically, once a month, he gets on a plane and flies it to Hawaii. He sits there on the beach for a week, comes back to the States, loads up another plane, goes back to Hawaii, and comes back home. A few weeks later, he does it all again.

"The reason why he has that route is because he's been with the company for nine years, and he has the seniority to choose the routes he wants. So what doesn't make sense is that Clark was on that route to Afghanistan. There's no way he would choose to go into that hell-hole, with the risk of being shot out of the sky every time he landed and took off without good reason."

"Yeah," Richter said, "like millions of dollars in gold?"

Wolf nodded. "Exactly. So my point is, your brother wouldn't have met Clark in Afghanistan. It had to have been somewhere here."

They stood in silence for a few moments, looking at each other.

"Was your brother into martial arts?" Brookhart asked.

Luke shook her head.

"How about a bar?" Wolf asked.

"He gave up drinking when he went into the service," Luke said.

"So he said," Richter said.

Luke rolled her eyes. "He gave it up, Danny."

"We need to go back into the databases," Wolf said. "Do some more digging. I don't know where else to go." He stared out of the sliding glass door at the fading light, feeling they'd just taken a step forward and five steps back.

CHAPTER 45

WOLF STARED out the passenger window, watching the businesses roll by as they drove down Grand Avenue in downtown Glenwood Springs, once again making their way to the field office. The sun had dropped lower behind the mountains, so Luke had the headlights on, but there was a cirrus cloud overhead that shone hot pink, bathing the tops of cars and the sidewalks in a rosy glow.

He pulled out his phone and called Jack.

It rang a few times and then he heard a blast of music in the earpiece.

"Hello?" Jack yelled into the phone.

"Hey how are you doing?"

Jack laughed. "Good! We're watching Terry's band. They're doing awesome."

"Who's we?" Wolf asked.

"What?"

"Who are you with?" Wolf asked louder.

"I'm with Pattie and Rachette," he said.

"Let me talk to Rachette, will you?" Wolf said.

Wolf heard Jack yell over the noise, then Rachette came on.

"Hello?"

"Hey, how you doing?" Wolf asked.

"What?" Rachette said. "I can barely hear you."

Wolf sighed and looked at Luke. Luke smiled and shook her head.

"I'll call you back. Get somewhere quieter," Wolf said, and he hung up.

Wolf looked out the window again.

"Well, sounds like they're at least having fun," Luke said.

"Yeah," Wolf said, glaring with unfocused eyes.

"What's wrong?"

"I'm just worried. They were coming after me last night. And I just don't like being away from Jack right now," Wolf said.

Luke nodded and kept silent. She sighed heavily, and Wolf could tell she was tearing herself up inside about her brother's involvement.

"You've got your son with your deputies, right?"

Wolf nodded.

"And they're at the most public, crowded place possible. I think it's the safest place for him. Safer than being with us, right? The action is following us. Like you said, they came after you last night."

Wolf didn't answer, just kept watching the passing buildings. He wondered how Sarah was faring after day two of around-the-clock protection of her son. He'd have to call her, too.

Wolf twisted in his seat so fast it nearly ripped the stitches out of his arm again.

"What?" Luke said. "What?"

"Turn around, turn here." Wolf grabbed the wheel and Luke slapped it away.

"Okay, okay. You gonna pull a gun on me again?"

"I'm serious—go back to the Mountain Goat Bar and Grill."

CHAPTER 46

RACHETTE WATCHED Sergeant McCall walk along the backside of the now swollen crowd toward him and Jack. McCall greeted concertgoers looking his way with warm smiles and nods. When a man chasing a hacky sack stumbled out in front of him, McCall simply stopped and smiled, watching patiently as the man hid a joint he was smoking in his hand and ran back into the crowd.

He reached Rachette and shook his head. "I'm still unclear on what we're supposed to do about pot in this state."

Rachette laughed. "Yeah, isn't everyone. I just turn the other cheek unless they're doing something stupid, like toking up in front of little guys like this." He ruffled Jack's hair, and Jack stood next to him with the same wide-eyed interest in McCall that Rachette had.

"You know better than to do that stuff, right, kid?" McCall asked with a serious expression.

Jack nodded like it was the dumbest question he'd ever

heard in his life. "Yeah, that crap's for losers. I play sports. That stuff makes you slow, and lazy."

McCall gave him a solid nod and held out his fist.

Jack knuckle bumped him, maintaining his serious expression.

"How's the music?" McCall asked, turning toward the stage in the distance.

Rachette shrugged. He hadn't been listening, really. "Pretty good."

"It's a local band. One of the guys is my friend's dad." Jack pointed to the stage. "The guy playing guitar. That's Jim Hughes. I'm friends with Zack, his son. We're in class together."

McCall looked at Jack's proud expression and smiled at Rachette. "Cool.".

They stood for a few more minutes, watching the crowd, and watching Jack dance like no one was watching, or more like everyone was watching. That's the way Jack liked things, Rachette had come to learn over the last couple days.

Rachette brought his radio to his lips. "Wilson, do you copy?"

"Go ahead." The voice was low coming out of his speaker, but loud on McCall's, so Rachette dialed up the volume and walked away a few steps.

"You doing all right up there? Anything we need to know about?"

"Doin' just fine. Crowd is still streaming in; there's quite a surge coming from the lot now."

"All right, I'll send Patterson up to join you when she gets back."

"Ten-four."

Rachette hung the radio back on his chest and walked to Jack and McCall.

Jack was looking up at McCall with the same worshipping gaze he gave Patterson, and telling an animated story over the noise.

McCall laughed with his head back, and then caught Rachette's eye. "Everything all right?" he asked.

Patterson came into view a short distance away, walking toward them through a puddle of light at the rear of the crowd.

"Yeah, as you probably just heard," Rachette said, "the crowd will be getting bigger. I really have no clue what to expect, since it's the first year and all. But so far, it seems to be going off without a hitch."

Patterson joined them and nodded without saying anything. Rachette gave her a quick nod, but otherwise ignored her, and McCall tipped his hat.

"How's it going?" McCall asked.

Patterson looked up at McCall and nodded, not saying a word.

Rachette frowned at the strange interaction.

"Hey, stay here. I have to call Sheriff Wolf real quick," Rachette said.

Rachette walked away, past the line of lit poles and up into the grass field toward the ski slope. He dialed the number and listened to the unanswered rings, then left a message.

"Hey, it's me again, finally somewhere quieter to talk." He looked back over at Patterson, McCall, and Jack. "Everything's fine. Jack's still showing off for Patterson. Give me a call."

When Rachette returned, Jack was hogging Patterson's attention, and she seemed to be fine with it, standing a few feet away from McCall.

Rachette shook his head and leaned to talk to McCall again. "I think it's going pretty well so far. I heard the condos and hotels are nearly sold out, and the camp grounds are completely booked."

McCall nodded, watching Patterson.

Rachette turned to her. "Hey, Patterson, I need you to go to the front gate and join Wilson."

Patterson turned and flicked a glance between Rachette and McCall. Then she nodded with a hint of resignation.

"Okay, I'll see you guys later." She turned and walked away.

Rachette watched her go for a few seconds.

"She's cute," McCall said.

Rachette turned and looked at McCall, and then smiled when he realized he might have been scowling at the remark.

"Uh, yeah. She's cute, I guess," Rachette said.

McCall laughed. "I mean, for you. I'm spoken for. I just think she probably likes you."

Rachette scoffed and frowned like he'd just whiffed a cow patty. "Yeah. Right."

"I have to take a whiz," Jack declared.

McCall raised his eyebrows and looked down at him. "Me, too."

"Ah, okay," Rachette said, looking up toward the merchandise tent.

"I can take him up," McCall said, looking at Rachette. "If you want. Seriously, I could use one, too."

Rachette felt like he was being asked to break some sort of rule, but he liked McCall and he trusted him. McCall had been at the hospital that morning with Wolf and Rachette, and had gone back up to the mountain with Wolf. It was like they had forged a bond through Wolf.

"All right." Rachette nodded. "Keep a good eye on him."

"You got it. All right, let's go."

They walked away around the back of the crowd and disappeared into the sea of bouncing heads.

A few seconds later Rachette turned his head at the sound of thumping feet.

"What the hell are you doing?" Patterson asked between labored breaths.

Rachette scrunched his face. "What? What the hell are you doing? You're supposed to be up with Wilson."

Patterson shook her head and looked past him. "I don't like that guy, and you're sending him off with Jack unattended?"

"That guy was helping Wolf investigate the shooting, Patterson. He's a sheriff's deputy, and a damn good one. They're going to take a leak, and they'll be right back. Chill out."

"Seriously, that guy gives me the creeps, I ..." She shuffled on her feet, and looked past Rachette. "They went to the bathrooms?"

Rachette nodded. "Yeah. They'll be right back."

Patterson was already walking away after them. Rachette rolled his eyes and felt his pulse race. This chick was really getting on his nerves, and now she was suggesting he wasn't doing his job. He turned and watched her go, started to walk after her, then stopped and waved his hand. *Fine. You go annoy someone else.*

CHAPTER 47

WOLF CRANED his neck to look out the Tahoe window when they pulled into the Mountain Goat Bar and Grill parking lot. The lit sign, perched high on the steel pole, was taunting something in his subconscious, and that something was clawing at a locked door in Wolf's mind.

The parking lot was full, so Luke drove around the back of the building to find an open spot. She parked and Wolf got out. He walked back around to the front and stood looking up.

Luke stood next to him. "What? For the love of God, speak."

Wolf stared at the neon sign. It was the profile of a mountain goat, standing in front of a tall peak. Wolf squinted, blurring the sign into a more basic shape—a tall triangle surrounded by a dark-blue circle.

"We have to go in here."

"Okay. And why?"

Wolf just shook his head. He didn't know why yet.

They threaded their way through two GCSD vehicles parked against the building and walked to the front door.

The air inside was warm and humid, thick with the smell of bar food. And it was loud. A lot of men, and only a smattering of women, stood around the bar, laughing, yelling, and drinking beers in thick mugs or dark bottles. Some wore uniforms, others loosened dress shirts and slacks, with only a few in plain clothes. Several patrons turned to look their direction, letting their gazes settle on Luke for a second, before finally returning to their conversations.

"Two?" an impatient looking hostess appeared, pulling out two menus from behind her podium. "Sir?"

Luke looked up at Wolf, and Wolf turned to the hostess. "We'll just be going to the bar, thanks."

"Okay, have a good time," she said, shoving the menus back in the slot. She walked away through the packed dining room area and disappeared into the kitchen.

Wolf stood still and looked around, taking in the interior of the place. There was a wood-framed glass case filled with merchandise next to his head. A dark-blue T-shirt was tacked to the wall inside it, blue coffee mugs, a blue hat, and a square handkerchief.

Wolf's eyes widened. "There."

Luke stood next to him.

"Jeffries was wearing that on the trail," Wolf said, pointing at the handkerchief. "I remember he pulled it up out of his coat to cover his face when he passed us. I remember the white logo pattern, and the dark-blue color. I'm sure of it."

Luke frowned. "This is a cop bar. And a lot of the guys at the field office hang here, too."

Wolf looked back toward the group at the bar. The conversation had dropped considerably, their attention drawn to Wolf and Luke.

"I'm sure," Wolf said and walked in.

"What are you doing?" Luke asked, following behind him.

"You come here a lot?" he asked over his shoulder.

"Been a few times, with my brother. And a few times with some guys from the office."

Wolf wormed his way past two guys who stepped aside, and another tough-type who didn't, and then leaned on the bar.

A fit-looking middle-aged bartender caught his eye and held up a finger.

Wolf waited patiently and scooted aside for Luke to come next to him. She pressed close and they looked around at the faces. More than a few men eyed Wolf with raised lips, looking like they wanted to start trouble. Bullies, looking at a big enough man who'd made a big entrance, with a beautiful girl, and an arm wound.

Wolf had been in the situation before, an outsider in another clan's territory. Suspicion was painted on each of their faces—they were wondering just what this duo was up to.

"What can I get you?" The bartender was looking at Luke.

"Who owns this place?" Wolf asked.

The bartender bent forward and pointed at Luke, ignoring his question. "I'm asking the lady."

"And he's asking you a question," Luke said.

The bartender looked meaningfully down the line of patrons on either side of Wolf, and leaned forward. "And who's asking?"

Wolf produced his badge. "I'm the sheriff of Sluice County."

Luke pulled out her ID badge. "And I'm Special Agent Luke of the FBI."

The conversation lowered to a murmur in the span of a second, and every eye was on them.

"Who owns this bar?" Wolf asked again, keeping his eyes on the bartender.

The other employee behind the bar looked up from scrubbing a glass.

"Why?" the bartender asked with a squint.

"What's going on, Luke?" a man in a white button-up shirt asked from a few feet away.

"We're conducting an investigation," Luke said with a raised voice, "and would like to know who owns this bar."

"T-A-M, LLC owns this bar," the bartender answered with a cool gaze.

Wolf noticed a closed wooden door beyond the bar, which would have been a perfect place for a managerial, or owner's, office.

Wolf tapped the guy next to him on the shoulder. "Hey, who owns this place?" The guy turned away and sipped his drink. Wolf looked down the line to the next man. "What's the other guy's name behind the bar? The guy who was sick yesterday?"

The man lowered his eyes and took a sip of his beer.

Wolf shook his head and looked around. "No one knows the owner of this bar? We're conducting an investigation here. A bunch of cops are just gonna keep tight-lipped?"

Wolf pushed himself away from the counter and threaded his way through the men. He heard Luke shuffle after him, pardoning herself with a hard voice as she did so.

One big guy in a GCSD uniform stepped in front of him. "Maybe we just don't like you," he said.

The man was a hand taller than Wolf, and probably a hundred pounds heavier. Wolf felt a pulse of impatience and briefly considered jabbing the man in the nose, then considered the ensuing brawl that would probably follow.

He nodded and turned away, and then walked back toward the hostess podium through curious glances all around. Luke stepped on light feet behind him.

"Wolf," she whispered. "Wolf."

Wolf ignored her, walked to the door, stepped outside, and then turned and walked along the exterior of the building.

"What's going on?" Luke said.

Wolf continued to the back of the building, and Luke broke off and headed for the Tahoe. Wolf didn't. He went to a flat red-painted door with no doorknob on it, and stopped.

Luke ran up next to him. "What the hell are you doing?" she hissed.

Wolf pressed his face against the thick glass of a window next to the door, and ran his eyes along its perimeter, eying the interior.

"Okay, what are you doing?"

He pulled his pistol and ejected the clip, then racked the slide to remove the round from the chamber. With the butt of his gun he smacked the window. It clanked with a high-pitched ring, but didn't budge.

"Jesus!" Luke whispered. "Wolf ..."

Then she grabbed his arm. Wolf pulled himself away and smacked the window again with a loud clang but, again, it didn't budge.

Luke pressed herself against the window and held up her hands. "Move. I'll do it," she said.

Wolf looked down at her and, with curiosity piqued, stepped aside.

She bent down and looked at the ground, searching for something. Then she found a small rock and picked it up, twisted it in the low light and then threw it on the ground. Then she picked up another one and took off her shoe. She flipped her shoe over and pressed the rock in between two square treads on her heel. Then she put her shoe on again, not bothering to tie it, and hopped on her left foot twice, positioning herself in front of the window.

"What are—"

She moved with lightning speed, twisting on her left leg until her back was to the window and thrusting a heel kick behind her, connecting in the center of the window.

The window thumped and spider webbed out from the impact point, shards dropping into the darkness of the room. The glass bounced off carpet inside and broke into smaller pieces.

Wolf put the sleeve of his jacket over his hand and smacked a few hanging sections, cracking them off and sending them inside.

He stuck his head in and froze. It was a dark office with a wooden desk in the middle of the space and a couch against the wall. The desk had a desktop computer on it and a laser printer set on the corner. There was a door with a sliver of light underneath it to the interior of the bar. Through it came loud, bellowing laughs, and what seemed to be more noise than ever. The men were probably hopped up and excited about the scene that'd just taken place.

Wolf kept still, waiting for an indication that they'd been heard.

"Any time, now," Luke said, pushing him from behind. "Someone's going to see us."

Wolf stepped in through the window, careful to keep his crotch unscathed, and then watched Luke glide in quickly after him.

He walked to the door and took a look. There were two twist locks, one on the knob and one above it—both locked, as evidenced by the light passing through the crack in the door. He flipped the light switch and the office lit up.

Luke looked over at him with wide eyes. "Are you sure you want to do that?"

"Keep an eye on these locks." Wolf walked around the desk and sat down.

"And if they start twisting?"

"Twist 'em back."

Wolf flipped on the computer and looked on the desk as he waited for it to power up. He leaned forward and picked through the contents strewn about.

"Plastic sheets of paper. Scissors. Wood glue."

He bent over and picked out a piece of the plastic from the trash bin on the floor. There was a circle cut out of it about the size of a fist. He held it up for Luke to see, and she gave him a puzzled look.

He stood and looked at the laser printer, and then pushed the power button. It came to life, beeping and sucking paper into its bowels with a loud whirring.

Luke looked down at the lock and shook her head as the electronic racket ensued for another few seconds, until the printer spat out a blank sheet of paper onto the floor.

"Jesus," she whispered.

Wolf shook the mouse, selected the printer icon, clicked through some options, and looked up at Luke.

"Are you good with computers?"

Luke shrugged. "Yeah, I'm decent, but who isn't?"

"Me. Come here."

Luke stepped over and looked at the screen. Wolf kept his eyes on the door locks and stood up. "Print the last document that was printed. Can you do that?"

"Yeah," she said, sitting down.

For thirty seconds, Wolf stood by the door, watching the locks, the punched-out window, the dark parking lot beyond it, and Luke clicking the mouse with growing frustration. Finally, she clicked a button and looked at the printer.

It came to life again, sucking a piece of paper. A few seconds later it was done, and spat out another sheet of paper. This time there was something on it.

Wolf bent down and picked it up. It was completely white except for a shiny black smudge on the bottom.

"A fingerprint," Luke said.

It looked different from a normal print. It was reversed —the spaces in between the ridges in black, the ridges in white. What resulted was a thick shiny blotch of ink.

Wolf set it down and looked at the wood glue and the scissors. "Shit," he breathed.

Then he looked at the computer screen. "Click on his email."

Luke looked at the screen and clicked on an icon on the bottom.

An email client opened up and loaded.

"There," Wolf said.

"I know, I know," Luke said, clicking on one of the emails. "Tyler McCall."

She looked up at Wolf and frowned.

Wolf's gut dropped a foot as he realized what that meant. *Tyler McCall. Sergeant McCall of the Garfield County Sheriff's Department. They were brothers.* And then he thought about Deputy Dan Richter coming back to check on his sister in the hospital, and he knew exactly where Sergeant McCall would be.

"Shit," he said again. Then he pulled his phone out of his pocket and dialed.

Luke looked at him with wide eyes. She stood and paced.

"Fuck," she whispered, biting her nails. Then she pulled out her own phone, pushed a number and put the cell to her ear.

Wolf stood still, listening to the ringing on the phone. The blood drained from his face and his skin itched. With every ring that went unanswered, his chest constricted more, and each breath accelerated faster than the last.

"Hi, you've reached Tom Rachette of—"

Wolf hung up and looked at Luke.

"Hey," she said into the phone, "who went to Rocky Points to cover for you?" She listened for a second, and then nodded at Wolf. "I have to go," she said, and hung up.

Wolf's phone vibrated in his hand and he pushed the button.

"Hey, sorry, I couldn't hear—"

"It's McCall, Sergeant McCall and his brother were the ones shooting at Jack and me that night!"

Rachette didn't speak. Wolf listened to a cacophony of music through the earpiece.

"Did you hear me?" Wolf screamed into the phone.

CHAPTER 48

I'M IN PLACE, *on the left side.*

McCall read the glowing screen and shoved the phone in his pocket.

His heart hammered in his chest as he watched the boy shuffle through the crowd in the merchandise tent, and out the other side toward the two lines of portable toilets.

People lined up everywhere, climbing in and out of the blue disease-boxes, letting the spring-loaded doors thwack shut behind them.

The boy looked over his shoulder and nodded at McCall, then beelined it to the right side.

"Hey!" McCall yelled.

The boy stopped and turned around.

McCall pointed to the far end on the left. "Over here."

The boy looked confused and furrowed his brow. Like, why the hell do you care where I'm taking a leak?

McCall smiled and waved him over, like he had something hilarious to tell him.

The boy smiled back and walked over.

"Over here. You've gotta see this first."

The boy hesitated, but McCall ignored him and walked forward, pointing in the distance.

"What?" the boy asked, this time with a little hesitation in his step.

McCall pulled his pistol and shoved it in the kid's back. He bent close to his ear and said, "Keep walking and stay quiet, or we'll kill your dad right now."

The boy slowed for a step, and McCall pushed him hard in the middle of his back with the barrel of his Glock.

"Don't test me, kid. All I have to do is make a quick phone call and your dad is dead."

The boy looked back, clearly scared shitless, and then looked forward, like he was resigned to his fate. It was an oddly mature expression, McCall thought. He'd expected more tears and whimpering from a twelve-year-old.

"Keep going," he said as they passed the final toilet and headed onto the darkened slope toward the derelict ski lift in the distance.

"Freeze, right now." The girl's voice was surprisingly close. They had barely walked ten yards into the clearing.

McCall ignored her, and watched the boy twist and look past him; then he watched the hope drain from the boy's face.

"Let's go," McCall said, pushing the boy forward.

Deputy Patterson walked past McCall and stepped in line with the boy. Tyler goaded her from behind with his own pistol, and winced as he pocketed Patterson's with his bad arm.

The boy looked back and nodded at Tyler. "That's the guy I shot in the arm."

"Shut up or we'll just shoot you," McCall said, poking his back harder.

"Just stay quiet, honey," Patterson said to the boy.

"Yeah, honey," McCall said, "stay quiet."

CHAPTER 49

"DID YOU HEAR ME?"

The panic in Wolf's voice jolted Rachette into action. He turned and sprinted, immediately barreling into a woman, making her fall face first on the ground.

"Ah, sorry. Yeah, I hear you!" Rachette's entire body was tingling and light, like his blood had been replaced with helium. "Shit. Shit."

"What? Where's Jack?"

"He's with McCall!" Rachette screamed, narrowly avoiding a toddler as he weaved in and out of the swarming crowd.

Wolf went silent on the other end of the line, and Rachette's stomach felt like it had been hit by a cannon ball.

"I ... he's with Patterson, too. She went after them," Rachette said in between frantic breaths.

"Where?" Wolf asked with a cracking voice.

"They went to the bathroom."

Rachette reached the merchandise tent and ran in, crashing through two lines of people purchasing concessions, and to the other side. He twisted and turned, and thumped into a man as he exited. The man cried out and went down onto his back, spilling his beer all over the woman next to him.

"Sorry!" he called out, not looking back. "Sorry," he said quieter, this time meaning it for Wolf's ears.

"Just get him," Wolf said.

Rachette reached the arena-like rectangle of portable bathrooms and stopped in the center.

"I'm at the bathrooms," he said, twisting in a circle. "I don't see them. Shit."

Wolf kept silent.

"They're not here," Rachette said.

"Check beyond ..." The connection cut out.

"What? What?" Rachette said. "Shit."

"... slopes." Wolf's voice came through. "The trees!"

"The trees?" Wolf said nothing. Rachette looked at the screen and saw the call was still connected but there was no answer from Wolf.

His hand was shaking and he almost dropped the phone. *Shit. Breathe,* he told himself. He took a deep breath and straightened his posture, realizing what Wolf was saying. He sprinted to the end of the bathrooms and looked out onto the darkened ski slope.

...

Kristen Luke's eyes glistened as she watched Wolf sit

down on the couch and grip his head. He pulled his hair with the fist of his injured arm, and looked through the carpet with wide, unblinking eyes. The mask of terror twisting his face startled her.

She heard a click on the door, and watched as the lower lock started jiggling. She stepped over and latched the top lock, watched as the knob twisted and the door pushed a millimeter toward her. Then a key entered the top latch again and she locked the knob below it.

There was a muffled conversation on the other side of the door, and then came a loud knock.

"Do you see them?" Wolf asked into the phone. His hand was out in front of him, shaking.

Luke sighed and flipped the lock, then swung open the door. Two cops were a foot away on the other side. At the sight of her they stepped back, raising their weapons.

"Freeze!" they screamed in unison, and Luke held up her hands.

The entire bar turned and swarmed toward them.

"Freeze!" another man yelled, and she saw another gun in her peripheral vision.

Luke stepped into the testosterone avalanche descending on her and closed the door behind her.

"Wait, wait! Stop! FBI! FBI!" Special Agent Brookhart jumped and climbed his way through the crowd flashing his ID. "Do not touch that woman, Officer!"

A uniformed man clamped a hand on her arm like a vice, but let up as he looked at Brookhart scrambling through the crowd. Luke twisted, ripping free, and the man turned back to her. She stepped into his face and glared him down.

"Easy," Brookhart said, stepping between them. "Calm down. Stand down, Officer." He turned to Luke. "What's going on?"

"That's my sister," Deputy Richter said from somewhere to Luke's left. "Don't touch her!"

Brookhart turned to Luke. "Luke, talk to me."

"Tyler McCall, the owner of this bar, is behind the whole thing. Arrest that man"—she pointed at the bartender—"and get your ass in here."

Luke watched for a second as the bartender shrunk away from the sudden glares, and then she opened the door and stepped back inside the office.

Brookhart followed closely, and Luke shut the door behind him.

"What's going—"

Luke put a hand on Brookhart's shoulder.

Brookhart took one look at Wolf and went quiet.

CHAPTER 50

"I SEE A LIGHT," Rachette said. "It's two lights, pointed away from me. Walking away."

"Follow them," Wolf said.

Rachette took off at a full sprint, instinctively trying to keep his footfalls quiet. His keys rattled every time he planted his left foot, so he pulled them out and dropped them, and then he put the phone in his left hand and pulled his gun.

"Okay," he said in between bouncing breaths, "I'm in pursuit."

"How far away are they?" Wolf asked.

"I don't know. Three hundred yards?"

"Where are they? On the catwalk above Sunshine Lift?"

Rachette shook his head. "I don't know. What is Sunshine Lift?"

"The lift at the bottom, the only lift over there."

"Yeah, yeah," he said. "On the catwalk. I think. You

mean, like a path? No, it's like a road cut into the mountain. Is that what you mean?"

"Okay. Listen, you have to calm your breaths. Breathe deeper."

His inhales were becoming loud wheezes, and would certainly give him away if he got any closer. His legs were holding up, and he realized Wolf was right. He had to calm down. He was in better physical shape than he was acting. Straight panic had taken hold of him.

But it was all his fault. All of this. Jack was out there, probably about to get shot, and it was all his fault.

"... neath them." Wolf's voice was breaking up again.

"What?" Rachette hissed.

"... walk along the base, underneath ..." Wolf's voice cut out again.

"Please repeat. Please repeat." There were three quick beeps in Rachette's ear, and he looked down at the glowing screen. The call had disconnected. He hit the button to call again, and listened to the phone ring until Wolf's voicemail answered.

"Fuck," he said under his heaving breath, and shoved the phone in his pocket. Then he pulled it back out, flipped down the button to silence it, and put it back. A little thing like that that could ruin everything—his phone ringing or beeping to tell him he had a message. That could get someone killed.

Rachette looked up at the dim flashlight beams. They were flicking in and out between the trees now, and would probably be completely obscured in the next few seconds.

He stumbled over a rock and cursed the low light.

Could he risk using his flashlight? Not if he kept following them. But if he went below them ... *that's what Wolf was saying.*

Rachette looked past the dark lower terminal of the chair lift and saw a gap in the trees. There were two ruts in the grass, barely visible in the moonlight above. They started just next to the chair lift and disappeared into the dark pines straight ahead.

He had a choice—go up after them, or go below them. If he went up after them, then what? He'd just get louder and louder as he approached, and they could just flip off their lights and pick him off at their leisure. But if he went below, would it take him where he needed to go?

Going up was suicide and failure. Going below was unknown, but still gave Rachette a glimmer of hope. And Wolf had said *go underneath them, along the base.* He was sure of it.

"That's what Wolf was saying, jackass. Let's go." He holstered his pistol and pulled his flashlight off of his duty belt. The flashlight beams above were now gone, completely out of sight. The observation was like a whip cracking into his side.

He flipped the Maglite on, sending shadows dancing across the slope, and took off in a full sprint toward the rutted road.

CHAPTER 51

WOLF LOOKED at his phone and dialed it again. The look on his face made Luke's breath jump—she couldn't help it. She cursed herself and fought to keep a straight face, knowing any break in her emotions would only make it that much worse for him.

There was a commotion going on in the bar, a flurry of arguments breaking out between the men on the other side of the door, but Luke didn't care. She heard her brother's booming voice giving orders, and another voice that seemed to be in agreement with him. She didn't need to be out there, confusing things.

She looked at Brookhart. He lifted his hands and his eyebrows. Luke closed her eyes and shook her head, and Brookhart, thankfully, had enough brains to just shut up.

A blue clock with a mountain goat painted on it ticked incessantly, as if taunting them that no matter what they did, time was passing by, and was going to keep passing by.

Wolf looked up at her with wide eyes. "We need your brother in here, now."

Luke ran to the door and opened it. Her brother was holding back another big guy, and it looked like they were going to come to blows any second.

"Dan!" she yelled.

Dan turned.

"Get in here, now!" Her tone spurred her brother into action.

"What?"

Luke closed the door behind them, suffocating the commotion outside once again, and looked to Wolf.

"I need Sergeant McCall's phone number." Wolf stood up, and held his finger ready over the screen of his phone.

Dan dug his out and gave him the number.

Wolf nodded and stepped to the door outside. Glass crunched underneath his feet as he stopped and twisted the lock, and then stepped out into the darkness, all the while pecking on his phone.

"What the hell is going on?" Brookhart whispered, turning back to Luke.

She shook her head. "We're praying, that's what's going on."

CHAPTER 52

Rachette's legs thumped underneath him with a driving rhythm. He took one strained breath for every two steps and the sound of his pumping blood hammered in his ears.

Every few seconds he looked up the hill, scrutinizing the overall direction of the path in front of him. It was turning gradually left and steepening, if only by a degree or two. He took both indications as good signs, and trusted that something would catch his eye, tip him off, present itself as the next thing to do.

For now, all he worried about was narrowing the gap between them and him. At the speed he'd been running, he doubted he was very far behind; in fact, he was pretty sure he'd passed them.

Distance from them vertically? He really had no clue. He wasn't a skier or a snowboarder, and wasn't familiar with the mountain. For the past two winters he'd spent in Rocky Points, the other deputies had made fun of him, calling him a flatlander. And that's exactly what he was. Growing up on a farm in Nebraska, the closest thing to a hill he'd spent any time on was a ten-foot gully into the creek that split his parents' property. Hurtling himself down a mountain on skies, wheels, or a board didn't appeal to him. But he vowed then and there he would learn how to ski the next winter. He would conquer every square foot of the mountain.

That is, if he was still around. Because what would he be known as if he let Jack die? If he was the sole reason Sheriff Wolf's son was buried next to his grandfather and his uncle? If that happened, there sure as hell wasn't going to be a *next winter* in Rocky Points.

Rachette shook his head, gritted his teeth, and fought through the burn in his lungs.

His flashlight beam bounced against the trees on either side—back and forth, back and forth—and just when he wondered whether he should stop and reassess his approach, the trees opened into a wide meadow, and he skidded to a stop.

Rachette shut off his flashlight, and then backed up a few paces and behind some trees. His chest heaved as he fought to control his breath. The sound of his breathing was too loud, he thought, and he shoved his mouth against his sleeve to muffle the noise. That only made him more desperate for air, so he lowered his arm and tried to pant as quietly as he could.

He scanned the meadow ahead and realized it wasn't a meadow but the base of the mountain where a bunch of runs met. There was another dark chair-lift terminal straight ahead, reflecting the moonlight. The gleaming cables stretched up the gradual slope to his left and then shot up for a thousand feet or more and out of sight.

There was no light ahead, no movement. No flashlight beams flickered through the trees. Over the thumping blood in his ears, he swore he heard the faint echo of a woman's voice. He held his breath, strained to listen, and heard it again.

Rachette squinted up the hill, but still saw nothing. There had to have been a reason why they'd taken the upper catwalk instead of the road he'd just run down, and that fact, along with the voice he'd just heard, was telling Rachette that he needed to climb. Fast.

The voice had come from up and to the left, so he was sure he was ahead of them now, and he aimed to keep it that way. Without further deliberation, he sprinted up the ski run.

After a hundred yards of climbing the slope, he slowed to a crawl, unable to force his legs to move any faster. His calf muscles were knots, and his hamstrings felt like they were severed. He slowed from a sprint to a fast hike and then, finally, as the slope steepened, to a hands-and-feet crawl. His breath was beginning to wheeze again. His vision was blurring. His body was at its physical limit, but he bared his teeth and let the hate for these men flow through his body like nitroglycerin.

Now he was nearing the catwalk they were on, he was sure of it. It was just at the top of the rise, above his head. Just ten more feet of clawing up and he would be there.

Just then he saw a flashlight beam sweep over the top

of him, and heard the voice of the woman again. It was Patterson, and she was talking incessantly.

"... without anyone ... or not," she said.

They were still too far away. Rachette couldn't understand anything. Rachette sucked his body close to the slope and continued to climb. Just five feet now separated him from the catwalk above, and it was as far as Rachette wanted to climb.

His phone vibrated in his pocket. It was probably Wolf calling. He had probably been calling continually for the past twenty minutes and Rachette must have finally climbed into reception.

He stilled his breath and fought to keep his left calf muscle from cramping, all the while the damn phone vibrating in his pocket. He steadied himself, reached into his pocket, and pushed a button to silence it. Something caught his eye to his right, off underneath the cables of the chair lift. It was a black SUV, parked in the middle of the ski run.

"... shoot a child? They're going to find out, I'm telling you. You can't shoot a child ..."

Patterson's voice and the scrape and thump of eight feet were so close now. Patterson was talking loudly and breathing rapidly, repeating her sentences over and over again. It was like she was trying to telegraph their position to some unknown rescuer, or she was just losing her mind. Probably both, Rachette thought.

Rachette squeezed the grip of his pistol. His palm was slick with sweat. He looked down at the fist-sized stones that reflected the moonlight, set his feet, and waited.

CHAPTER 53

McCALL'S PHONE vibrated again in his hand, and another text message came up on the screen. He shoved it in his pocket and clenched his teeth.

"Shit," he said under his breath. Or maybe he'd screamed it, because Tyler, the boy, and Deputy Patterson all looked at him.

He was losing control. No, he was well past the point of losing control; he'd already lost it. How the hell could they have found out? They should have killed Wolf. They should have finished the deed, and moved on to the easier prey of his son.

"You can't kill a little boy."

The little bitch was talking and talking. It was enough to drive him mad.

He stepped in front of Tyler and poked the gun into the back of her head. "Shut! Up! Or I'll spray you with this kid's brains. Turn around."

That shut her up. He stepped back behind the boy and

looked over at Tyler. Even in the darkness, he could read the concern on his brother's face.

"What?" Tyler mouthed.

McCall looked his brother in the eye for a moment, and then to the black forest, searching his thoughts for answers.

Everything was unraveling too fast. Options grew to plans in his mind, then popped like bubbles.

They were going to survive this. That was a certainty in his mind. He had to think about the positives, and about what he wanted, not what he didn't want.

Deputy Patterson being there had been an unforeseen complication, but this was good. The plan was originally for the boy to disappear, with Tyler, alone. McCall was going to stay, wait a few minutes, and then go berserk with the rest of law enforcement, steering them in a false direction while Tyler took care of the dirty work. But Patterson had followed, so now McCall was out here in the woods. There was no way his brother would have been able to handle the two alone, not with his bad arm.

This was good, he told himself again. Because now Wolf had somehow found out about them, and if Patterson hadn't followed, McCall would have stayed, and would be sitting in handcuffs right now, or dead after a bloody shootout. Now McCall and Tyler had escaped the lion's den, and had two hostages for insurance. It was all good fortune.

Shit. Panic flooded him, and for a second it seemed there was no way he could hold it back. He was too smart to kid himself anymore. Standoff hostage situations never worked out well for the hostage takers. Never. Not in America. Not in this century.

They had to run, and do so intelligently. Wolf had already warned them that there was no way to escape in a vehicle. In the last text message, he'd even used the road name Tyler had driven up here on. McCall thought Wolf was bluffing because the bulk of the Sluice County law enforcement was a mile behind them, at the festival grounds.

McCall liked their chances for escape, but they would need to be quick. They'd packed a few bars of gold in the SUV, just as an insurance policy in case something did go wrong. *And it had gone very wrong.* The stash would be enough dead weight to carry without hauling these two around on top of it. He felt nothing for the boy. The kid had had a loving father, and that was more than he'd ever had. But he did feel a twinge of regret about having to kill the cute little Deputy Patterson, though he could put the blame squarely on that kid renting out the mountain bikes.

"All right. Just a second, stop," McCall said.

They all stopped, and the girl turned around with a defiant look.

"Just leave us alone," she said in an icy tone.

"Shoot them," he said. He'd have killed them himself, but his brother had the sound suppressor.

He turned to look into the woods, and waited for the deed to be over.

Three thumps, in quick succession, came from the catwalk behind them, as if someone was running up fast.

McCall twisted and pointed his flashlight just in time to see a rock bounce to a stop.

"Wha—"

A horrific animal noise came from in front of them, and McCall spun around with his flashlight. It was a man coming straight at them, screaming psychotically with a pistol pointed forward.

McCall raised his pistol and shot as quick as he could. He could hear the spits of Tyler's gun next to him between the deafening flashes of brilliant light kicking the barrel of his own gun.

Then something connected with his arm, pushing his aim to the right, just as he fired another shot. He watched in agony as his pistol erupted with fire, and his brother's head jerked away.

McCall reeled in horror as his brother's body crumpled, hit in the temple by his own round! He pointed his flashlight beam for an instant, studying Tyler's lifeless body, and then he turned with a surge of fury. Before he could raise his gun again, something hit the side of his head. It was so loud in his skull and so jarring that his whole body went limp for a second. The next thing he knew, he tasted dirt, and something hot stung his temple. Then a spear of pain ripped through his head, and then there was nothing.

CHAPTER 54

WOLF, Luke, and Patterson followed the doctor into the bright room. The shades were pulled up, letting the morning light reflecting off the mountains through the windows. Machines beeped and pumped, and tubes snaked off them to the bed and underneath blue sheets where Rachette was laid out.

At the sight of his deputy, Wolf felt a sense of pride so strong that tears began to pool in his eyes.

Rachette woke when they reached his bed. "Hey," he said with a dry voice. His face dropped when he saw Wolf. "I'm sorry."

Wolf shook his head. "For what?"

"It was my fault all this happened," he said, clamping his eyes shut, like the thought hurt him more than the three gunshot wounds to his body.

"You saved my son's life, Tom." Wolf used such a loud and clear tone that Rachette opened his eyes.

A tear spilled down Wolf's cheek and he made no

attempt to hide it. Instead, he reached up and patted Rachette on the head. "You didn't get shot here, did you?" he asked.

Rachette broke into a smile and winced the instant he started laughing.

"Careful, son," Doctor Sobel said, and he gently pulled Patterson out of the way and stepped close to Rachette. After checking the various monitors, he turned to Wolf and looked over his glasses. "Let's try to keep the jokes to a minimum. The staples in his abdomen are rated for grins only."

"I'm all right, Doc," Rachette said. "I'm all right."

Doctor Sobel stepped away and picked up his clipboard off the food tray.

"I don't remember much." Rachette looked at Patterson. "You gonna tell me what happened up there?"

Patterson gave a sideways glance to Wolf, then looked at Rachette. "You redeemed your idiocy just in time. They were just about to shoot us. If you hadn't come out of the trees and thrown yourself into three bullets, Jack and I would be dead."

Rachette closed his eyes and leaned his head back. "I just remember yelling and then dying."

Patterson and Wolf exchanged looks.

"You lost a lot of blood," Wolf said. "You got a personal chopper ride here."

Rachette nodded. "And what happened to them? McCall and whoever that asshole was with him?"

"It was his brother. And they're dead," Wolf said, glancing at Patterson.

Rachette watched Wolf's eyes, and then shifted his gaze to Patterson. "Good job, Patterson," said Rachette. He eyed her with a hint of devotion.

Patterson looked unnerved. "Uh, sure. Hey, that's what we do, right?"

They stood in silence, listening to the ticks, beeps, and hisses of the medical equipment.

Luke gently gripped Wolf's arm and held up her phone, which was lit up with the name *Brookhart*. Wolf nodded.

"Good job," Luke said to Rachette, and then she turned and walked out.

Rachette and Patterson watched Luke leave the room. "Who was that?" Rachette asked with a confused look.

"Special Agent Luke, FBI, Glenwood Springs. She's helping with the case."

"Ah, nice." Rachette looked back at Wolf, and then bounced his eyebrows.

"And the idiocy returns," Patterson said, "and so soon."

"This idiot saved you from certain death." Rachette sniffed and looked at Wolf. "Don't you forget it."

"My hero," she said.

"Where's Jack?" Rachette asked.

"Out in the lobby with Sarah."

"And he's okay?"

Wolf nodded, and laid his hand on Rachette's shoulder. "Good job. I'm gonna go now. You rest, and I'll be back."

Rachette's eyes glistened with tears, and he nodded.

Patterson hovered a hand over Rachette's shoulder,

then over the other one, and then settled for patting him on the head. "Good job."

Rachette closed his eyes and took a deep breath. Wolf and Patterson turned to leave.

"You have to teach me to ski this winter."

They turned around and saw Rachette craning his neck forward, glaring at Patterson with utter seriousness.

"Me?"

"Yeah, you."

"Okay. What? Why?"

Rachette closed his eyes and leaned his head back. "Because you're my partner." Rachette huffed another deep breath and fell dead asleep.

Patterson pulled down the corners of her mouth and left the room.

"Doctor." Wolf motioned, and Doctor Sobel followed him out of the room.

When they got out into the hall, Wolf turned to him. "How's it looking?"

Doctor Sobel lifted his glasses onto his gray head of hair and nodded. "It's looking good. The abdomen shot missed the liver and stomach, and we got the bullet out without complications. The leg will heal, but I'm afraid it could take a long time, and he may have a slight limp. I'm not so sure about that last skiing comment, let's put it that way. The arm will be fine. It was a clean through-and-through shot on the top of his forearm, and missed all the tendons."

Wolf nodded, and shook his hand.

The waiting area was full of deputies, all looking exhausted, hanging on Patterson's hushed words.

"So? What did the doctor say?" Wilson asked Wolf.

Wolf nodded. "He'll be fine. Let's give him some time to rest, everybody. He needs it. And the music festival goes on."

The room bustled as the deputies stood and streamed out.

Wolf walked through the waiting room into the bright entryway of the hospital, and was greeted with a sight he wasn't prepared for.

Special Agent Luke was talking with Jack and Sarah. Sarah was smiling wide and nodding, gripping Jack next to her as if he would blow away in the wind if she let go.

Wolf took a deep breath and approached.

"Hi," Sarah said. Her blonde hair was pulled back in a messy ponytail and she wore flannel pants. Despite being ripped from slumber in the middle of the night with uncertain news about her son for the second time that week, she looked surprisingly chipper and as flawless as ever.

"Hi," Wolf said, feeling his face flush a little. Exactly why, he wasn't sure. "I see you've met Special Agent Luke."

"Yes, and I was just meeting Jack, here," Luke said with a flash in her eye. "What a beautiful son you two have."

Jack gave an aw-shucks grin and leaned against his mother.

"Hi David," a deep voice said behind him.

Wolf turned around and stepped aside for Mark Wilson. "Hello, Mark."

Mark passed by, holding two cups of styrofoam coffee. He handed one to Sarah, stepped close, and wrapped an arm around her shoulder.

"Is Deputy Rachette going to be all right?" Mark asked.

Wolf nodded and looked down at Jack. "He's going to be fine."

Jack was glaring into nothing. Wolf reached down and brushed his hair. "You okay, buddy?"

Jack looked up and nodded.

He didn't look it. He'd experienced a lot more first-hand violence in the past week than most people would in a lifetime, and he wasn't even thirteen yet.

The five of them stood in awkward silence for a beat.

"Well, it was nice meeting you. I've gotta get back." Luke gave a quick wave and walked away.

Sarah, Mark, and Jack watched her leave through the glass doors and then looked at Wolf. Sarah's lip turned up a little.

"I'll be back," Wolf said, and walked outside.

It was sunny outside and a warm breeze pressed his T-shirt against his chest. There were a few people walking in the parking lot, but Luke was nowhere in sight. He sighed and adjusted his sling, which sent a wisp of air into his shirt that tickled his arm bandage and the rest of his scabbed-over wounds.

"Looking for me?"

Wolf turned and saw Luke on the sidewalk. Her head

was tilted, and her brown hair flowed behind her in the wind.

"Yeah," Wolf said, "actually I was."

"She's beautiful, your ex-wife."

Wolf nodded. "Yeah, she is."

Luke brushed her hair behind her ear and smiled.

"What did Brookhart have to say?" Wolf asked.

Luke pursed her lips and shoved her hands in her pockets. "They found a shit load of gold in a safe at McCall's house. Took them all night to crack it, but when they opened it, it was full of gold kilo bars. Over a hundred and fifty of them."

Wolf whistled. "Wow."

They started walking down the sidewalk.

"At least five point seven six million worth. And that's not including the stuff in the SUV."

Wolf whistled again.

Luke nodded. "Yeah. And they found a lot of stones and gems in the safe, too. According to Brookhart, they look really old, with carvings in them. Then there were a few pieces with the gold and gems still intact. Old bracelets and a dagger. They took some pictures and sent them to DC, and some analysts think the dagger is part of the Bactrian stuff, like you were talking about, and the others are probably part of what was looted from the National Museum during the civil war."

"Too bad for Clark and the McCalls," Wolf said.

"They also found out that our pilot, Ryan Clark, was a cousin of Tyler and Adam McCall," said Luke.

Wolf nodded. "It was the McCalls next to Clark in

that picture. It took me the drive from Glenwood last night, then a few hours to sleep on it, but I think I've got everything figured out by now."

Luke stopped and turned to him. She nodded. "I think I do too." Her eyes welled up and tears started to drip down her cheeks. "They found that my brother's fingerprints at my house, and the one on the container, were too big to be real. Both sets were the same exact dimensions, just under two microns too big to be my brother's real prints."

"The old reverse-relief printout slathered with wood glue trick." Wolf shook his head. "Clever enough to fool us, I guess."

"But getting the resolution right, and pixels per inch, and whatever else they didn't know, meant they were off by two microns. I would like to think we'd have caught it eventually."

She looked down at her feet and then looked up at Wolf. "Thank you so much."

Wolf shrugged. "Why?"

"Brookhart also said you called last night asking to compare the writing on the note to Jeffries's army application."

Wolf lifted his chin. "And?"

She nodded, and let the tears flow freely down her cheeks. "And now I don't think my brother was involved in this."

"No, he wasn't. The way I see it is that's why the guy on the EOD team made that statement ... that your brother had gone after the other three the next day. Because that's exactly what he did. Your brother wasn't in on the whole thing; he was trying to stop them, trying to reel in his men. I think he tracked them down, and the only way forward for Jeffries, Hartley, and Quinn was to kill him, and then bury his body in that explosion. We'll never know exactly what happened, but your brother didn't fit the profile of these other guys. They were all a bunch of misfits, with nothing to live for here."

Luke exhaled. "Ask Danny, and he'll tell you Brian was like that."

"But you know that's not true," Wolf said. "You knew Brian. Was he like that? Would he fake his own death for some gold?"

Luke sniffed and shook her head. "No, he wouldn't."

Wolf nodded. "It was Wade Jeffries who wrote that note. The note was a confession and the gold bars an atonement for what they did. He regretted what they'd done to your brother. *You deserve some of this, too. I'm sorry,* it said. The note explains it all."

Luke wiped her eyes and nodded, her expression steely now. "So I think it all started with Ryan Clark and Wade Jeffries, right?"

"That's what I think," Wolf said. "It fits. They went to the same high school in Delta and must have been friends. Jeffries comes across the gold somehow in Afghanistan, and he knows just the guy to help him get it out—his cargo pilot buddy, Clark. So they meet and go over their plan, probably right there at the Mountain Goat while Jeffries is in Colorado on leave. Clark agrees to help the team, for an equal cut, and then he goes and tells his cousins, the McCalls, which was bad news for the EOD team.

"Because the McCalls come up with a better plan. It's a perfect opportunity that lands in their laps. These guys fake their own deaths seven thousand miles away, and all they have to do is wait for them to bring them their load of gold—with really no risk of bringing suspicion on themselves, because who would miss a bunch of already dead guys?"

"Jeffries's mother and sister would," Luke said.

Wolf nodded. "They would."

"Best-laid plans of mice and men often go awry," said Luke in a lofty voice.

Wolf looked up in thought. "Or *shit happens*?"

Luke smiled.

"And, yes," Wolf said, "things like Wade Jeffries contacting his mother and sister, and Jack and I walking into one of their executions, unraveled their perfect plan in a hurry."

Luke looked up at Wolf and then down at her feet; then she stepped into Wolf, got on her toes, and before Wolf could react, pressed her warm lips against his.

Wolf stood still in shock for a second, and then he returned the kiss, meeting her swirling tongue with his own. He pulled his hand out of his pocket and wrapped it around her waist, and she pressed herself close.

A few seconds later they parted, and Luke stared him in the eye. "My hero," she said. "Thank you."

Wolf chuckled and shook his head.

Luke's face dropped. "What?"

"Nothing," Wolf said. "You're welcome."

Luke pulled down her blouse and pulled her hair behind her ear. "When are you coming to get your truck?"

Wolf nodded. His SCSD SUV was finally out of the FBI lot and back in his hands, but the Toyota still sat at the Garfield County Sheriff's Department building in Glenwood Springs, helpless and abandoned. "Oh yeah, I probably need to come get that."

"Want a ride?"

"Not today," Wolf said. "There's too much happening here this weekend for me to go killing more time running around with you."

Luke nodded and smiled. "Well, maybe you'll give me a call when things let up?"

Wolf smiled. "That sounds good."

Luke nodded again and turned around. "Okay, I'll let you get back to your—" She spun around on her heels. "Hey, wait. I almost forgot. You're a complete asshole."

Wolf peaked his eyebrows. "And why is that?"

"I just met your son inside, and that picture you showed me, that night you almost ran me off the road? That wasn't your son. That kid in the picture was younger and had black hair. Totally different looking."

Wolf squinted. "Oh yeah, that was Wilson's kid. He has a ton of pictures all over his desk."

Luke grinned ear-to-ear and then turned around. "On second thought, don't call me."

Wolf watched her swaying hips as she walked down the sidewalk toward her Tahoe.

"I'll come over and we can have a beer again," he said.

Luke popped open her door and stepped one foot inside. She stopped and looked him up and down, then covered her mouth, stifling a laugh.

"What?" Wolf's face dropped.

"I was just thinking about the last time you came over for a beer."

Wolf stood dumbly. "You're thinking about me naked."

She whipped her head to the sky and climbed in. "You're trouble, David Wolf," she said, and shut the door.

CHAPTER 55

Wolf stood alone in a vast park in Aspen, sweating through the armpits of his T-shirt. Alone, yet surrounded by tens of attentive parents and over a hundred scrambling pre- and post-pubescent kids in full football gear. It was mid-July, without a breath of wind, in the mountains of Colorado, which meant it was dry and hot—not good weather for full pads. Despite the skin-scorching sun, the two-day football camp was scheduled to end in authentic fashion, and so it did for all age groups—with a full-length scrimmage, with referees and everything.

Wolf couldn't help but think back on that fateful night for the thousandth time since, and Jack and Wolf's conversation. Though Jack still hadn't grown a lick since then—it had only been a month—Wolf felt somehow more assured for his son's safety. Then again, as he watched three of the largest kids on the opposite team lumber onto the field, he decided he could have been jumping the gun.

"Your son on black or yellow?" a female voice asked from a few feet away.

Wolf turned and saw an attractive woman hanging on the muscular arms of a tan, gold-adorned man behind her.

"Yellow," Wolf said.

The man and woman turned back to the field without a response. *Black.*

Wolf studied the happy-looking couple for a moment and then turned back to the field. He couldn't help it; the sight of the big guy draping his arms around that beautiful woman had him thinking of Sarah and Mark. *Again.* Mark, and his unshakable presence in their lives—and apparently Wolf's thoughts. Not that Wolf was necessarily trying to shake him—mentally or physically. Not that Wolf didn't appreciate the help and the positive influence in Sarah's life. After all, Mark was keeping her straight and healthy. *And happy.* Hell, Mark had even driven Jack the hour and a half to this football camp when Wolf had been stuck at work the day before.

Wolf supposed that if he hadn't had Special Agent Kristen Luke as a prospect in his life at the moment, he'd be a hell of a lot more depressed when he saw big guys with beautiful women on their arms. But Luke was a prospect. They'd enjoyed dinner together on a few occasions in the past month. It was clear they liked each other's company, and it was more lately discovered that they were extremely compatible in other ways.

Wolf couldn't help but smile a little and exhale as he daydreamed about their recent date. It was a shame she was so close, just thirty minutes up the road, but couldn't make it down to visit.

A month later, she was still wrapping up the case —*their case*. Apparently, some bigwigs from DC had flown in earlier that day, and she was debriefing them on one of the more high-profile crimes the mountains of Colorado had seen in over thirty years.

Looking into the lives of the McCalls was turning out to be quite a candle-burner for Luke and the FBI. Forensic accountants had uncovered that Adam and Tyler McCall not only jointly owned the Mountain Goat Bar and Grill, but had been deeply involved in the distribution and sale of cocaine and marijuana in the valley Wolf stood in at the moment. The McCalls had been millionaires before the gold, and had apparently used Sergeant McCall's position of authority to keep suspicion off themselves.

The fact that they'd run a cop and FBI bar as a front establishment was turning out to be an embarrassing and unrelenting topic in the local papers, which were raising questions about the effectiveness of law enforcement and local FBI. The illegal drug underground was another hot topic in print—just where they burrowed, and whether there were more corrupt men of authority, and, if so, where. Wolf had to admit being intrigued by it all and was keeping up with the news with the rest of the population.

Luke was compounding her own work by ruffling buzz cuts, trying to get someone in the army to help her look for her brother's body in Tora Bora. It wasn't working, and Wolf found there was little in the way of his contacts either. All he could do was point to the mounting evidence that Brian Richter had been killed, completely detaching him from the whole incident, and console her.

"Set, hut! Hut!" The field of boys broke into a swarm of movement and ground to a halt after the whistle, with half the kids ending up in a pile.

Wolf took a deep breath and searched through the kids for Jack. He was a good head shorter than most, but zoomed around the field and was easy to spot.

Just a heartbeat of panic hit him, wondering whether he'd done the right thing by convincing Sarah that Jack was ready, despite his size. But Wolf was sure of it—he would be okay. He'd seen Jack get through hell, albeit with a healthy dose of fear, but with zero hesitation and a clearer head than a few soldiers Wolf had served with. Jack could take care of himself, and Wolf didn't want to deny his son something that made him so happy.

"Hut!" Grunts and the dull plastic thud of helmets filled the air, and then the thump of cleats as two wide receivers and their defensive counterparts flew by, sending a swirl of wind into Wolf.

Just when the chaos behind the line of scrimmage looked to be collapsing into another heap of motionless bodies, a tight spiral sailed into the blue sky.

Wolf watched the trajectory of the pass and flicked his eyes to where it would land—smack into a group of players with black jerseys. One huge defensive player shuffled backwards, and may as well have been licking his lips as he eyed the ball, while another tall kid slowed his trot to get underneath the ill-aimed pass. The ball dropped lower, and before it reached the group of defensemen with outstretched arms, a yellow jersey streaked in and bounced out of the sea of black, snagged the ball with two hands, twisted, and dipped down out of sight.

A barrage of shouting erupted from the sidelines, and the black jerseys began dropping like dominos as they tripped over themselves and mowed into one another, trying desperately to catch Jack, who was now sprinting his way past defenders, down the line of orange cones, and into the end zone.

Jack dropped the ball and gave some of his teammates five, ignoring the slaps on his helmet, acting like it was just another touchdown, like he was used to it.

"Damn, that kid's got some skills," the man next to Wolf said, still gripping the woman tight.

Wolf made eye contact with Jack and nodded, unable to hold back his smile anymore. "Yeah," he said. "He does."

THE END

ACKNOWLEDGEMENTS

Thank you so much for reading Alive and Killing. I hope you enjoyed the story, and if you did, thank you for taking a few moments to leave a review. As an independent author, exposure is everything, and positive reviews help so much to get that exposure. If you'd be so kind as to leave an honest review, I'd appreciate it very much.

I love interacting with readers so please feel free to email me at jeff@jeffcarson.co so I can thank you personally. Otherwise, thank you very much for your support by other means, such as sharing or lending the books with your friends/family/book clubs/the weird guy who wears tight women's yoga pants at the golf course, or anyone else you think might be interested in reading the David Wolf series. Thanks again and I hope to see you again inside another Wolf story.

Would you like to know about future David Wolf books the moment they are published? You can visit my blog and sign up for the New Release Newsletter at this link – http://www.jeffcarson.co/p/newsletter.html.

As a gift for signing up you'll receive a complimentary copy of Gut Decision—A David Wolf Short Story, which is a harrowing tale that takes place years ago during David Wolf's first days in the Sluice County Sheriff's Department.

THE MAN LEANED over the wheel, squinting through the windshield as another powdery gust of wind hit the side of his truck.

All he saw was a swarm of snowflakes illuminated by his headlights, and he felt his eyeballs twitch back and forth as he tried desperately to get his bearings. When he instinctively let off the gas, the truck lurched and stuttered, rocking him in the seat. He kicked the clutch and down-shifted to first, and then he felt the truck meander to the side, though to which side was impossible to tell.

It was useless trying to orient himself. Like looking through the eyepiece of a twisting kaleidoscope. Just as he was about to stomp the brakes, the whiteout let up and the two pinpoints of red light flitted back into view on the otherwise deserted county road ahead.

Dammit. He turned the wheel left and got back into the twin ruts in the snow he'd been following, hoping to God they were somewhere near the center and safe from drainage ditches, roadside boulders, and anything else hidden under the blanket of ever-thickening white that could derail his plans.

County 15 was a desolate, winding dirt thoroughfare with steep drops off the left shoulder in a few spots. Houses were few and far between. If a driver got in trouble here, it was a long walk to get help, and an even longer one in weather like this—overall a stupid place to be driving tonight.

He was waiting for his quarry to call it quits, turn around, and coast back down the hill before the deepening drifts stranded them. Maybe they would take the girl back to one of their places or go to a hotel or something.

He looked at his watch—11:26 p.m., Saturday night, on the eve of surely the biggest powder day on the mountain in years. Fat chance of getting a hotel room. Out-of-town skiers on the mountain today would have sensed the opportunity and snatched up any vacancies after the big gala.

What a night to have a big event on the mountain, he thought with a shake of his head. It was going to be mayhem for people getting back down the gondola and to their homes and hotel rooms.

He scratched his nose and grasped the wheel with a two-hand white-knuckle grip. The defroster howled, blowing hot air on the highest setting against the windshield. Regardless of the wipers' speed, an immovable arc of water remained on the glass. The red taillights ahead illuminated it, and it reminded him of oozing fresh blood.

For the past day he'd seen red, and the way this girl

was acting was only driving him madder as the seconds ticked by. Picking up two men in the span of half an hour? She'd simultaneously proven herself a bigger whore than he'd already thought and killed his entire plan in one slutty move.

He shook his head and gripped the wheel even tighter, and then spat onto the floor of the passenger seat and growled aloud. He'd never felt more disgust with any human beings than with those conniving behind the scenes of Rocky Points.

Well, he'd felt a similar disgust once before. And that? That had ended badly. Was he going to remember anything after this? Or was he going to wake up in blood again? The thought made him nervous and his hands were slick on the wheel.

Because the memory of his first time was buried deep in the cave of his mind and he didn't have a map to find it, he knew this was going to be like his first time all over again. It had to be done. He would not fail. He turned the heater knob down and the cab quieted. The digital clock changed to 11:30. This was looking to be futile. They were going to her house, if they could make the last mile, and then what? It was sure to be full of roommates, and the neighbors who lived in that line of six houses in the middle of nowhere, and no opportunity. The driver bared his teeth and shook his head.

Ahead, the taillights rounded the corner and disappeared from sight. All he could see was the thick curtain of swollen flakes flying into the lights, the windshield and the twin tire grooves.

Damn, it was deep, he thought, looking to the left and barely seeing the trees in the forest. The snow had started at sundown, and really ramped up after nine. By the looks of the ruts, at least twenty inches had accumulated already, and the storm was still coming in full force.

Enough was enough. He should quit and get back home while he could. He started scanning for the widest part of the road to turn around.

Ahead, the lights flared red and he jammed his foot down on his own brake. The truck had stopped.

He shut off his headlights and the chaotic scene outside went black. He squinted and blinked as his eyes adjusted to the darkness. Finally, he could see the twin grooves running up the road, disappearing into a television-static night, and then the faint lights of the motionless truck.

It was almost impossible to see—the snow and wind were relentless—but he swore that the cab light flicked on and then off. The tail lights shone as the truck backed and K-turned, and then the truck's headlights were coming straight at him.

His pulse jumped as he considered his next play. He flicked on his headlights and shifted into first. His knobby tires spun briefly and then caught. He shifted into second, following the tracks ahead. Less than a minute later the truck's headlamps glared into his cab as it passed. He squinted and held up his hand to cover his face, figuring the truck's occupants might be pressed against their windows and wondering who in their right mind was out in this weather along with them.

He sighed and looked in his rearview mirror. The tail-lights disappeared around the corner without braking.

It was over, he decided. He followed the ruts to the point where the truck had turned around. There was no sense breaking new ground and risking falling over the edge of the road, sitting in a snowdrift overnight, and possibly dying for his carelessness.

As he drove, he tested the high beams. Visibility was worse, so he shut them off.

He leaned forward again and squinted. When he'd flicked off his lights, he could have sworn he'd glimpsed a dark figure along the right shoulder several yards ahead.

He blinked rapidly, then squinted again. And when the shape moved, his pulse jumped. *It was a person.*

"Holy shit," he whispered to himself, and sat up straighter in his seat.

It was her. There was no mistake. She was waving, and then she held up a gloved thumb.

The man swallowed, letting his brain process the opportunity standing in front of him. His mission, melting away moments ago, had now dropped in his lap, and he found himself wondering what to do.

He slowed down and stopped next to her. Before he knew it, her face had filled the passenger window. As she pressed against the glass and peered inside, the driver opened up the center console, grabbed the gun's rough plastic handle, and pulled it out.

If he shot her when she opened the door, would he black out and wake up a few hours later? Just sitting in a car, engine running, door open, and a bloody corpse lying nearby, waiting for early-morning plows to discover them? Was he even conscious now? Was he dreaming?

His breathing was frantic, and his skin tingled as sweat glands opened up all over his body.

She pounded on the window and yelled something too muffled to hear.

He clicked the lock and she opened the door. The dome light went on and a blast of snow and cold swirled into the cab as she bent inside. He tucked the revolver in between his legs way too late, but she didn't seem to notice.

"Hey, it's you! What the hell are you doing up here? Don't answer, I don't care. Can I get a ride?"

"Yeah, get in," he said. His voice sounded a mile away in his own ears. He reached into the center console again, pulled out his leather gloves, and put them on.

She jumped up onto the seat butt-first and knocked her feet together out the door to drop off the snow, and then twisted into the chair and shut the door.

The cab was suddenly filled with her sniffling and breathing and a flowery scent. She pulled off her wool hat, flipping snow all over the dashboard.

"Oh, I'm sorry. Shit. Thank God you're up here. Oh, man ... do you think you can get up the rest of this hill to my house? Do you know where I live?"

The driver stared at her and smiled. Or was he sneering? He couldn't tell.

She looked at him and frowned. "Are you okay?" she asked.

The driver picked up the revolver and pointed it at her face.

"Oh, God!" She twisted and grabbed for the handle, and then put her hands up and shut her eyes. "Please. Please. Don't hurt me. What are you doing?"

"You know you killed her, right?"

"What?" she said, still cowering against the door. "What?"

Every muscle in his body tensed as rage overtook him.

"Unzip your coat," he said, flipping on the cab light.

Her eyes were wild and wide, pupils tiny, mascara running down her cheeks. She nodded profusely. "Yeah, okay," she said, fumbling to take off her gloves. At first, she moved quickly to unzip her jacket. Then she looked up at him as if a sudden brainstorm had given her an idea, and she slowed down, arching her back a little and taking a calming breath. "Yeah, let's get comfortable."

He set his jaw and inhaled deeply to contain his rage. It figured this whore would think if she puts out, he would punch her ticket out of this. He kept his aim steady and pulled up on the emergency brake, shifted into neutral, and let up his feet from the clutch and brake.

"Now pull open your jacket with both hands, and pull it down your back, and push out your boobs again."

She smiled and gave him a wink, and then slowly did as she was told.

He unbuckled his seatbelt and scooted his chair all the way back, watching her closely. She was now sitting with her hands effectively wrapped against her sides, but he would need to make sure she couldn't fight back, so he put the gun to her head and climbed on top of her, and then put his knees on her arms.

She gave him a smile and closed her eyes, trying to look like she was enjoying it, unconvincingly so.

He dropped the gun on the driver's side seat and grasped her neck. First, he just gripped her and started squeezing. And then she started to squirm.

There was no preparing for this moment, and her fierce counter-attack startled him. She thrashed and twisted underneath him, and he tightened his grip until his muscles shook, and then he gripped harder still.

She sagged down in the seat, like she was trying to escape by sliding underneath his legs, but he just leaned on her harder and a gurgling sound bubbled from her lips. Even through the leather gloves, he could feel the pounding of the blood in her neck. Then, after what seemed like an eternity, she went still, and the pounding stopped.

He gripped her for a while longer, knowing she was already dead, but just wanting to make sure. He finally eased his grip, the leather of his gloves peeling off her skin as he pulled away.

He had almost forgotten. With a quick movement, he opened the center console again and pulled out the tube of Ruby Fire lipstick. He removed the cap, carefully twisted the tube's base to expose the right height of color, and then applied the mark to her forehead. He leaned back and assessed his work. *Maybe not exactly like the original,* he thought, *but close enough.*

He wiped a tear from his cheek before it dropped onto the warm lifeless body. It was strange. As the seconds ticked by and he replayed images of the past few minutes, a persisting adrenaline spike spawned an airy sense of wonder. *I did it. I strangled her. I killed this pathetic excuse for a human being. Maybe my mind is playing tricks on me,* he thought. *Maybe I am out cold, lying on a dead woman in a running vehicle on a deserted road in the middle of the night.*

He slowed his breathing and looked around, watching the flying flakes and listening to the windshield wipers squeal behind him. Then he felt the warmth on his knee and jumped over onto the driver's side. She had pissed herself, and it was all over the seat.

He reached over, pulled on the door handle, and then shoved her out. She ended up hanging out the door with her legs still jammed inside on the floor, so he crawled onto the passenger seat, feeling the warm liquid soak through his jeans, and then rolled her out into the deep snow.

For a few seconds he stared, watching the snow cover her body like a lace veil, and he again wondered if this surreal scene was a dream. The bitter-cold wind and his sticky wet jeans reeking of urine convinced him otherwise. It seemed real because it was real.

He climbed back in the driver's seat and decided that even if it were a dream, the prudent thing would be to dream about getting the hell out of there. So, he turned the truck around and did just that.

THE ANTICIPATION on the pass was electric. If Wolf had not been cocooned in his winter duty gear—hat, gloves, fully zipped coat, pants, boots—he was sure his body hair would have been standing on end.

"Waiting on you, Sheriff," the distant-sounding voice crackled through everyone's radios.

Wolf looked at the other bundled faces and wide eyes of the people around him, and then shifted his gaze up the snow-blanketed highway that bent out of sight behind the pillowed pines. It was the day after a huge dump of snow, and a beautiful morning on a bluebird day, as skiers called it—a cloudless, radiant sky. Despite the crowd surrounding him, Wolf regarded the scene as desolate and peaceful. For the moment.

He turned to look past the congregation of official personnel that surrounded him. A few hundred yards down the highway, a line of still vehicles puffed exhaust behind a closed gate arm. For five minutes now, people had been abandoning their vehicles and huddling on the roadside next to the fresh wall of plowed snow, jockeying for position to see, cell-phone cameras swinging between the bright mountaintop and the congregation of Sluice County sheriff's deputies, Rocky Points Rescue volunteers, and Colorado Department of Transportation workers milling in the cold shaded road above them.

An RKPT-News 8 crew had set up next to the road gate, with an expensive camera mounted on a tripod, lens aimed high up the mountain.

"Stand by!" Wolf shouted, a puff of cloud jetting from his mouth. He thumbed the radio button and brought it to his lips. "All clear."

The uniformed men and women surrounding Wolf swiveled in unison to look up, and he gave a final glance to the line of vehicles down the road. They reacted to the synchronized commotion and stared up. He watched as motorists nearest the front shouted down the line and people began sprinting toward the gate for a better view.

Wolf felt like he had just opened a cage containing a wild beast.

"Fire in the hole," Bob Duke, longtime director of the resort's ski patrol, said through the radio.

Even through the tiny speaker, Wolf could hear Bob's high-pitched excitement, and it coaxed Wolf's body to tense and tingle. He resigned himself to the moment, and assured himself that they'd taken every precaution so that no one would be in harm's path. Wolf had taken CDOT's recommended perimeter around the slide zone and doubled it. He had discussed the terrain above the motorists in detail with the avalanche specialists. There was nothing more to do but ...

Two sharp-edged blasts thumped the air, and Wolf looked up.

The deputies nearby started to whoop as a white cloud began billowing from the bowl high above.

On a normal blast day, when the conditions on the resort's southernmost bowl were just right to slide, a triggered avalanche would make its way down a third of the mountain, and stop in the relatively flat zone at the bottom of Brecker Bowl along the southern boundary of the resort.

But if snow conditions were just right (or just wrong) and an especially deep layer of powder lay over a weak layer of sugar snow, the slide could ride through the flat zone and spill into the treeless chute that had been gouged out over the millennia by other slides. An especially big avalanche could get as far as the highway. That specific zone was a safe distance up the road, clearly discernable by smaller, younger trees and an open glade.

According to Duke's earlier assessment, backed by over thirty years of experience with the Rocky Points Resort ski patrol, there was a small chance they were going to see a slide reach the road, or something even bigger. The official accumulation from last night's storm was twenty-seven inches at the peak, and conditions had conspired to prevent CDOT and ski patrol from preemptively blasting the bowl. Topping that, the wind had shifted and come strong out of the north all night, loading at least nine feet of wind-deposited snow underneath a freshly sculpted cornice, all on top of a layer of depth-hoar crystals, or sugar snow, a result of the resort's dry and sunny conditions over the past month.

For ski conditions on the rest of the mountain, and the skiers who would be enjoying them all day, the new snow was a godsend. But as Wolf watched the white cloud explode from the bowl above, he wondered if this wasn't something sent from hell.

Go to Amazon.com to continue the next David Wolf adventure!

Gut Decision – Sign up for the new release newsletter at http://www.jeffcarson.co/p/newsletter.html and receive a complimentary copy.